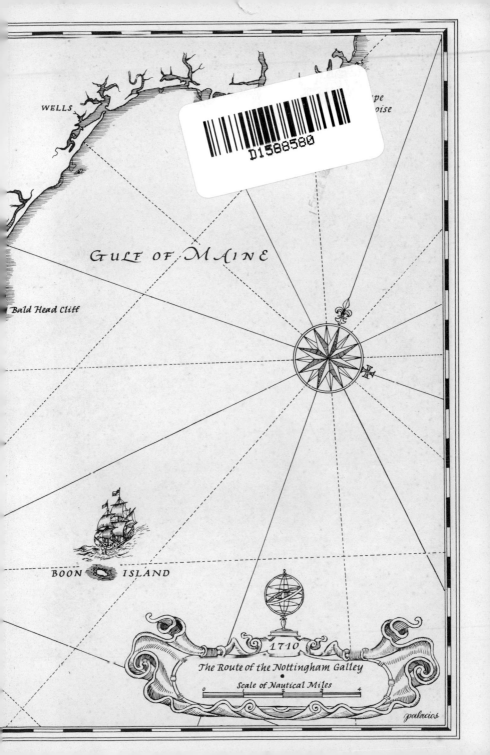

WELLS

pe
oise

GULF OF MAINE

Bald Head Cliff

BOON ISLAND

1710

The Route of the Nottingham Galley

Scale of Nautical Miles

0   2   4

palacios

To Auntie Kath

With love
From Richard
May 1954

BOON ISLAND

Kenneth Roberts' new novel—the first for nine years
—tells the story of two friends, Miles Whitworth and
Neal Butler, who sailed across the Atlantic in the
year 1710. Miles lived with his father in Greenwich.
Down from Oxford, his chief absorption was the
theatre. A chance encounter with a strange young
lad, fishing for whitebait in the river, led to a firm
friendship. Neal, the fisher for whitebait, was himself a minor player in Penkethman's celebrated
Greenwich summer company; and his father, a
former player, whom men called Swede because of
his yellow hair, met Whitworth senior and enlisted
his aid to improve Neal's future. Events were to
confound those plans, however. Neal, playing the
part of a young girl, had the attention of a corrupt
fop forced upon him; and Neal, in defending himself, killed the fop. Thus it was that Miles, Swede
and Neal fled England on the *Nottingham* galley with
a motley crew. What befell them when the ship was
wrecked on ice-covered Boon Island in a howling
north-easter is recounted graphically and excitingly
by the famous author of *Northwest Passage.*

Kenneth Roberts

BOON ISLAND

COLLINS
St James's Place, London
1956

PRINTED IN GREAT BRITAIN
COLLINS CLEAR-TYPE PRESS : LONDON AND GLASGOW

To Stephen Nason
Vicar of St. Alfege, Greenwich
with the gratitude and admiration of
his American cousin

Chapter One

GREENWICH, for all its faults, was a fascinating place, and I always left it with regret, especially at Trinity Term, to go up to Oxford.

Twice a year I protested to my father that I'd be better off in Greenwich; but he wouldn't have it so. Roughly speaking, our wrangling went around and around, like moles in their devious underground wanderings; but, after the fashion of mole-holes, they seemed to arrive nowhere.

The sum of all my contentions was that an Oxford education, so called because of the strange professors, dons, fellows and tutors to whom we were exposed, was a waste of time, if not downright dangerous.

My father, however, insisted that no matter how much of a drunken sot a don or a tutor might be, education somehow worthy was bound to be achieved by my mere presence within the stone walls of my college, which was Christ Church, by my daily exposure to the portraits in Christ Church Hall, and to the conversations of those drunken dons, those barnacle-like fellows, all waiting for someone to die and provide them with a Living—and I often wondered what idiot first applied the word "Living" to a bare existence in a miserable parsonage at the end of a muddy lane.

"Look here, Miles," my father would say, "you defeat your own arguments against Oxford without realising what you're doing. You want to study the writing of plays, and you complain that you're not allowed to do it, so Oxford

is a bore and a waste of time. But you *do* do it! You belong
to that Buskin Club of yours! You know Colley Cibber
made a better play out of *Richard III* than Shakespeare did!
' Off with his head!' 'Richard is himself again.' That's
Cibber: not Shakespeare!

"You say your tutors are morose, profligate, insipid asses
—and you've learned it by yourself! That's a whole lot
better than believing some old fool of a professor who tells
you that a knowledge of chemistry is an elegant and desir-
able accomplishment because it was revealed to Adam by
Heaven! To Adam, for God's sake! And by Heaven! Pish!
Nobody's educated by that sort of teaching! All anybody
does in college—if he's fortunate—is to learn how to make
a start at educating himself: to change his mind if his mind
needs changing."

He was right, of course. If I'd never numbed my feet and
fingers and nose in the cubicles of the Bodleian, reading the
nice nastiness of Mrs. Aphra Behn and the humourless
comedies of a score of imitation Shakespeares, I'd never have
struck up a friendship with Neal Butler. Whether that was
a good thing or a bad thing, I can't say, because it's possible
that something worse than Boon Island might have happened
to me.

That's what I hope those who read this book will bear in
mind: no matter what dreadful thing a man may encounter,
he might, but for the grace of God, be overwhelmed by
something even more awful. I can't endure people who
complain about this or that little thing; but I only reached
that state of mind by sad experience.

In the beginning, I had small use for Oxford, and its
dreary dullness and monotony. I copied Dr. Atterbury's
sermons until I was physically ill; I pored over grammar
and rhetoric until my eyelids seemed glued together—and
I looked forward to nothing but returning to Greenwich at

the end of Trinty Term—to its life and its bustle, its palaces and taverns and parks, its endless traffic on the Thames.

One of my reasons for disliking Oxford—and how I laughed, in later years, at such unreasoning folly—was the fact that Trinity Term made it impossible for me to see the great fair held in Greenwich at Whitsuntide. I never reached home until weeks after Whitsuntide, and to me a three-day fair was of more importance than anything—except, naturally, my father and my dinghy.

So at the end of Trinity Term, in that memorable summer of 1710, my father had my dinghy waiting for me at the yard of the Naval Hospital, and within an hour after he had welcomed me home, I had pushed her out on the river and was being foully cursed by a hundred rivermen.

A failing wind and the incoming tide carried me to Deptford Steps, where the river makes its great bend to the south—the bend that holds, as in a bag, the palaces and the Naval Hospital and all the taverns so famous for their whitebait dinners.

Even before the dinghy had touched the stone, a boy reached out for her bow, turned her sideways and drew her to the bottom step with no apparent effort. This takes strength, and it surprised me, for at first sight the boy didn't look overly strong; but when I climbed from the dinghy and we lifted her from the water to set her on the step, so that she'd be out of the way of the innumerable fishermen who were constantly on the move, he made it seem as easy as lifting out a broomstick.

All these fisherfolk were concentrated between Ballast Quay and Billingsgate—the stretch where the incoming tide pushes whitebait by the millions against the abutments of the Naval Hospital.

Seemingly every one of those thousands—sailors, girls, gipsies, old women, dock workers—had some sort of white-bait basket-trap, and was lowering it into the brown waters of the Thames and flipping it out again, so that the whole waterfront was a flurry of splashing spray.

Above this spray hung a sort of medley of sound, caused by the groans, shouts, curses and shrieks of those who were either successful or unsuccessful in the yankings and jerkings of their traps. Their facial contortions, as they thus toiled, were something remarkable; but this particular boy would flip his wire basket from the water: then, whether the basket was empty or whether it held a glimmering flicker of those succulent little spratlings, he would glance at the whitebait fishers on either side with a sort of disarming concentration of amusement, generosity, amiability, apology . . . apology, perhaps, for the smallness of his catch, or for his good fortune, or for his ineptitude, or perhaps for looking so much cleaner and neater than any of the men or boys who were sousing their baskets down and up, down and up, with dour determination and scowling ferocity.

If I seem to talk overmuch of Greenwich whitebait, it's because those insignificant minnows, in season, were Greenwich's most important product. People came from miles around, especially from London, to dine on them, even to have official whitebait banquets, such as were never held elsewhere—and for an excellent reason. No place in the world produced such delectable morsels as the whitebait brought ashore at Greenwich; and whitebait at its finest arouses a sort of frenzy in the breasts of those who know it. Nobody ate mutton in Greenwich during the whitebait season, nor fowl, nor beef—not if he could get whitebait.

When the boy went back to his fishing-station, I saw that he had been fortunate; for on a square of wet sacking close behind him were perhaps two-thirds of a bushel of whitebait, a good part of them still flopping and shimmering; so as a reward to him for helping me, as well as a home-coming gift for my father, I thought to buy some of them at a generous price. To that end I put my hand on his arm to get his attention.

To my amazement he shied away from my outstretched hand, as a puppy might shrink from a threatening foot, and the look he darted at me was almost violent in its wariness. Then, in a moment, he was merely a polite boy again, snapping his trap from the river, bringing with it a score of wriggling, glittering minnows which he dumped skilfully on his square of sacking.

"There's already enough for a dozen suppers," I said. "Spare me a few—two shillings' worth, perhaps?" Two shillings should have been enough to buy half a bushel, but the boy only concentrated silently on the submerging of his little trap.

Not wishing to embarrass him by too much talk, I told him to bring all he could to my father's house on Church Lane, two streets beyond the Naval Hospital. "If you have difficulty finding the house," I said, "ask for Magistrate Whitworth. I'm Miles Whitworth."

"I can't, sir," he said. "I'm fishing for Mr. Langman."

"Nonsense!" I said. "I'll pay you two shillings for a quart, and I'll bet your Mr. Langman, whoever he is, doesn't do as well for you!"

"No, sir," he said. "Mr. Langman pays a shilling for four quarts, but I made a contract with Mr. Langman. On the days I don't work for Mr. Penkethman, I catch whitebait for Mr. Langman." He twitched his trap from the water, swung it deftly within hand's reach, spilled another shower of whitebait into his burlap container; then looked apologetic as he lowered his trap to the water again.

"Penkethman!" I cried. "Penkethman of the Haymarket? The actor-manager?"

The boy gave me a look of approval. "Comedian, sir," he said. "He moved his players here this month—some from the Haymarket and some from Drury Lane."

I studied him more carefully. There was almost a look of elation about him, such as young girls so often have, but boys almost never. When he stood, he had an air of being about to rise on his toes. In short, he looked happy.

"Don't tell me," I said, "that you're an actor! Not at *your* age."

"Well, sir," the boy said, "I'm not exactly an actor, but Mr. Penkethman prints my name on the bills—Neal Butler. I'm only the prompter's call boy for Mr. Penkethman; but my father taught me how to write, so I write parts as well, forty-two lines to a length, and a penny for each one. Whatever I write, I remember, so I'm a quick study."

"How old are you, Neal?" I asked.

"Mr. Penkethman said I wasn't to tell my age," the boy said. "When I play female parts, he says it helps him with the rakes if we leave 'em guessing."

"Rakes?" I said. "Female parts? You play female parts?"

"Oh, yes, sir," the boy said. "There was an accident one night, and Mr. Penkethman let me play the page in Mr. Otway's *Orphan*." He proudly repeated, "I'm a quick study," and he had good reason to be proud, as I had learned at Oxford, when I spent long hours struggling to memorise wordy speeches from *The Fair Quaker of Deal*.

He snatched his fish trap from the water, found only two minnows flopping on it, gave me a look of pretended haughtiness that was vastly amusing; then dropped the trap back into the river. "Once he let me recite Mr. Cibber's epilogue about the Italian singers, and when I'm better at Italian, he'll let me do it again."

Female parts! A quick study! They helped him with the rakes! A penny for a length of forty-two lines! Mr. Otway! Mr. Cibber! Better at Italian! This boy, only a little more than half my age, was a real actor, even though his modesty prevented him from saying so.

"You're learning to speak Italian?" I asked.

"Oh, no, sir, just something that sounds like Italian." He placed his free hand on his breast, regarded me with candid wide eyes, and from his lips there gushed a stream of foreign syllables among which English words were dropped disconcertingly. The whole effect was foreign, but falsely foreign: the words seemed to have meaning; yet they meant nothing, and were merely excruciatingly droll, especially when, as if emphasising his strange flood of nonsense, he hauled up violently on his fish trap to find it brimming with whitebait. As he swung it sideways, to deposit the minnows on his square of burlap, one of the four cords broke: the basket slipped, and all his minnows spilled back into the brown Thames water.

"Step my vitals," Neal cried, and I knew he was quoting Otway. He dropped his broken trap beside him on the stone steps, and suddenly and surprisingly he held in his hand a long, thin-bladed knife, with which he went at the broken cord, trimming and splicing it as neatly as any bos'n on the river.

"Where'd you get that knife?" I asked. I held out my hand for it, but the boy made a quick movement and the knife vanished.

"It belonged to my father," he said. "My father says even big men'll shy away from a knife."

His reference to big men floored me, but somehow the mention of his father made his possession of that long thin knife seem excusable, if not exactly reasonable; so I forgot the knife and sat there beside him on the steps of Ballast Quay with the cool scent of the sea drifting past us, borne by the swift tide, which held the bows and the riding sails of all the brigs and schooners and frigates and ships-of-the-line, lying off the Naval Hospital, as steady and true as though carved and mathematically placed there by one of the hospital's ancient pensioners.

Neal's father, he said, had once been a strolling player.

Then, when Neal's mother died, his father enlisted in the St. George's Light Dragoons. Later his father joined the Navy because he thought it offered more opportunities for prize money. After he had been wounded in an engagement, he was admitted to the Naval Hospital, where his scanty allowance barely enabled him to buy tobacco for himself and supply Neal with a weekly two shillings on which to live in a room on Fisher's Alley.

Thus, Neal said, he counted himself fortunate to receive seven shillings a week from Mr. Penkethman, even though that pay was three weeks in arrears.

When the tide was wrong, so that the fops and rakes couldn't sail down from London to Greenwich and sail back again to London the same night, the theatre was closed and he was free to fish for Mr. Langman. On theatre days he fished for himself and turned over his catch to Mr. Penkethman's players, who repaid him by teaching him how to walk and enunciate and have stage manners.

There was something about the way he said the words "fops" and "rakes" that made me wonder what he or his father had endured at their hands; but when I asked him that question, he said abruptly that the whitebait had stopped running. Would I, he asked me, take him as far as Watling Stairs? When I said Yes, he neatly slid the dinghy off the step without any help from me. Watling Stairs, Neal said, was where Langman daily went to collect the catches of his fisherboys.

I saw Neal meet Langman—a swarthy tall man with a dubious half-smile on one side of his mouth; and I never dreamed, as I watched him empty Neal's little bag of fish into a larger sack and give him a few coins from a leather wallet, that I'd ever see that troublesome man again.

Chapter Two

THROUGH ALL my boyhood and youth Greenwich and its waterfront had been my stamping ground.

Everything about the river was familiar and fascinating to me—the merchantmen and ships of war that moved perpetually or lay at anchor all around the tip of the Isle of Dogs and up past Deptford on the one hand and down past Woolwich on the other: the constant movement of watermen bearing gentlemen on an outing to see the beauties of the palaces; the watermen's hoarse crying of "Oars, Sculls! Sculls, Oars!"; the sloops, loaded with brightly dressed men and women, who, screaming like seagulls, waved at me as I passed; the towering three-deckers, with their carved and gilded stern galleries and their bright red sides: their fluttering lines of newly washed sailormen's togs: the never ending passage up and down gangplanks of women and hucksters, wives, trulls, boatmen, visitors: the vessels battered from long voyages beating up to their anchorages; those setting off for unknown ports with new canvas gleaming from their squared yards and noisy with the shouts of angry mates and drunken sailors.

They were sights and sounds to which I looked forward all through each long winter, when I crouched beside my sea-coal fire in Christ Church, reading and forever reading those tiresome books that had been preserved for generations in the Bodleian's underground caverns.

Greenwich being what it was, I never defied my father's

orders to stay indoors after dark; for sailors, whether King's men or merchant seamen, were a scurvy lot, and one who ventured on the streets at night too often found himself in the grip of a press gang, beaten black and blue, stripped of his clothes, and thrown into a vermin-ridden cable tier so far below the water line that his cries were as nothing compared with the gurgle of the tide against the bow.

Greenwich, the life of the river and particularly the life of the theatre, concerning which Neal Butler had spoken so familiarly, was heaven to me by comparison with Oxford.

My professors, my tutors, seemed to me like drone bees, living on some invisible college pollen; whereas actors from Drury Lane and the Haymarket, greatest of England's theatres, by contrast were truly alive.

Even at Oxford I suffered with those actors from the influx of Italian opera singers, who squalled so loudly as to threaten the existence of English players whose education in squalling was neglected.

The truth was, I was stage-struck. Aristophanes to me was a long-dead shadow who had written about frogs; but Penkethman, known by reputation to all of us in the Buskin Club, was Pinky, a genius who now was doubly a genius for having conceived the idea of coming to Greenwich for the summer with scenery such as had been first invented at Christ Church by Inigo Jones, and with all the machines, devices and appurtenances necessary to cause sprites to fly through the air and demons to rise from the earth.

When, that night, I guardedly told my father about Neal Butler, I emphasised his association with Penkethman's players more than I did his aptitude as a catcher of whitebait or his association with Langman; for my father said, "Pah!" and immediately used the very words that Neal himself had used, "Fops and rakes!"

"This boy isn't a fop or a rake," I said. "He's no more a fop or a rake than I was at his age—or than I am now."

"He's an actor, isn't he?" my father asked, putting his hands on the table and thrusting his head towards me, as he did when he'd caught a witness in an outrageous evasion of the truth. "That's what actors are forever representing, isn't it?" he demanded. "Pint-sized clowns in tatters and tarnished gold lace, making faces and laughing like hyenas at their damned dull witlessness. Overdressed harridans with breasts half exposed, pretending to be Sir Courtly Nice's mistress, or aping a droopy doll, all prunes and prisms, fainting if a man says, 'Split me'! Players with perukes two feet high and scented with pulvillio and essence, screeching and squalling, 'A harse! A harse! My kingdom for a harse!' Otway had the right word for 'em! Punks, my dear Miles, corrupting the morals and principles of the youth!"

"But, sir," I protested, "this boy isn't that sort. If I had a brother, I'd be proud if he were like Neal Butler: looked like him: behaved like him. He's as uncorrupted as can be!"

I told him how the boy had shied away from me—not frightened exactly, but wary, as if he'd had occasion to question the motives of someone.

"I liked him the moment I saw him," I said, "and so would you, unless I'm greatly mistaken. There's something about him—something that makes you sure he'd be good at anything to which he turned his hand. Even the white-bait seemed to be attracted to him. He had a little trap with the edges bent up—a sort of wire platter with a cord at each corner. The four cords were lashed to a larger cord, and the large cord was fastened to a short pole. I think it must have been instinct that told him when to pull that trap! He certainly couldn't see the whitebait—at least I couldn't. The water was brown, as it always is when the tide first turns. I think he might become a great actor."

My father snorted. "He'll probably grow up to rewrite

Shakespeare, like so many damned fools—Dryden and Tate and D'Urfey, for example!"

"Or like Cibber," I said. "The *Tatler* seems to like Cibber, and the Butler boy mentioned Otway with a good deal of respect. Was Otway a damned fool?"

"No," my father said, "not when he wasn't rewriting *Romeo and Juliet*. He was no Shakespeare, any more than Shakespeare was, but he makes people talk like people instead of gingerbread mannikins. Come to think of it, so does Vanbrugh."

He pulled off his tie-wig to rub his short grey hair with an impatient hand. "I've no objection to buying this boy's whitebait—have 'em every day for a week if you'd like; but don't for God's sake take a child's opinions about the stage and about actors. They're punks, all of 'em, just as Otway said. Punks, my boy!"

He cogitated for a moment. "Well, not all of 'em exactly. I saw Betterton as Falstaff once, and damn near died laughing!"

I left my dinghy at the Hospital Yard the following afternoon with no thought of Neal Butler except that, with the tide flowing an hour earlier, he had probably netted enough whitebait to let me have as much as I wanted.

He hadn't though. When I caught a barge to Deptford Steps, Neal was where I'd seen him the day before, and on the step above him, in the blue-sleeved summer waistcoat and blue yarn socks of a pensioner of the Naval Hospital, was a lopsided man with a long yellow moustache and clumps of yellow fuzz protruding so far below the round, flat-topped black hat that they covered his ears. His look of being overloaded on one side was due to the way he carried his right shoulder somewhat lower than his left, as if he were about to reach down with his right hand and haul up an anchor.

Neal gave me that quick smile of his, but before he could speak, the lopsided man leaned forward, looked almost fiercely at me and spoke my name.

"Yes," I said, "I'm Miles Whitworth, and you must be Mr. Butler."

"Swede, not 'mister,'" the yellow-haired man said. "Swede Butler. Moses was my name; Neal's too; but they called me Swede because of my hair. I never thought much of Moses. There must have been something wrong with him if it took him forty years to get the Children of Israel out of the Wilderness. Neal dropped the Moses because Penkethman told him to."

That name-changing habit of actor-managers had often touched me on the raw. They never had the brains to understand that the actor makes the name; not the name the actor. Moses Butler—Neal Butler—what's the difference! It's the inner fire that an audience sees and feels: not the label by which a bailiff knows him!

"I wonder what Anne Bracegirdle's real name is?" I asked Swede.

"I won't even try to guess," Swede said, "I only want to know who my boy takes up with."

"I don't wonder," I said. "Your boy has a knack for catching whitebait. He has a way with him, too."

"Aye," Swede said. "He tells me your father's a magistrate. He tells me you're a member of Christ Church, *in statu pupillari*." He paused, as if surprised at his use of the Latin phrase: then again stared at me almost fiercely. "And he says he thinks you're an actor."

"That's putting it too strongly, Swede," I said. "We have a club at Christ Church—the Buskin Club. We read plays, and once or twice we've staged one in the Hall; but I hope to write 'em rather than recite 'em."

"Good!" Swede said. "You need fish to fry and I need the advice of someone who isn't an actor. I've been an actor myself, and I wouldn't take an actor's advice any more than I'd take a sailor's. Do you suppose your father would trade a bit of advice for some of Neal's whitebait?"

"I'm sure he would," I said. "He'll take to Neal just as quickly as I did."

Swede put a big hand on his son's shoulders. "Pick up your fishes, boy. We'll go see Mr. Whitworth. Perhaps he can work out a future for you—one that won't leave you rolling in a gutter or living like a beggar in a naval hospital."

Chapter Three

JOHN DEAN was an old friend of my family, a sea captain from Twickenham, a little upriver from London, but he loaded and unloaded his cargoes at Greenwich, and always came to our house, before starting on a cruise, to have vessel and cargo insured. I know my father thought highly of him, and frequently ventured a moderate sum, which Dean would invest in coffee or tea or spices, thus providing education-money to be used by me at Oxford.

Behind our house on Church Lane was a walled arbour from which we caught glimpses of the river; and my father and Captain Dean were sitting there when I brought Neal and Swede Butler to the garden.

When Captain Dean saw us, he folded a paper and got up to go, but my father stopped him. "Unless I'm mistaken," my father said, "Miles has found us some whitebait, and we'll have it for supper, with pickle sauce. You'll get no dish to touch it on your *Nottingham* Galley nor in any tavern, for that matter. Maybe, after you've let out your belt a fathom or two, you'll stretch that insurance by a hundred pounds or so."

Dean, a large calm man, smiled at us, and settled back comfortably in his chair. "Whitebait!" he exclaimed. "I'd run a mile a day for a platterful, but I've got a mate who cheats fisherboys out of nearly all they can net—makes a small fortune selling it to taverns for ten times what he pays for it—so there's never any left over for me. Yes,

I'll stay with pleasure, Charles, and you ought to put your chopped pickle in sour cream if you want a proper sauce."

I shook hands with Captain Dean, and my father got up to look at Neal Butler, who made him the politest of bows and held out his poke of whitebait-filled sacking.

When my father fumbled in his pocket, Swede Butler stepped forward and touched his hat. "Sir," he said, "my boy and I ask you to accept it in place of a fee."

"This is Swede, Neal's father," I explained. "He asked me whether you'd trade him some advice in return for Neal's catch. He wants the advice for Neal. Neal's a good boy, and I told Swede you would."

"You did, did you?" my father asked. "That's the value you put on my advice, is it? A sack of minnows?"

"No," I said. "I thought you might earn two people's affection, and some entertainment as well—if Neal recites his Italian epilogue for you. That's fairly good pay, isn't it?"

My father put his hand on Neal's shoulder. "I'm mighty pleased with your whitebait," he said. "I'll ask you to take it to the kitchen and give it to Mrs. Buddage. She's our cook. She'll rinse your piece of sacking, so you can have it to use again. Oh, and could you remember to tell her that Captain Dean says to make the sauce out of chopped pickle and sour cream?"

"And just a little chopped onion," Captain Dean said.

"Sour cream, chopped pickle, chopped onion," Neal repeated, and somehow he enunciated the words in such a way as to make my mouth water.

He marched obediently toward the kitchen, and even his manner of walking, though unaffected, was a pleasure to the eye.

"Quite a boy," my father said to Swede.

"Yes, sir," Swede said. "I don't know where he gets it.

Maybe from his mother. She'd have been a player herself, and a good one, too, if a gallery hadn't fallen on her when we were playing the Angel Inn—Duke of Norfolk's servants, sir. I couldn't bring up a baby, Mr. Whitworth, so I left Neal with his grampa and granma outside of Norwich and took to the Army. Then I tried the Navy and got to be captain of the foretop on the *Minerva* till a French musket ball caught me in the shoulder and put me in the hospital yonder." He nodded in the general direction of the palaces on the waterfront.

"What's your problem, Mr. Butler?" my father asked.

"Well, sir, here it is," Swede said. "This boy has something I've never put to proper use. I've taught him to read and write: he's the quickest study I ever saw, and I've seen some good ones. If I could be in the theatre with him, I wouldn't mind so much; but I'm too banged up to be any good to a young man like Penkethman. So Neal's going it alone in the theatre, paid about half the time if he's lucky, and nothing much ahead of him but getting to be a beggar, depending on benefit performances, which is charity, no matter how you look at it. I know the end of it—work a fifth of the year, and never save a penny: get spoiled by the women and the men, too, and wind up in rags or drudging for some rat like Langman."

Captain Dean leaned forward. "What's that? What about Langman?"

"Oh," Swede said, "he's a mate on one of these merchant vessels. She's laid up for repairs. He weaves nets for boys to catch whitebait with: then he collects 'em and sells 'em and makes a good thing out of it."

"Why, that's my mate," Captain Dean said. "That's Christopher Langman!" To my father he explained, "He beats anything I ever saw! Every minute of the day he's figuring how to make money, and he doesn't care how he does it."

"Sounds caddish to me," my father said carelessly. "Why don't you get rid of him?"

"The truth is," Captain Dean said hesitantly, "I can't."

"Since when," my father asked, "has a captain been unable to get rid of a mate when his vessel's in port? I can see how it might be a little difficult if you're halfway across the Atlantic, but you aren't. You're seizing spars, or fishing ropes or sheets—whatever it is you nautical people fish and seize—and you'll be lucky to get to sea inside of another two months."

"I know," Captain Dean said, "but it's a long story."

"Well, give me a hint," my father said. "I'm interested in this Langman and his whitebait ventures. First thing we know, he'll be making it into one of these stock companies —selling shares on 'Change Alley and ruining thousands just like the stock jobbers. How does it happen you can't get rid of Langman, John?"

"Well," Dean said, "he sailed on one of Woodes Rogers' ships two years ago."

"Woodes Rogers! Why, he's a buccaneer," my father said quickly.

"No, no," Dean said. "Not a buccaneer, Charles! He's a privateer. Privateers carry government commissions, and a tenth of their takings go to the state."

"Oh, don't try to tell me the law," my father said. "I know what the law is, and most of these privateers are nothing but buccaneers, no matter what the law says."

"Well, I don't know about that," Captain Dean said, "but I do know that Langman says he sailed with Woodes Rogers; and around the Gulf of Guayaquil, when Rogers was busy capturing some footling town or other, Langman went off in a small boat with a few of his seamen, came across a smart-looking galley and captured her. Then somehow he was separated from Rogers, couldn't find him again, and decided the safest thing he could do was sail home.

He had no money, and his men hadn't been paid, so he hunted up my brother Jasper and offered to sell him the galley at a bargain, provided he was retained as first mate."

He stirred uneasily beneath my father's scrutiny.

"Sounds fishy to me," my father said. "What happened to the crew that was in the galley when she was taken?"

Captain Dean looked more uncomfortable. "I asked him that, and he said they just went ashore, all but two men that he persuaded Jasper to hire."

Neal Butler came back from the kitchen to stand beside his father.

My father snorted, raised incredulous eyes to the sky; then spoke to Neal. "What did Mrs. Buddage say, young man?"

"She said Captain Dean came here just in the nick of time," Neal said. "She said she'd just been thinking of making some cheese out of her sour cream." He sounded exactly like Mrs. Buddage.

"Good," my father said, "good. Now, Neal, this Langman you're working for: did you undertake to work for him for a certain length of time?"

"Yes, sir," Neal said, "I promised, when he gave me the trap, to fish for him every day when I had nothing else to do. He pays me threepence a quart."

"You know that's not a fair price?" my father asked.

"Yes, sir," Neal said. "If I had time to peddle 'em around, I could get more; but if I took out time to peddle them, I wouldn't be able to catch enough."

"Yes," my father said, "there's something in what you say, but I'm a magistrate and I herewith declare your contract with Mr. Langman to be null and void. I have friends who'll be glad to pay a shilling a quart for them, and that's what I'll pay you—a shilling a quart and guarantee to dispose of all you catch. Understand? As for Langman,

I'll give him a talking-to. He sounds to me like a slippery customer."

My father turned to Swede. "Now, Swede," he said, "does it make you easier in your mind to know your boy's having no further dealings with Langman?"

"Yes, sir," Swede said, "that'll help, but I'd like to get him out of the theatre. When Penkethman finishes with Greenwich, he'll take his players back to London; and if Neal goes with them—well, Mr. Whitworth, he's too young to be around a theatre. I know what it means. He'll buy a periwig and become a fop—learn to drawl and take snuff: strut and cock his cravat strings. Ten to one he'll go to the Groom Porter's and run into debt over the turn of a dirty deuce."

"How do you feel about it, Neal?" my father asked.

"Don't ask him," Swede said hastily. "He thinks these actors are angels right out of heaven. He can already walk like 'em and talk like 'em, and the only thing he doesn't yet do, thank God, is *think* like 'em. He thinks like a human being, and I don't want him spoiled."

"It's understandable," I told my father. "There's something about the theatre that's mighty exciting."

"It can be mighty destructive, too," my father said. "What are the plays all about? Whoring, drinking, gaming! What are the manners of the fine ladies you see represented? Those of the tavern and the brothel, without relation to life or art!"

He turned to Neal. "See here, my boy: Miles tells me you recited one of Mr. Cibber's epilogues. Will you do it for us now?"

Neal said quickly that he would, but that he'd like a costume. My father went into the house and I heard him calling to Mrs. Buddage to bring him a shawl and a soiled tablecloth. How Neal wrapped those two pieces of cloth so deftly about him, I couldn't see, but he turned in a moment from a young boy to a girl, wide-eyed, pleading, provocative, looking at us over his shoulder as he spoke, and smoothing the tablecloth over his narrow hips.

I can't remember Cibber's lines; but the verses told how, eventually, English actors would be forced to imitate Italians, and it's impossible to reproduce the strange quarter English, quarter Latin and half imitation Italian that followed the line, "I give you raptures while I squall despair." There was something overwhelmingly ludicrous about this meaningless twaddle, so earnestly delivered, and with such coy and fetching gestures. My father snorted and Captain Dean said, "Haw!" but Neal seemed not to hear them.

"'If this won't do,'" he quoted, coquettishly touching his fingertips to his lips, "'I'll try another touch—half French, some English, and a spice of Dutch'"... and immediately he broke into another utterly meaningless song that made no sense although it seemed constantly on the verge of doing so.

When it came to an end, all too soon, my father slapped his leg delightedly, Captain Dean's face was red from repressed laughter. Swede was the only one who didn't laugh.

"I think I see what you mean," my father said to Swede, as I helped Neal fold the shawl and the tablecloth. "I see what you mean. It isn't easy to divert a talent like that. It isn't even safe. If I were you—if Neal were a few years older —I'd advise you not to try to do it, but as I say, I think I know exactly how you feel."

He seemed to think aloud. "It's London you're afraid of. Now suppose Neal had a profession to support him. We've had some good professional men in the theatre and they've done well. Take Sir John Vanbrugh. He was an architect. When Miles goes up to Oxford, I might be able to use Neal.

He'd be a help to me writing briefs—writing insurance. What would you say to that, Swede?"

"I'd be forever in your debt, Mr. Whitworth," Swede said.

"Yes," my father said. "Well, that's one way of looking at it, so if you've been uneasy in your mind, you'll probably feel better. All of us can keep an eye on Neal till it's time for him to go to work for me in the autumn—and the work he's doing now is training of a sort: teaches him how to hold a tea-cup—how to seem to be at ease when he isn't."

When Swede looked dubious, my father seized his hand and shook it, tapped Neal lightly on the shoulder, and said, "See them to the door, Miles."

To Neal he added, "I'll remember to speak to Langman, so don't forget to bring us whitebait whenever you can."

Captain Dean got to his feet. "Just a moment," he said. "I've been thinking about that mate of mine, and about Swede's experience on the *Minerva*. How do you spend your days in the Naval Hospital, Swede?"

Swede laughed. "I spend 'em in the hardest kind of work, Captain. Doing nothing. Describing my aches and pains to others who have worse aches and pains."

"*Do* you have aches and pains?" Captain Dean asked.

"Everybody who does nothing has aches and pains."

"You don't look to me as if you had as many aches and pains as any one of my crew has. How'd you like to ship with me on the *Nottingham* Galley? I'd be glad to have you along, just to have the benefit of your advice. I'd sign you on as first lieutenant. We've got ten guns and a gunner who contrived to blow his eyes full of powder."

Swede looked from Captain Dean to Neal and back again. "Why," he said slowly, "I think that might be a good thing if my boy's going to help Mr. Whitworth. I felt like being a pensioner before my shoulder healed, but I don't feel like it any more. I think it would be a good thing all around if Neal had a first lieutenant as a father instead of a pensioner."

I thought, as I led Neal and his father to the street, how odd it was that, because the tide had thrust my dinghy against Deptford Steps, the lives of two people had been altered—and greatly for the better, I earnestly hoped. How many people's lives that tide had altered, I couldn't dream. We never know: we never know!

Chapter Four

THAT WAS the beginning for my father, as well as for Captain Dean and me, of a course in the most popular of London's plays. Penkethman's playhouse was next door to the Hospital Tavern, and I'm bound to say Penkethman did well as a manager, for he went out of his way to add to his Drury Lane and Haymarket regulars, bringing in promising drifters from strolling companies like those in Dublin, Bath and Bristol. The plays he presented were held to be the best, and certainly Penkethman knew how to read his lines in such a way as to make words of no consequence seem irresistibly droll.

The curtain rose at five or six o'clock three times a week, and for a guinea apiece, the three of us had tickets that entitled us to see twenty-one plays. We by no means saw twenty-one, for our playgoing came to a sudden and unexpected end with the production of *The Walking Statue* on the last Saturday in July, the twenty-ninth; but until that day we talked theatre as though we ourselves were actors: of Penkethman as Daniel in *Oroonoko*, of Penkethman as Calico in *Sir Courtly Nice*, with Powell playing Sir Courtly: of Penkethman as Squib in *Tunbridge Walks*, of Penkethman as the painfully comical shepherd in *The Libertine Destroyed:* of Mrs. Kent's artistry as Caliban in *The Tempest* and of Mrs. Baker's beauty as Miranda: of the vast promise of Lacy Ryan in *The Fair Quaker of Deal:* of Penkethman as

Fribble in *Epsom Wells*, and Spiller in *The Emperor of the Moon* and *The Recruiting Officer*.

If I were an artist, I could have drawn pictures by the score of those play nights in Greenwich: of wherries, barges and galleys unloading their tumultuous, half-drunken pleasure-seekers at Kings' Head Stairs while the hot July sun was still high enough to make the massed vessels in the river stand out sharply in black and white, and while the fishermen along the quays were still turbulent and noisy: of Londoners, both men and women, outside the doors of the innumerable Greenwich taverns, some standing, some sitting at little tables because the taverns were so crowded, each with a dish of whitebait and a tankard of ale before him, and each one tossing crisp morsels into himself with a great show of daintiness and refinement.

Even the sounds and odours of Greenwich on those play nights were fascinating—over everything the savoury fragrance of the whitebait: and in the foreground the peculiar mangled gabbling of Londoners, who think of everyone beyond the sound of Bow Bells as being half-witless and speaking a language incomprehensible to gentlefolk: the penetrating perfumes of the silk-clad playgoers: the squealing of orange and apple women who pushed through the crowds, crying their wares and reminding all hearers that there was nothing like an orange for throwing at actors: the common sailors in blue and white striped trousers and coats always too big or too small, and caps made from pieces of stocking: the naval officers with tangled golden swabs on their shoulders, and half-moon hats the size and shape of the shallops that are forever running errands between barges and docks.

To me the most memorable of play-night pictures were those of the playhouse itself—the shouting, catcalling, orange-throwing roisterers in the gallery, the subdued and honourable citizens of Greenwich in the pit, the affected ladies in the boxes above the stage, and the incredible fops grouped on either side of the stage itself, and frequently all across the front of the stage, so that occupants of the pit had difficulty in seeing the movements of the actors. Some nights those wretched fops formed a background entirely around the rear of the stage, if the play was one that had made a reputation for itself at Drury Lane.

Some of these fops became as well known to us, by sight, as Penkethman, Powell, Spiller or Neal. All of them affected little mannerisms and great ones, too, for that matter. Their wigs without exception were enormous, sometimes tinted in strange blues and reds. Their speech seemed to be marked with peculiar sibilances and lisps; their gestures, as when they tossed back the lace from their wrists, or took snuff with a flourish such as a dancer makes when she poises herself for a pirouette, were airy and womanly. They were forever making play with perfumed handkerchiefs, touching them to their lips, or whisking imaginary nothings from their sleeves or waistcoats.

Sometimes they travelled in pairs, and sometimes singly, but even in the latter case they made a pretence of being disdainfully amused by those about them, bowing here: bowing there: staring out at those of us in the pit through quizzing glasses, as at animals in cages.

We had names for them—Sugar-leg for one who was constantly admiring his not too slender ankle: Jackdaw for one who was constantly bursting into cackles of laughter: Tintoretto for a little man with painted cheeks and lips who stood motionless for long periods of time, staring, so far as we could see, at nothing, his face a mask that never moved.

Only twice in all the nights we watched Mr. Penkethman's players in their antics did we see Neal on the stage, and on both occasions he recited that epilogue of Cibber's about the Italian opera singers, reading his lines in a way that brought

smiles to the faces of those who listened, and downright
guffaws when he lapsed from his lines into that queer
running outburst of imitation Italian. On each occasion he
was got up in the same costume: a blue gown, voluminous
around the hips, with a pointed stomacher, a high collar
that rose almost to the top of his head in black, and on his
wig of auburn curls a little cap that looked as though made
of pearls.

Mr. Penkethman, he told us, had begged the cap from
some lady of title, for the especial purpose of being worn
by the person who recited this epilogue. His youth and the
soft brown of his face gave him the look of an Italian
beauty; and when, at the close of the epilogue, he gathered
up those full skirts and curtsied deep to the audience, he
was as pretty a picture as a Rembrandt portrait of a young
girl, glowing with reflected light—as pretty, surely, as
Anne Gracegirdle was supposed to be. I found it difficult
to believe that he was the same boy who had pulled whitebait from the Thames with his little four-cornered trap and
had shied away from my outstretched hand on the afternoon
when I had first seen him.

Sometimes, after the play, we waited for Neal and he
walked home with us to tell us some of the many things
concerning which my father, both as a magistrate and as
an interested human being, was profoundly curious. He
probed into Neal's mind to discover how some of the plays
we had seen had impressed him, and we soon learned that
allusions which seemed offensive to my father had appeared
to Neal to be simply amusing, or just so many words written
by an author and recited by an actor in order to further the
action of the play.

"I suppose it's amusing in *Venice Preserv'd*," my father
asked politely, "when an actor says, ' In what whore's lap
have you been lolling? Give but an Englishman his whore
and ease, beef and a sea coal fire, he's yours for ever.'"

B

"Sir," Neal said, "that was a Frenchman said that. The answer was 'Frenchman, you are saucy!'" He seemed puzzled that my father should have questioned the speech.

We discovered how Penkethman's players had built up their wardrobes by begging discarded gowns and gentlemen's silks from such people of high station as were fascinated by theatrical matters—as so many of them were.

We learned how benefits were arranged to increase the pay of various actors—benefits to which the actors themselves sold tickets, running after the carriages of rich folks, begging them to subscribe, or calling at houses to sell tickets as a fishmonger might solicit patronage.

Such a benefit, Neal said, might bring as much as one hundred guineas to an actor, and make all the difference between a season without profit, or one that would let him live in comfort for two months or more if he were so unfortunate as to be unable to obtain work.

On one subject he was silent. He recognised, from our descriptions, the fops who had caught our attention by their posturings and grimacings as they stood in the stage entrances. He nodded understandingly at our imitations of Sugar-leg and Jackdaw; but when my father described the mask-like face of the little man we called Tintoretto, Neal's face and eyes were expressionless. He seemed almost to have stopped breathing.

We found out nothing at all from Neal when we first mentioned Tintoretto to him; but we learned a little more —not much, but more than enough—about him on the twenty-ninth of July, when Penkethman's company performed *The Gamester* and, as "a cup of tea," threw in a second play, *The Walking Statue*, with the gibberish-interlarded epilogue which Neal recited to appreciative laughter. *The Walking Statue* had been a great favourite at Drury Lane and was equally so in Greenwich. The words "a cup of tea," we knew from Neal, had come to be actors' slang for anything likeable. Tintoretto, obviously, was not Neal's "cup of tea."

Probably my father and Captain Dean and I would have waited for Neal, the night of July 29th, and walked him home with us if it hadn't been for that epilogue, which made it necessary for Neal to get out of his costume and make-up. Unfortunately the night was warm and all three of us were eager for a bottle of chilled claret; so home we went.

When we got there, we did something we seldom did— opened our downstairs windows. This was a dangerous practice in Greenwich, as it was in any naval town, because of the almost unbelievable number of thieves, streetwalkers, wandering Jews, irresponsible sailors and light-fingered dockyard workers who roamed the streets at all hours of the night, alert to snatch anything from an unguarded room, provided only that the anything was small enough to be lifted through an open window.

We sat there in the semi-dark, listening to Captain Dean's comments on his *Nottingham* and his forthcoming voyage to America. Every sea captain considers his own vessel somehow superior to every other vessel, no matter how much larger; and I could sense how Captain Dean felt because of knowing how much finer my own dinghy was, in sailing qualities and clean lines, than larger shallops and even some yachts.

Since the *Nottingham* was a galley, Captain Dean explained, she was fitted with oars for rowing when necessary, and with guns so that she could fight if forced to do so, and she was faster than a running vessel, which is fast enough to sail without convoy. That meant she was designed to make quick voyages with small cargoes.

Behind Captain Dean's talk I was conscious of all the night-sounds of Greenwich—the bells from the vessels in

the river; the distant shouting from taverns; the clatter of
hoofs: the rattling of wheels of after-theatre carriages on
the cobbles of the river front—when suddenly I heard something I didn't like at all. Captain Dean and my father heard
it too, and liked it as little as I; for their heads turned
slowly and questioningly toward each other.

What we heard was half-way between a gasp and a gurgle,
as though someone had started to shout, and had been
prevented by a gash of liquid in his throat.

But if that sound was repeated, it was lost in all the other
noises that made Greenwich, in summer, so difficult a place
in which to sleep.

I pulled the curtain to one side, leaning from the window
to listen. I thought I saw a blob of darkness on our front
steps. When I stared at it half-sideways, to see it more
clearly, I decided it was nothing—there was no movement
from it—and then, suddenly, I heard a long-drawn, quivering
inhalation, such as one might make after holding his breath
until his lungs are on the verge of bursting.

I ran to the front door and drew it open.

Neal Butler fell into the hallway as if he had been leaning
against the door.

I pulled him to his feet. His appearance horrified me.

"What's the matter with you? You look sick!"

I took him by the arm and turned him toward the front
room. My father and Captain Dean were on their feet,
staring at us, and Neal's appearance led my father to hurry
to the windows, draw them down and close the shutters.

He struck a light, and helped me put Neal in a chair.

We saw it was no ordinary sickness that troubled Neal,
but some sort of mental disturbance that had left him half-
conscious. He seemed unwilling to look at either of us. His
breathing was quick and shallow, with a deep shuddering
breath at unexpected intervals.

"What happened to you, Neal?" my father asked. "Speak up! We're your friends."

When Neal didn't answer, my father reached for a claret bottle and filled a glass. "Here," he said, "drink this and tell us what happened to you."

When Neal continued to stare into space, my father grasped his chin, and put the glass to his lips. Neal choked; then drew two of those long, shuddering sighs.

"He was waiting for me after the play," he said flatly.

"Who was?" my father asked.

"The one with the white face," Neal said. "The painted one."

"You mean the one we call Tintoretto?" my father asked.

Neal nodded. "He pulled at me—pulled at my clothes. I tried to walk around him so to get to you and Miles."

"This man—this Tintoretto. He'd pulled at you before?" my father asked.

"I had that knife," Neal said. "That one I'd sharpened. When we were almost at your house, I ran. He ran after me. When he caught up with me, I showed him the knife. He pushed it away. He—he laughed! That white face! That painted fish mouth! I never thought the knife would go into him so quick—so smooth!"

For the first time he looked directly at me and at my father. "When he fell over against me, I was glad I did it. I had to do it. You'd have done it if you'd been me! Then I was afraid."

My father put his hand on Neal's shoulder. "Had Tintoretto ever done this before?" Neal seemed to have run out of words. My father shook him. "I asked you whether he'd ever done this to you before to-night."

Neal gulped. "No, sir. The first time I recited Mr. Cibber's epilogue I could hardly get past him in the wings. He squeezed me, and my hand smelled of perfume. I couldn't get around him."

"Listen carefully," my father said. "Do you think others saw him squeeze you, as you put it?"

Neal nodded and swallowed hard.

Captain Dean got to his feet. "Let's see about this," he said. "Charles, you sit here with Neal while Miles and I go out on the street for a few minutes. Neal, you're not to move! Understand?"

Neal nodded.

Captain Dean and I went out on to the street and turned toward the river. We found Tintoretto near London Street, between our house and the park. He was huddled against a hedge, a crumpled shadow of a man.

"The man's drunk," Captain Dean said loudly. "This is no place for him! We'll put him where he can sleep it off. You take him under one arm, Miles, and I'll take him by the other. We'll walk him toward the park."

When we pulled him to his feet, his head hung slack on his shoulders, and even in the dim light his painted face had the blank look of a clown's. The handle of Neal's knife still protruded from the black silk front of his coat. His garments had an abominably musky odour.

"Take out that knife, Miles," Captain Dean whispered. "We can't leave that in him. Toss it into your yard. We'll pick it up in the morning—if we can't find it to-night."

We supported Tintoretto draggingly toward the park, and it seemed to me that we did it so successfully that anyone who saw us would think we were merely doing a Christian act for a gentleman who had been oversedulous with the port.

At least, that's what I thought until two men came toward us from the direction of the park. Then I knew that Tintoretto's body was limper than any mere drunken man could be or could look.

As they drew nearer to us, Captain Dean muttered, "Better do some acting!"

He took Tintoretto around the waist and hung him, doubled up, over his arm; then bent over him solicitously. I bent over too and made retching sounds.

The two men halted beside us. One said, "Want any help?" I thought I recognised the voice of Lacy Ryan, one of Penkethman's young players.

"No, indeed," Captain Dean said heartily. To Tintoretto's body he said cheerfully, "Try hard! Better out than in." Again I uttered retching sounds and made play with my handkerchief.

The two men went slowly on, laughing; and when they were dim in the darkness, we carried Tintoretto to a wooded spot and left him there.

I was sweating, and with good reason, because I had no way of knowing how much the eyes of a keen young man like Lacy Ryan might have seen.

"Well," my father said, when we told him that Tintoretto was dead with a knife wound under his ribs, and that Lacy Ryan and another man had spoken to us when we were getting rid of the body, "there's nothing like an occurrence of this nature to help a man make up his mind. And there's one sure thing about it: we've got to get Miles and Neal Butler out of here before somebody starts asking too many questions."

He looked at Captain Dean. "How long before you'll be ready to sail, John?"

"Two weeks, maybe," Captain Dean said. "Our cordage is at Gravesend, ready to go aboard, but I've done nothing about the butter and cheese. I'm only taking on a little: just enough for a quick turnover in Portsmouth or Boston —Portsmouth probably."

"Get 'em in Donegal," my father said promptly. "Go north-about around Scotland and Ireland: come down to the island of Aran, and just beyond it you'll see the red

cliffs of Donegal. The best butter and cheese in the world
come from those fields around Donegal Bay. They're the
greenest fields you'll ever find. I'll tell you what to do,
John: drop down to Gravesend on the early tide to-morrow
morning, and pick up your butter and cheese when you get
to Ireland."

When Captain Dean started to protest, my father jumped
up to wag a magisterial finger before his nose. "Now listen,
John! I can't have Miles mixed up in anything like this,
and if Lacy Ryan recognised him, he certainly *will* be
mixed up in it. So now I've told you what to do, I'll tell
you what *I'll* do: I'll provide enough money to double your
purchases, the profit from my part to be divided between
us.

"I make this stipulation, though: Miles must go along
as supercargo, and you'll make Neal your apprentice. He's
a good boy, John. We can't let him start off in life with
a murder charge against him—and that's what it'll look
like to most London magistrates, no matter how it looks
to us."

"It seems to me," Captain Dean said, "that this killing
was justifiable."

"Bah!" my father cried. "Justifiable homicide: most
dangerous thing in the world! What *is* justifiable homicide
of a private nature? It's the defence against force of a man's
person, house or goods. Ah! But how do you interpret the
word 'justifiable'? Put all the judges in Britain in one
room, and ask 'em to interpret a homicide you consider
justifiable, and they'd argue for years! Take it to court, and
Lord Itchpate, C.J., would press a bunch of flowers to his
nose and mumble that we are certainly not prepared to
suggest that necessity should in every case be a justification.
And what, to the mind of a learned judge with his nose in
a bouquet, is necessity, for God's sake? Not the same thing
that it would be to Neal Butler, harried, horrified and

frightened half out of his wits by the insane maulings of a —a creature so frenzied that he impales himself upon a knife. No, no! I can hear Itchpate now!

"'It is therefore our duty to declare that the prisoner's act in this case was wilful murder, that the facts as stated are no legal justification of the homicide '—and the honourable Court, in a hurry to down two dozen oysters and a bottle of port, would briskly proceed to pass sentence of death upon the prisoner! No, John: you do as I tell you! Get the *Nottingham* to sea with Swede and Neal and Miles aboard, and with no loss of time!"

Captain Dean nodded thoughtfully. "Why not? With Neal aboard, Swede will work twice as hard. It'll let me have decent company aft, in place of Langman. It gives me an excuse to send Langman forward with the men. Your idea's a good one, Charles. You won't make a fortune on the venture, but we ought to clear enough to take on a good load of salt codfish in America. It smells, but it's a sure seller in England or France."

"Well, now, look," my father said. "There's a lot to be done to-night." He laughed ruefully. "Doesn't it beat hell how much inconvenience and downright misery just one misguided brute—one betwattled male doxy—who deserves nothing but to be officially and legally removed from this world, can cause by getting himself unofficially killed!

"Anyway, go on back to the *Nottingham*, John. Go to-night—now! Take Neal with you. Stow him away in your own quarters where nobody'll see him. Keep him out of Langman's way until you're clear of the land. I hunted out Langman, hard at work at his fishmongering, and gave him a talking-to he'll never forget. I doubt that he knows which way is up, as the saying goes, but we can't take chances. He's Malice personified."

He put his hand on Neal's shoulder. "Are you hearing

all this, Neal? We're doing this for your own good. Your father will agree."

Neal just stared at him.

"You go along with Captain Dean," my father said, "and try to forget everything that happened to you to-night, as well as everything we've said. Under Captain Dean you'll learn to be a mariner—a credit to your father and to all of us."

Captain Dean emptied his glass of claret and got to his feet.

"There's one more thing," my father said. "Swede hasn't boarded the *Nottingham* yet."

"He's signed on," Captain Dean said.

"I know," my father said, "but the hospital authorities don't know about it. I can notify 'em and make everything all legal sometime to-morrow afternoon; but we'll avoid any chance of delay by having Miles go to the hospital first thing in the morning."

To me he said, "The doors open at five o'clock. Find Swede and bring him to me. Tell him I'll arrange things with the hospital authorities after the ship has sailed. There'll be clothes for him here, and we should have him aboard the *Nottingham* by six o'clock."

To Captain Dean he added, "I'll send the money for the cheese and butter by Miles."

I followed my father's instructions to the letter. Swede, when I told him the *Nottingham* must sail that day, and the reason why, looked almost relieved. "This is the way I've always wanted it," he said: "A way for us to be together. Ever since I signed on with Captain Dean, I've been like a fish out of water in this damned hospital, with all the political pensioners that don't know a futtock shroud from a wallpiece. If Neal killed a man, he did it for a good reason. I'd have done it for him if I could—but he wouldn't talk about such things. They made him freeze up inside. I suppose it was my fault for giving him the knife, but I'm glad I did it all the same."

He felt his shoulder and seemed pleased. "Damp mornings like this, my shoulder used to feel sore, but since I signed on with Captain Dean, it's been all right! Yes, sir, I can pull my weight!"

My father had two seamen's bags ready for us. "Get to the quay as fast as you can—and don't look so glum, Miles. Remember what I told you: a smile is the best ticket to Heaven that any man can carry."

He pushed us toward the door. "Get out of here before somebody finds that piece of carrion and comes running to me to do something about it."

He put my bag on my shoulder, kissed me lightly and coughed as if to show me he wasn't overly concerned at my departure. "Every young man ought to travel, and any kind of travel is uncomfortable; so you'll be no worse off aboard the *Nottingham* than all the other young Englishmen who run off to France and Italy every summer."

I knew how my father felt. I was always low in my mind when I left him to go up to Oxford; but now I was even more unhappy, because he showed so clearly that he *was* concerned, and deeply. For the life of me I couldn't say a word: could only hope that some day I could show my feelings in a proper manner.

As we went down the steps and turned toward the oily, misty river, my father called after us, "Watch over him, Swede, as though he were your own boy." I always remembered his words, and Swede never forgot them either.

Chapter Five

AN ARGUMENT was in progress between Langman and Captain Dean, when we came over the *Nottingham's* bulwarks that morning of July 30th. Langman was protesting because Captain Dean had ordered him to remove his dunnage from the after cabin so that there might be room for other passengers—the others being his younger brother Henry, Neal Butler, Swede and me.

Probably for those of us who don't have villainy in our hearts—and villainy, of course, includes jealousy, which is responsible for most of the ills that beset this world—stupidity is our besetting sin. I have never been jealous of any man, but I have been stupid far too often. I was stupid not to see why Langman was so determined to retain a foothold in the after cabin.

"You made an agreement with me," he told Captain Dean. "I was to have a cabin, same as yours. I was captain of my own ship under Woodes Rogers, and captain of this vessel, too, before I sold her to your brother, and you've got no right——"

"Now just a minute," Captain Dean said. "My brother Jasper made a gentleman's agreement with you. He bought your ship and paid three hundred pounds for it, and no questions asked. He made just one concession to you, and that was that you were to sail on her as first mate under me as captain, and could ship Mellen and White along with you."

"All those other things are in the contract," Langman said. "He promised me——"

"Come now, Langman," Captain Dean said moderately, "my brother has no secrets from me. He told me exactly the arrangements he made with you, and I've followed them precisely. You're first mate of this ship, and you'll continue to be so, no matter how many lies you tell me. Nicholas Mellen and George White were signed on as sailors on this ship at your insistence. First you said I'd promised you a berth in the after cabin. I didn't. Then you said my brother guaranteed you the same. He didn't, any more than he guaranteed Mellen and White any specific quarters. Through no fault of my own, there's no room for you in the after cabin, so you're to get forward and bunk with the men. If you find this too uncomfortable or too inconvenient, you can feel free to leave the ship at any moment."

"Now you're not only breaking your brother's solemn covenant, but you're trying to deprive me of a chance to make a living," Langman said.

"Stow it," Captain Dean said. "Stow all that guff about solemn covenants. I'm breaking nothing and I'm depriving you of nothing. I'd be within my rights if I discharged you for insubordination; but even if I did, you'd get along anywhere on the Thames Estuary as long as you could scrape up little boys to catch whitebait for you. Go forward, Mr. Langman, and light a dozen sulphur candles in the fo'c'sle —a matter you should have attended to long ago, by the way. The place has enough bugs to stock half a dozen of those Woodes Rogers ships you're always talking about."

Langman stared at Captain Dean with that characteristic little one-sided smile of his—one that I soon came to recognise as a sneer: not a smile at all. "First thing I know," Langman said, "these passengers of yours will rank me. And if they do, I won't be first mate any more. Then you'll have broken your brother's solemn covenant again."

"Don't worry, Mr. Langman," Captain Dean said. "You're still first mate, but you'll be subordinate to these two gentlemen. Mr. Whitworth is supercargo and Swede here is first lieutenant, having served as captain of the foretop on one of Her Majesty's ships. As soon as I've got Mr. Whitworth settled in the cabin, I'll thank you to give him whatever help he needs to get our cordage aboard and stowed away. We've got to be out of this river in two days."

"She's not fit to sail," Langman said, "and you know it."

"I know nothing of the sort," Captain Dean said. "She's fit to sail as far as Ireland; and whatever needs doing, we'll have done when we get there."

"Four of our guns are worthless," Langman said. "You can't protect yourself if you get chased by a privateer."

Captain Dean looked surprised. "That's news to me," he said. "You fired all ten of 'em?"

"Well, not exactly," Langman said, "but I can tell."

"If they're guns and hold together," Swede said, "you only need to scale 'em and prick out their touch-holes. I'll make 'em worth something to you."

"We've got no water," Langman protested.

"We've got enough water to take us to Donegal," Captain Dean said, "and the best mineral spring in Great Britain is at Killybegs. Do as I tell you and do it quick."

Captain Dean pushed us into the after cabin. "Thank God you're aboard," he said. "That damned Langman! I'll bet your father was right when he suspected Langman of being a buccaneer! Remember how he said ' most of these privateers are buccaneers, no matter what the law says '? That would account for the way Langman fights me at every turn. That's a buccaneer to the life. A privateersman has order aboard his ship, but buccaneers live without government, spend all the money they capture, make no distinction between captain and crew, and are forever changing officers and fighting among themselves like tomcats."

He introduced us to his brother Henry, contenting himself with saying that Henry was the gambler of the family, and travelling for his health: wishful, too, of studying the methods of American merchants. Henry was a smaller silent copy of the captain, done in weaker colours, and he was an epileptic.

"Where's my boy?" Swede asked.

"I've got him copying something," Captain Dean said. "I'll keep him at it until we're safe away. He laid awake all last night, gritting his teeth. I probably gritted mine, too, because I had a lot of thinking to do—some about Neal and Miles, but more about this Langman."

We stowed our dunnage as instructed. Captain Dean put me with Henry Dean in one of the three small rooms, Neal Butler in a second room with Swede. The captain bunked by himself in the third and smallest room. There was a fourth room answering as a head for those occupying the great cabin—though the term "great" could only be applied to it out of courtesy. Neal was hard at work copying *The Seaman's Secrets* on to sheets of paper stitched together, but Captain Dean took me by the arm and urged me toward the deck when I stopped to look at Neal's writing.

"Don't waste a minute," the captain said. "This Langman is a troublemaker. He hates your father for giving him a dressing down, and somehow—probably by keeping his ears open at the Riverside Tavern—he found out that I insured this vessel and our cargo with your father. He's been gabbing about it all over the ship. Insured for vast sums, he's telling the men. Vast sums, for God's sakes! You probably know how much insurance I took out—two hundred and fifty pounds!"

He halted me at the top of the companion ladder. "That's why I'm so anxious to stow that cordage, and get to sea before Langman has a chance to go ashore and talk. If he ever hears about that dead man, he'll put two and two together, and he'd be bound to figure ten as the answer."

For a time I feared that Langman might inflict some of his contrariness on Neal, but apparently he had been made wary by my father's protest against his employment of boys at small wages. He walked widely around Neal, but I often caught him looking at the boy out of the corners of his eyes, as one watches a thunderhead that may become dangerous.

Of course I couldn't be sure, but I felt that Langman didn't know that Neal had ever been in any way connected with Penkethman's players. Even so, I was apprehensive, and Captain Dean was equally fearful; so the two of us worked the men hard at loading the cordage, and I had my first look at the company with whom I was to spend the most important days of my life.

Sailors to me are a mystery, always, and I shall forever be at a loss as to why men of their own free will take to the sea. To my way of thinking a ship is no better than a prison, and those who sail upon her, barring the captain, do so out of desperation or out of their inability to make a living on the land.

Our ship's cook, for example, Cooky Sipper, could never have been a cook anywhere except on a merchant vessel, where there's little to eat save salt pork, salt beef and ship's biscuit. As a seaman and a stower of cordage he was useless; and being a fat man, he succeeded at only two things: perspiring easily and getting in everyone's way. He was of so little use to us that I asked Langman to send him back to his galley.

The *Nottingham* accidentally—and because of Langman's insistence when he sold the *Nottingham* to the Deans—carried two bos'ns, George White and Nicholas Mellen, both former shipmates of Langman. A bos'n, because he has charge of all sails, rigging, canvas, colours, anchors, cables and cordage, must of necessity be an able seaman, and White and Mellen certainly were able, even though they were thick as thieves with Langman. White had a depression at the end of his nose, like the stem-end of a peach, and Mellen was so cross-eyed that I didn't see how he could steer a boat.

The carpenter, Chips Bullock, looked a little like his name, for he would stand with head lowered, staring at a task to be done, then rush at it like a bull, pushing and heaving and grunting.

The other men in the crew—William Saver, Christopher Gray, Charles Graystock and Harry Hallion—were about the same sort of sailors that every resident of Greenwich was accustomed to see in taverns, or wandering aimlessly along the streets: people who seemed to have come from nowhere and to be bound for nowhere.

Saver had enormous ears and never smiled except when he heard of trouble occurring to someone. He wasn't particular. Anyone would do.

Christopher Gray was a gunner who had lost two fingers and had his eyelids blown full of powder grains. I doubted that he could lay a gun effectively, but I never found out, fortunately.

Graystock was a small man with a drooping lower lip. Whatever he was set to do, he always left it half done in order to talk to and interfere with someone who was doing well enough without assistance.

Hallion was a reckless sort, forever getting hurt because he did things in ways they shouldn't be done. He had a positive genius for doing things wrong, poor wretch.

Their faces were wrinkled and drab, as if they'd been salted in a beef barrel, instead of exposed to the sun. Yet all of them worked to the best of their ability, perhaps because that pale gambler Henry Dean worked with them, as did Swede and even the captain, except when the latter was

ashore, getting the cordage into barges and making sure
that it reached us with a minimum of delay. Only Neal
Butler remained in the cabin, copying and copying *The
Seaman's Secrets* on to his stitched sheets.

"We'll take no chances," Captain Dean said, "and I won't
feel safe if anyone—anyone at all—catches a glimpse of that
boy while we're still at this anchorage."

So every one of the five of us in the *Nottingham's* cabin
heaved a sigh of relief when, on the morning of August
2nd, the last bargeload of cordage came aboard. Even before
it was lowered into the hold, our anchors were aweigh, and
we were headed downstream for the Nore, that sandy islet
at the mouth of the Thames where outbound merchantmen
assemble to wait for warships assigned to convoy them out
of England's privateer-infested narrow waters and in the
general direction of their desired havens.

As we came down among the sixty-odd vessels anchored
at the Nore, Captain Dean eyed them disparagingly. "Look
at their hulls," he told me. "Hardly a galley among 'em:
bluff bows, like tubs. If we get many like that in our
convoy, we'll have to strike out on our own."

"If you strike out on your own," Langman warned, "this
ship'll have another owner in a week's time."

"Is that a threat, Mr. Langman?" Captain Dean asked
mildly.

Langman's face was a dusky red. "No!" he shouted. "But
I took this ship myself when I was with Woodes Rogers,
and I know how easy she is to take! You let a French
privateer lay her aboard and where'll *you* be?"

"I'll be awake, Mr. Langman," Captain Dean said. "I
think perhaps her crew was asleep when *you* took her."

Langman went forward, seething.

That passage between Langman and Captain Dean was
characteristic of their attitudes. Captain Dean's idol, whom
he quoted and to whom he referred more frequently than

did Langman to Woodes Rogers, was Sir Isaac Newton. Dean had corresponded with Newton regarding an improved method of finding the longitude of a ship at sea; and he admired Newton immeasurably for his invention of the reflecting telescope.

But at any mention of either of these additions to human knowledge, Langman became not only outrageous, but almost incoherent with fury.

"Longitude!" he'd sputter. "What do you want of more longitude! All you need is latitude! If this Newton finds out what you're hoping he'll learn about longitude, he'll take the bread right out of the mouths of sailors. Any damn' fool will be able to navigate. I say let well enough alone! Why foul your own nest?"

His attitude toward Newton's reflecting telescope was even worse, and he went so far as to insist that such a telescope was impossible. Nonsense, he called it.

Captain Dean listened to his tirades against Newton and his reflecting telescope with a placid face. "Mr. Langman," he said, "I've looked through Sir Isaac Newton's reflecting telescope. By using prisms, he makes it possible to see things that you couldn't see at all through an ordinary telescope."

"Prisms!" Langman snorted. "There's no such thing! Even if there was, you couldn't clog a telescope with one of 'em and still use it!"

"Seeing is believing," the captain said.

"Like hell it is," Langman said. "I've seen ships sailing upside down! I've seen sun dogs, with four suns around a central sun! That doesn't mean ships sail upside down, does it, or that there's five suns? Prisms, for God's sake! You'd never get me to look through a telescope full of prisms! This Newton must be crazy!" His look implied that Captain Dean as well was more than touched with insanity. He stalked away, his neck swollen with suppressed anger.

"What makes him like that?" I asked Captain Dean.

He shrugged his shoulders. "Who knows? The world is full of Langmans, believing in all sorts of worthless tarradiddle, but condemning things that might help mankind. Newton's a case in point. He's shown the world something new and valuable, so the ignorant attack him. Like all ignorant people, they're stubborn about it, and angry for fear they may have to eat their words. The Langmans always refuse to look through the telescope."

"Maybe so," I said, "but if I were captain of this ship, I'd make Langman keep a civil tongue in his head."

"Well, you *aren't* captain, Miles," Captain Dean said, "and to be frank about it, I wish *I* weren't. I'm captain to please my brother Jasper. I'd rather be of some service to my country in foreign parts—in America: Holland: Sweden, where I wouldn't be dealing day and night with sailors, who're forever seeing sea-serpents or the Flying Dutchman or privateers, and condemning everything decent like Isaac Newton or the reading of books."

He eyed me quizzically. "How would *you* make Langman keep a civil tongue in his head, Miles?"

"With a belaying pin, if I had to."

Captain Dean shook his head. "No, Miles. That wouldn't do. There's two ways of running a ship. One's by violence. The other's by letting the men think they're being consulted. I can't use violence, Miles, because I don't like violence. I'm afraid of it. I'm strong, and if I hit any man on this ship, I'd put my heart in it and wouldn't be able to keep my mind on my work for fear he'd be hurt—killed, maybe. Besides, Miles, we're shorthanded. A galley, by rights, should have a crew of twenty-five. We have fourteen, including you and me. I can't leave the quarter-deck to hand sails, and I can't risk losing a man for any reason. Don't expect heroics out of me, Miles. I'm just an ordinary individual, who has to go to the head like everyone else, makes mistakes like all the rest of the world, and is mighty glad he doesn't have to be

burdened with listening to as many damned fools as
surrounded Oliver Cromwell or Charles II."

On the seventh of August two sloops of war made signals
indicating that they would convoy all merchant vessels
wishing to proceed to northern Scotland or northern Ireland,
and we soon learned that Captain Dean was right about the
sailing qualities of the twelve vessels that moved off to the
eastward to cluster around the sloops of war like fat goslings
between two proud parent geese. They were slow, and by
the time we had rounded the bulge of Norfolk and borne
up into the North Sea, Captain Dean was in as much of a
frenzy as a man so placid could be. His irritation was understandable, because in order to sail as slowly as the other
tubs in the convoy, we carried nothing except topsails and
headsails.

By the time we had reached the latitude of the north
riding of York, with Whitby off our larboard beam, he
sniffed the warm west breeze and could stand it no longer.
"Get the rest of the sails on her, Mr. Langman," he shouted.
"We've been five days coming this far, and alone we could
have done it in two. Crowd on the canvas. We'll have this
convoy hull-down by midafternoon, and be off the Orkneys
to-morrow, sure as shooting."

Langman seemed horrified. "What do you want to do,"
he demanded, "throw this vessel away? What'll you do if
you run into a privateer?"

"Do?" Captain Dean asked. "Why, I'll do what any
sailor'd do. I'll run from her. Before I ran, though, I'd
want to make sure she *was* a privateer. One thing I learned
long ago, Mr. Langman, is that nearly every time a sailorman thinks he sees a Black Flag, it turns out to be the
captain's overcoat hung up to dry. Get those sails on her."

"The men won't like it," Langman protested.

"You mean Mellen and White won't like it," the captain

said. "They won't if you tell them not to, so don't tell 'em. A few days ago you were howling we shouldn't sail because of not having enough water: now you're screaming we oughtn't to make a run for Killybegs, where there's plenty of fine water to be had. Get on with those sails."

That was the beginning of an oft-renewed argument between Langman and Captain Dean—an argument that came to one of its many heads when we did in fact round the northern tip of Scotland, slip through the narrow waters between the mainland and the Hebrides, swiftly skirt the north of Ireland and start down toward the Isle of Aran and Donegal Bay.

We were still short of Aran by a few miles when the lookout sighted two vessels in a bay near the tip of Aran. As soon as Langman heard the word, he went half-way up the mizzen ratlins to see for himself: then called down to Mellen and White.

"Privateers," he bawled. He came down the ratlins like a squirrel and ran to the quarter-deck. "Those are privateers," he told the captain. "All the men say so."

"What do the men know about it?" Captain Dean asked. "I know, and they probably don't, that Donegal Bay is full of British naval vessels and fishermen. This is no place for French privateers."

"I say they're privateers," Langman said. "I can tell by the cut of their jibs."

A voice reached us from the waist. "He wants us to be captured."

"Hear that?" Langman demanded. "That's what they're all saying: you want to be captured by a privateer."

"That's the silliest thing I ever heard," Captain Dean said. "Why in God's name would I want to be captured by a Frenchman?"

"You wouldn't act the way you're acting—you wouldn't run toward two privateers—unless you wanted to be taken."

"Look here," Captain Dean said. "This ship cost money, as you well know. So did the cordage we're carrying. We're within a few hours of a port where we'll take on another expensive cargo. I'd be the last one to run risks with this ship."

Langman was supercilious. "You insured the cordage, didn't you?"

"Of course I did," Captain Dean said. "Only a fool would fail to insure his cargo."

"Well," Langman persisted, "if you turned the ship over to a privateer, your brother Jasper'd get the insurance money, wouldn't he?"

"Certainly he would," Captain Dean said. "Also, all of us, including me and my brother Henry, would land in a French prison. If I thought I was in danger of being captured, I'd run the ship ashore."

Langman wouldn't stop worrying the subject. "If you *did* run her ashore, both you and your brother would get the money."

Captain Dean turned away from him and took the wheel from Harry Hallion. "Harry," he said, "go forward and tell the men we're running between Aran and the main, and that we'll neither abandon this ship nor let any Frenchman have her."

Hallion went forward and spoke to White and Mellen, the two bos'ns. At his words both Mellen and White burst into derisive laughter.

"This has gone far enough," Captain Dean said. "Take the wheel, Miles! Keep her steady as she goes."

He ran from the quarter-deck to the waist, stepping in front of Mellen and White, who stared sullenly at the deck.

"What are you damned fools preaching to these men?" Captain Dean demanded.

Mellen gave him a sullen answer. "We're not preaching

anything. We just don't propose to be turned over to the damned French."

"Do you know what you're saying?" Captain Dean said. "You're implying I'm a traitor."

When neither Mellen nor White answered, Captain Dean's two big hands shot out, seized them by the collars of their jackets and banged their heads together so that the sound came clearly to us on the quarter-deck. "I'll have common sense on this ship, and not a lot of buccaneery blathering about things you don't understand! Such as privateers! Such as insurance!" He threw them to the deck between two of the guns.

He didn't like violence, he had told me, and he had meant it. Both White and Mellen were able to get to their feet. The cracking together of their heads had been no more violent than the caning a schoolmaster gives a boy for writing verses on the wall of a privy. If the captain had treated them with the violence their conduct deserved, their skulls would have cracked like plover eggs.

It was easy to see that Langman, Mellen and White had conspired together. They used the same words: the same impossible false arguments, and I, like a fool, still couldn't understand why. I thought they behaved as they did because they were wrong-headed. God only knows why so many humans are afflicted with that terrible disease, or failing, or whatever it is; but I did know that wrong-headed men are responsible for nearly all the world's troubles; and so I thought Langman, Mellen and White were wrong-headed because they couldn't help themselves.

The captain had been right all the time, for the two ships paid no more attention to us than as though we'd been a fishing schooner. We ran safely through the strait that separates Aran from the main, and next day, August 13th, we rounded the red cliffs at the northern entrance of

Donegal Bay. By nightfall we were anchored in the snug harbour of Killybegs, surrounded by the greenest hills I ever hope to see. On the slopes of all the hills were black and white cattle on whose milk and cream and butter, which even Cooky Sipper couldn't spoil, we lived in luxury.

We lay in the harbour of Killybegs for six weeks, not from choice, but because Captain Dean said we had to wait for cool weather before loading a thousand firkins of butter and the three hundred cheeses which he proposed to sell to the citizens of Portsmouth, New Hampshire. Otherwise both cheese and butter might spoil.

Portsmouth people, Captain Dean claimed, were the best people in the world—the kindest, the most hospitable, the most generous, the most appreciative, the most civilised of any people anywhere in America and he'd run no risk of offering them rancid butter.

England, he said, except for its Langmans and gipsies, its beggars and whores, its thieves, snobs, toadies, fops, rakes, gambling schemes, press gangs, wasn't half bad; but if it weren't for his brother Jasper and his obligation to sail ships in accordance with Jasper's plans, he would get himself a home in Portsmouth.

"Sometimes," he said in his solid, mild way, "I think Englishmen are all a pack of bastards; but Portsmouth people aren't. They don't think the way we do. It's something about the climate, probably. Those who can stand it have something happen to them. Even the lobsters grow two big claws."

For the first time since that terrible twenty-ninth of July, Neal Butler's smile came back to him in Killybegs. When he finished his copying of *The Seaman's Secrets*, Captain Dean set him to drawing the coast line of America from a worn Mercator's Projection, starting with Cape Sable in Nova Scotia and working as far south as New York.

Perhaps the prospect of America helped Neal to forget the happenings of July 29th: perhaps the scents and the sights and the sounds—the calmness and remoteness—of that placid pretty harbour of Killybegs started him talking to the captain about fish. But talk he did, and soon, with the captain's permission, he and Swede were thick as porridge with a dozen fishermen, so that they knew where to go to fish, and kept the galley well supplied.

Soon, too, except for one thing, he was himself again. When he wasn't running errands for Captain Dean and cleaning our cabins, or carefully laying off the American coast in his notebook, he was helping Swede scale the guns, or learning the care and the use of a plane and an adze from Chips Bullock, giving him a hand at knocking together the water casks; or he was in the galley, peering at the messes Cooky Sipper concocted.

Yes, he was himself again except for just one thing. He wouldn't talk about the theatre or anything that had happened to him during his life in Greenwich. Swede and Captain Dean and I knew why this was, and were careful to make no reference to matters that Neal with good reason found painful. But not Langman. I'll never forget the glittering September morning when Neal was stowing fishing tackle in the *Nottingham's* small tender, and Langman stood at the top of the ladder, looking down at him with that derisive half-smile of his. Just what Langman said, we on the quarter-deck couldn't distinguish; but we heard him mockingly call Neal "Whitebait."

Captain Dean and I simultaneously started for Langman; but though we were quick, we were too slow. Swede, darting from the after-cabin, swung his long right arm scythe-like at Langman. Langman rose a little to fall across the top of the bulwarks, his arms flailing, hung there a moment; then rolled over and into the harbour with a gratifying splash.

Neal, ironically enough, gaffed him and pulled him out; and as Langman mounted the ladder to stand dripping on the ladder grating, Captain Dean eyed him impassively and told him to be more careful of his footing.

For once Langman, as his glance went from Captain Dean's face to Swede's and mine, looked apprehensive, and he set off for the fo'c'sle without his usual disdainful reply. Neal, I was sure, would be free of Langman's attentions for some time to come.

The last of sixty thousand pounds of the best Donegal butter, all packed in firkins, and three hundred Donegal cheeses had come aboard when we set sail on September 25th on a voyage that for devilishness was enough to make me wonder again and again why any man went to sea of his own free will.

During all the time the *Nottingham* sailed the great circle, we saw nothing but mountainous waves—ran into winds so contrary that we spent more time blundering backward than we did wallowing forward. The men, forever shortening sail, making sail, battening everything down to ride out storms that seemed to have no ending, manning the pumps, were constantly complaining, and like all men everywhere, they blamed their misfortunes on Captain Dean until I marvelled at his patience.

Our water casks sprung leaks so that we had to go on short rations: our beef turned sour.

October was a villainous cold month: November was worse; and in December the sun apparently disappeared for good in a gurry of fog and dirty grey clouds.

Early in December we sighted a ship—the only sail we sighted in all that time—and spoke her, at which Langman set up his now familiar squealing that she was a French privateer.

She proved to be the ship *Pompey*, London bound, and her

captain told us only two things: that we were off the Banks
of Newfoundland, and that the weather where he'd come
from was worse than what we'd had, no matter how bad
that had been.

On Monday, December 4th, we caught a glimpse of Cape
Sable in Nova Scotia. Then the weather turned dirtier
than ever.

"We could make Portsmouth in a day," Captain Dean
told us, "but I've got to see the sun just once before I take
any chances."

So we stood off and on, and a week passed before we saw
the sun.

The wind was frigid and bitter, and in the north-east, and
the seas kicked up by that north-east gale seemed to run at
us from every direction, instead of from the north-east. The
waves, too, were dirty and grey, as if they'd gone down deep
and dredged up all the sand and seaweed from the bottom.

I well remember that Monday morning when we finally
caught sight of the sun. Usually a glimpse of it after a
north-east blow, Captain Dean said, meant that we'd have
a little decent weather. Instead of that, the sun stayed out
just long enough for us to stand in toward the land and sight
the long, low coast line of New England, with tree-covered
points thrust out toward us, and all the ledges and hills
covered with snow.

Captain Dean was elated. "That's Cape Porpoise," he said.
"Now I know exactly where we are. We'll head due south,
and we'll be in Portsmouth to-morrow morning."

He'd no sooner spoken than the sun disappeared again
behind a driving wall of snow.

December 11th, Monday

I REMEMBER that day for other things. Our food, bad to begin with, had become steadily worse; and on that morning of December 11th there was none at all. Cooky Sipper, Langman told the captain, was sick, with a throat so full of phlegm that he could hardly swallow, and none of the other men knew how to cook.

So Swede volunteered to do the cooking until we reached Portsmouth; and when he went to the galley, Neal went along with him to help, not only to carry food to the after cabin, but to dish out to the men forward when they came to the galley with their mess kids.

We wallowed creakingly south, with those dirty grey seas and stinging snow squalls hissing all around us, until nightfall, when the captain turned over the deck to Mr. Langman, and Neal brought us boiled beef, boiled potatoes and ship's bread; then disappeared. We ate our supper as well as we could in that heaving, lurching cabin beneath the dim lights swinging in their gimbals.

The cabin felt empty without Swede and Neal, and as time went on I worried about them and so climbed on deck to go forward to the cookhouse. The quarter-deck, except for the helmsman, was empty; and when I half slid, half skated forward to the galley, I found Langman braced in the doorway of that narrow cubicle. Inside it the lamp cast a flickering light on Swede and Neal, both of whom were staring at Langman with eyes so shadowed that they seemed sunk in their heads.

When, to steady myself, I caught hold of the doorpost beside Langman, he opened his mouth as if to say something: then shut it again, turned, and worked his way back to the quarter-deck.

"Miles," Swede said, "something smells around here, and it's not the cheese. Langman's been in the hold after extra meat for White and Mellen."

"He's got no business tampering with the provisions," I said. "That's for the captain to do."

"Yes," Swede said, "and he also wants to head straight out to sea."

I couldn't believe my ears. "Straight out to sea! What for, for God's sake! We're running south-west before a north-easter. If we turn at right angles, we'll be in the trough and on our beam-ends before you can say Scat! Why would anyone want to take her straight out, anyway?"

"Tell him what you heard, Neal," Swede said.

"It was when he gave Mellen the meat," Neal said. "He said, 'If we can't wait for this blow to let up, we'll be in Portsmouth to-morrow.' Then he said, 'Tell 'em I'll get 'em more water too.'"

"That's what Neal heard," Swede said, "and as I see it, there's no two ways about it. Langman wants this ship for himself. He's waited till the last minute, all along, hoping for a fair wind and blue skies that would make it safe for him to take her over on one excuse or another. Well, he'll never get a fair wind or blue skies to-morrow, and he knows the only way to get 'em is to put straight out to sea and wait for the wind to turn. If he doesn't, we'll be in Portsmouth, and he'll have lost his chance."

I stared at him; and only now did I see clearly what I should have seen long ago. "Of course," I said. "And the extra meat and the extra water would be for bribes to get the others to side with him."

"What else?" Swede asked.

I told Swede to dowse the lantern, lock the galley and get back to the cabin with Neal as quickly as he could—and because I didn't like the way Langman had abandoned the quarter-deck to argue with Swede and Neal in the galley, I went behind them to make sure they got there.

When I reached the quarter-deck, I could just make out Langman in the snowy dark.

"I didn't see a lookout up forward," I told him.

"Lookout! What's the good of a lookout on a night like this?" I could sense the contempt on his swarthy thin face.

In the snug cabin Captain Dean had his coat off, readying himself for bed: but when I followed Neal and Swede through the door and started telling him what they had told me, he reached behind him for his coat.

Henry Dean, lying fully dressed on his bunk, climbed out heavily and pulled a knitted cap down over his ears.

They heard me out: then Captain Dean angrily pulled on his own hat, picked up the loggerhead from beside the cabin stove; and all of us went out again into the whirling snowflakes.

Langman wasn't on the quarter-deck. Captain Dean spoke to the helmsman, "Where's the mate?"

Gray, the helmsman, said, "He went forward, Captain."

"He went to the hold," Swede said. "That's where he went: to the hold for water."

The door to the hold swung open and Langman, carrying a lantern in one hand and a water jug in the other, stepped out on the snowy deck.

"You're supposed to be on watch, Mr. Langman," Captain Dean said. "Where's your lookout? You have no business in the hold. What are you doing with that water jug? You know everyone on this ship is on a strict water ration!"

"That ain't so," Langman said. "You have all the water you want, and the crew gets half enough! They're sick of you and your ways. They say you're aiming to run this ship ashore, now, to-night! They say you've got to alter your course and take her straight out to sea if you want to prove you're not aiming to wreck her."

"Wreck her?" Captain Dean shouted. "In a north-easter? Are you crazy, Langman? Do you think I want to commit suicide? I took my bearings from Cape Porpoise! There's no place to wreck her unless I steer due west. Wreck her at night? Wreck her in a north-easter? Wreck her in a snow-storm? Talk sense, Langman! And get a lookout forward!"

"By God," Langman said, "you'll take her out to sea or we'll know the reason why!"

Captain Dean raised his head and seemed to sniff the air. "Swede!" he shouted. "Go forward! Keep your eyes peeled!"

Swede left us, scrambling, his right arm hanging low, ape-like, as if to keep himself from falling on the scum of slush amidships.

To Langman Captain Dean said, "I'll take no orders from you, Christopher Langman. You'll stop inciting this crew to rebellion! If you don't start acting like the mate of this ship, I'll take steps! What in God's name are you running without a lookout for?"

"How can a lookout keep his eyes open in gurry like this?" Langman demanded.

"He could hear, couldn't he?" the captain snapped.

Langman turned contemptuously away, and found himself squarely confronted by Henry Dean, who reached out and took the water jug, almost as though he took a child from his mother's arms. Langman resisted, shouting, "Mellen! White!"

On this Captain Dean stepped forward and brought the loggerhead down on Langman's skull. When Langman swayed but didn't fall, Captain Dean hit him again. Langman dropped to his knees, but, unfortunately for all of us, staggered to his feet again and reeled toward the cabin.

We heard Swede shouting something from the bow.

The captain ran forward, sliding precariously on the sloppy planks. Almost immediately he ran back past us to climb to the quarter-deck again and I was conscious of a hoarseness in the air about me, a sort of raucous wet humming that seemed to fill me with a deadening fright and turn my arms and legs to water.

"Starboard!" Captain Dean shouted to the helmsman. "Hard to starboard!"

The deck surged up beneath us. The whole ship lurched and seemed to cough, as a man, coughing, convulses himself.

The bow fell off to larboard, and the vessel sickeningly rolled and rose up and up on a monstrous wave.

"Get your helm to *starboard*! *Starboard!*" Captain Dean screamed.

The raucous wet humming all around us deepened to a menacing all-pervasive rumble, overwhelming, stomach-shaking—and the enormous comber on which the ship was riding seemed to hurl her forward.

She struck with a crash that threw me to the deck—a crash so loud that my brain crackled, and among the splinter was a faint hope that if any man lived within a mile of where we struck, he would be wakened by that dreadful sound and hurry to help us.

The rumbling, roaring thunder of which we seemed to be the centre was the sound of breakers pounding at the unseen rocks on which the *Nottingham* shuddered and grated; and even in my despairing panic I had quick thoughts— if the disjointed fragments that flutter in a man's mind in an emergency can be called thoughts:

. . . that Langman's repeated insistence that Captain Dean

C

had all along intended to run the *Nottingham* ashore now seemed to be true, but was in truth more untrue than ever:

. . . that never, in all our weeks of sailing against adverse winds, had we ever heard anything approaching the deafening tumult that now surrounded us:

. . . that nothing made by man could withstand the hammer blows that beat upon the *Nottingham*'s weather side to pour torrents of icy water and slashing spray across her canted deck—and yet that this shore upon which we had struck, had been here unharmed, since the world began, in spite of innumerable storms—that among the crevices of those rocks were living things that would survive these pounding waves . . . and that perhaps we ourselves would similarly survive.

The *Nottingham*'s stern was higher than the bow, as if bent on thrusting her stern more solidly against the shore, and the waist of the ship seemed filled with struggling figures, striving to reach the after cabin.

I found Neal pushing at Swede's buttocks: found a rope-end to which to cling: ran into Chips Bullock, with an axe and a hammer in one hand and his work bag in the other, making his way along the weather rail.

A breaker curled over the bulwarks, hit him squarely, and sent him sliding down the steep deck, and into a gun carriage. My rope-end let me reach him, take his axe and hammer and pull him to his feet.

"My work bag!" he shouted. "Spikes! Nails!" He fell to his knees, scrabbling in the scuppers for his work bag. Another wash of icy foam struck us. By the grace of my rope-end we clawed free of the scuppers and pushed and pulled each other to the cabin companion.

The cabin was like a room insecurely poised on one of its corners, and something about a structure so tilted throws a man off balance, both physically and mentally. Every person in it is dizzy and, unless he holds to something, falls down: his mind, too, is so addled that he thinks he can stand, and so gets to his feet only to fall immediately, like a wounded pigeon.

The dark deck had been bad enough, what with waves, the icy torrents that drenched us, the crunching of the ship as she thumped upon the rocks; but the inside of the cabin was worse, and for the first time in my life I knew terror, as I think each of the fourteen of us knew it, even though some concealed it.

A single lamp still burned dimly, shuddering in its gimbals. Only Captain Dean was on his feet, supporting himself by the rudder case. The others were on the floor, some trying to rise, only to reel down again: the others just lying there. Cooky Sipper was moaning.

I found that if I closed my eyes the strange tilt of the room had next to no effect upon me. I could crawl to the cabin wall and pull myself erect by clinging to it. I made my discovery known to Neal and Swede and Chips.

Langman, when we crawled in, was striving to make himself heard by Captain Dean. "You were bound to do it from the very first!" he was shouting. "You've been looking for a chance to run her ashore since the day we left the convoy! You planned it!"

"Don't be a damn' fool!" Captain Dean shouted back. "This is no time for such stuff as that! I want every man in this cabin to pray."

"Pray?" Langman demanded, and his voice was a squeal. "You think God's going to come down here and pull us off these rocks after you've put us on them?"

Captain Dean smashed his fist against the rudder case. "All right! All right! I put you here! All I know is there was no land on the course I plotted from Cape Porpoise, and there was no lookout forward when you had the deck. Now pray!"

"Pray?" Langman shouted again. "How's that going to

help us? Nothing can help us, now you've gone and run us ashore!"

"Don't pray for help!" the captain told him. "Pray for the strength to help yourself! Strength!"

The whole ship sagged sickeningly to one side: reeled even more sickeningly to the other: a sea that must have been enormous struck her side with such force that my eardrums felt thrust against my throbbing brain. A splitting sound came from beneath us, and the cabin floor fluttered.

"Oh, God!" Captain Dean said, "give each man the strength to stand upon his feet and stretch out a helping hand to every other man. Say it, every last one of you, and mean it! God give me strength! Say it, Langman."

"God give me strength," Langman said.

"Again!" Captain Dean shouted. "Everyone! God give me strength!"

The men's voices quivered, thin and bird-like through the sounds of the smashing seas.

The whole after part of the ship straightened a little, then seemed to slide downhill.

"Get on deck," Captain Dean cried. "Get up and get out before she breaks in two or slides off." He reached out and pulled Chips to his feet. "Use your axe! Swede! Miles! Go with him! Cut the weather shrouds and ratlins! If the masts fall toward the land, we may have a chance! If they don't fall, chop the foremast!" He flung Chips toward the companionway. Swede and I followed him.

Behind us Captain Dean stormed among the men, kicking them and hauling them to their feet.

The task of cutting those shrouds and ratlins—of keeping a foothold on that steep and slippery deck—was difficult beyond belief. We couldn't trust ourselves on the chains because of the smashing of the waves against the side. For a time Chips insisted he could stand on the bulwarks and swing his axe. We hoisted him up to let him thrust a foot through the ratlins. He hooked his other leg around a stay, but when he swung his axe, one of those roaring towering breakers foamed against him and blinded us. When the foam subsided, Chips was in the scuppers once more, but still clinging to his axe.

We tried holding Chips pinned against the bulwarks with our shoulders; but the unending slash of icy foam and the driving snow numbed me: must have numbed Chips, too, for he couldn't seem to swing the axe.

"Give me that axe," Swede shouted. "We've got to get ashore somehow! Stand under me. When I fall, catch me if you can."

He pushed the axe handle inside his breeches, put an arm around Neal's shoulders, bellowed, "We'll be all right"; then went up the inside of the ratlins like a big spider. We lost him at once in the snow and the flying spray, but felt the jarring of his axe against the rigging—and then, suddenly, he came sprawling down among us. Almost in the same moment the foremast went over the side with a splintering crash. Then the mainmast went, and the ship rolled on her side to surge soggily as if agonised by the pounding of those roaring breakers.

"Look for the axe!" Swede said. "I threw it to leeward when I fell!"

"To hell with the axe," Chips said. "Get ashore! Wherever people live we can find another axe."

I agreed with him. We could have hunted forever for that axe or for Chips's work bag in the darkness and on that glacial deck.

"I'll go first," Swede said. "I want Neal close behind me. I want Miles behind Neal."

He left us, and we felt rather than saw him inching along the mast. We crawled out after him. Ratlins and shrouds were tangled around it. The foretop was like a fence to be climbed, but we climbed it.

The tip of the mast rested against something solid. That something was seaweed, and beneath the seaweed were rocks —solid, immovable rocks.

We were safe, I thought, secure from those bellowing breakers; and even as I write the words "safe" and "secure," I feel a sort of shame for those who, like myself, could let themselves think that there is ever any such thing as safety and security.

The seaweed was so slippery that if a person upon it was unable to see where to step, he staggered, he lurched, his feet went out from under him, pitching him upon his face or, even worse, wrenchingly upon his back.

Under the thick mop of seaweed that covered the rocks against which the foremast truck rested there were countless barnacles. When we put out our hands to break our falls, which were constant, the barnacles slashed our fingers, wrists and knees.

Eventually slipping and feeling our way up that treacherous shore, hopeful of removing ourselves from the unending roaring of the breakers, we came to naked ice-covered rocks on which no seaweed grew. To me that meant we were above high-water mark. Now we were truly safe—or so I idiotically thought again.

I caught at Swede's wet coat. "Swede," I said, "we'll have to find shelter from this snow and wind." Not only was the snow plastering itself against our faces with a force that numbed us, but the snow was mixed with spindrift, so that it seemed twice as cold as anything could be.

"Go to the left," I told Swede. "I'll go to the right. Chips can walk straight ahead. Let's leave Neal here to shout to us in case we're lost. Leave Chips's hammer with Neal, too, so Chips won't lose it when he falls. Hunt for trees or bushes—any kind of shelter. Anything—anything at all. Even an old shed, or a pigpen, or an overhanging ledge. Or a fence or a clump of thick grass. Or a hill. If you can find a hill, we can get in its lee. That would be better than nothing."

We blundered off into the thick roaring dark. The tumultuous sea seemed to thunder from every direction. The footing, in that darkness, was nothing but rock—round boulders; sharp boulders; low irregular ledges, all slippery with a half-inch coat of ice.

Rocks turned beneath my feet; spilled me into pockets between them. The pockets had razor-like crushed seashells at their bottoms. The naked rocks were worse than the sea-weed-covered ones on which we had landed, for when I fell I had the feeling that a leg or an arm must break.

These rocks, I thought, must lead to some sort of beach, or a marsh, or a field. Instead of that, my groping hands again felt seaweed. Either the coast had turned, or I had become confused and turned myself. I bore more sharply to the left, to escape that damnable seaweed that was even more slippery than ice, though more cushiony.

After all this exertion, this fever of activity, this terror of the pelting snow and flying foam—yes, and of the un-ending menacing crashing of the sea—my mouth and throat were like leather. In desperation I chipped ice from one of the boulders and sucked at it. It was almost fresh, with only the faintest trace of saltiness.

While I stood there, chipping more ice and crunching it to bits, I heard a thin piping ahead—a faint wailing or squeaking, dim amid all the uproar of the breakers. It might have been a sea bird: it might have been the screaking of one rock driven by a breaker against another.

I held my breath and listened—and heard it again: a faint call.

I crawled even more to my left, feeling for boulders, cutting my hands on barnacles, skirting ledges; easing my-self head first to the tops of rocks: then lowering myself feet first on the far side.

On thus mounting a ledge I found myself looking down into a black cavity in which there was noise and movement and from which, as I balanced there, burst a desperate bellow, a prolonged "Hullooo!" from many voices.

"I'm Whitworth," I shouted into that black void.

I heard Langman's voice. "Whitworth makes nine. Where's Captain Dean? Where's Neal Butler? Where's Swede? Where's Chips? Where's Cooky Sipper?"

"I know where Neal is," I said. "I'll get him. I sent Swede to the left to hunt shelter when we got above high-water mark. I sent Chips straight out."

"Shout," Langman said. "One, two, three: Hulloooo!"

I joined in their shout with all my heart and strength, realising horribly, as I did so, that the faint sound I had heard a few short minutes before had been the concerted bellowing of eight men, yet that outcry had carried only a matter of ten paces because of the wailing of the north-easter and the terrifying unending noise of that savage ocean.

There was a clatter and a cry of pain from the dark hollow. I heard Captain Dean's voice. "I've got Cooky Sipper! How many's here?"

"Nine," Langman said. "Eleven with you and Cooky." Swede's voice came to us throbbingly, half strangled by the snow and the wind. "I'm twelve. I've lost my bearings! Where's the boy?"

"Thank God," the captain said. "The boy's back there a rod and a half. He said Whitworth told him to stay. He wouldn't come along with me."

I shouted to Swede that I'd get him, and went lurching off into the teeth of the storm. The going seemed easier when I had a known goal. Maybe I'd learned how to handle myself more skilfully on those ice-covered rocks and ledges.

As I went I called Neal's name, and when at length I heard

him answer, I had the first moment of mental peace I'd had since Captain Dean brought down the loggerhead on Christopher Langman's skull.

When I reached him he sank to his knees and huddled down into himself. "I haven't moved," he said. I could hardly understand his words, his voice was so shaken with cold. They came from him in shuddering gasps, most distressing.

"The captain found Cooky," he said. "The captain lost his coat. He cut his hands on the rocks. Where's my father?"

"He'll be all right," I said. I hoped to God I was telling the truth. "Everybody's safe in a hole in the rocks. We'll go there now."

"Did anybody find a house?" Neal asked. Shudderingly he added, "Place to get warm?"

I didn't have the heart to answer. "You'll have to crawl, Neal," I said. "You'll fall if you don't. The rocks are icy. If you're thirsty you can eat the ice."

He still held Chips's hammer. I took it from him and with it pounded ice from a boulder. It came off in curved slabs about an inch thick. We bit into them as into slices of solid frosted bread. I could hear Neal crunch the ice. He would stop, overcome by a spasm of shivering: then go on crunching again.

When we got to the depression where Langman, Captain Dean and the other ten were huddled, I knocked more ice from a boulder and brought the slabs into the depression.

When I told them that the ice was nearly fresh, Langman protested that it couldn't be fresh: that it was nothing but frozen salt water and that those who ate it would lose their reason.

"How much have you eaten?" I asked.

"I haven't eaten *any*," Langman said. "I don't have to! It stands to reason it's got to be salt."

"I've eaten it," I said. "So has Neal. It's *not* salt. Didn't you hear me say it's fresh—almost?"

"Yes, I heard you," Langman said. "I heard another thing, too: heard Captain Dean say he didn't aim to run the ship ashore. Look at us now!"

Unseen hands fumbled at me and relieved me of my load of ice. Sounds of crunching came from all around.

"Has anybody got anything I can put on my head?" Captain Dean asked. "When I came to get off, the ship had slipped. To get ashore I laid off my coat and wig and had to jump. I can't see my hands, but I think I tore off some fingernails on the rock."

Nobody answered.

Swede called out, "Send Neal over here to me."

"I'll come too," I said.

The men were huddled together in an irregular oval between two outcroppings of ledge. The outcroppings were perhaps three feet high—no shelter at all until one rose to his feet and got the full force of the wind, snow and spray in his face.

No one stood up except from necessity, as when someone moved a boulder from beneath him and hoisted it to the top of the ledge.

To remove a boulder seemed to create more boulders. Underneath them was a hodgepodge of wet grit compounded of a million dead seashells.

"What did you find, Swede?" I asked.

"Same as Chips," Swede said. "Nothing. Just rocks and ledge. Then more seaweed."

"I think this is an island," Chips said. "When we get the spring tide——"

"Shut up!" Swede shouted. "Don't talk about things unless you're sure of 'em! Most of the hell in this world comes from loose talk!"

"Now look," Captain Dean said hoarsely. "We can't go

on this way, or we'll freeze to death. My feet are numb already. I can't move or think as fast as I could before we went ashore. It took me quite a time to realise the mate was again implying that I ran the ship ashore on purpose."

Langman cursed him.

The captain's voice was as mild as it could be in such a tumult. "That's neither here nor there. I'm still captain, and I still give orders. To-morrow you can elect a new captain if you think it's necessary. Right now I've got to do everything I can to see that there *is* a to-morrow for us. If we can last until daylight, and see where to put our feet, we'll find a better shelter. We can be warm. We'll be able to sleep. Maybe the ship will hold together. Maybe there'll be part of her left. What we've got to do is keep moving, two at a time, all night."

Langman spoke up at once. "I say No! If anybody moves around over those ice-covered rocks, he'll break a leg."

"Nobody's asking anyone to do so," Captain Dean said. "As near as I can tell from your voice, you're opposite me. All right: get to your feet. I'll get to *my* feet. All the rest start counting out loud. Count slow. Count to a hundred. While you count, the mate and I'll stamp up and down, standing in one place, and slap our arms across our chests. When the count is one hundred, the mate and I'll help those beside us to stand up. The rest of us'll count a hundred, while they stamp their feet and swing their arms, same as we did."

We had barely started when one of our number screamed horribly, and our rock hollow became a turmoil of flying arms and legs. "It's Henry," Captain Dean shouted. "Catch him and hold him!" Never before had I heard or felt a man in the throes of epilepsy, and when at last Henry Dean was pinioned and lay gurgling and groaning beneath us, I thought I had plumbed the depths of horror, and knew I couldn't endure another night like this.

All that night I rose, hunched my shoulders to the driving storm, stamped my feet, swung my arms, then pulled Neal to his feet and sank down to count to a hundred over and over again. It was like thunderous eternity, something beyond the power of a mere man to bear. If I'd been alone, I couldn't have borne it. I knew if I stopped that agony of struggling up, facing the driving snow that blistered my face—that added to the wet weight of my clammy clothes—Neal might stop.

The others might stop as well; so I couldn't stop. I could only hope and pray.

My prayers were as formless as my hopes—Oh God Oh God Oh God Oh God, over and over.

Deep within me, underneath the counting aloud and the praying, were other vagrant longings for warmth, for shelter, for an end to the deafening crashing of the waves: flashes of my father and his distress if he could know of our plight; of how he would blame himself for it; of how I, like a fool, had protested at being sent to Oxford; of how I would never again find fault with anything provided I could be warm and dry and have friends about me. . . .

December 12th, Tuesday

THE TIME came, eventually, when, on stooping to pull Neal to his feet, I could see him dimly. Snow, mixed with rain, pelted us from the north-east, but the wet rocks on which we had ached and shivered through that long, long night were visible. All of us had ceased suddenly to be disembodied voices and were human beings once more—human but wild-eyed at the sights revealed to us by that pallid dawn.

We were on an island, as all of us had feared since Chips Bullock had dared hazard that awful suspicion after hunting for shelter the night before—an island, but *what* an island!

It lay low in the water, like the back of a whale. In a long-gone age it might have been a rounded mountaintop of solid rock, but one that a demonic force had smashed with giant hammers and made into a shattered travesty of flatness. On it there wasn't a handful of soil, or a bush, or any growing thing.

The sea was all around us, so close that from the hollow where we stood I could have thrown a rock into the raging breakers to north, south, east or west. Rimming the island was a border of blackness—the seaweed on which we had slithered and fallen the night before. Beyond the black weed the white breakers raced out of the north to spurt up in spray on the north side: then go galloping and bellowing down the west and east sides of the island; swinging around to pound the south side with a sort of ferocious maelstrom of foam.

Of the *Nottingham* there wasn't a trace—not that we could see.

Fourteen of us had spent the night in that rocky depression, and all but three of us were on our feet. Cooky Sipper lay on his face, shuddering and sobbing, great racking sobs that were frightening. Two seamen, William Saver and Charles Graystock, just lay there with eyes closed. Their faces were greenish.

"Please God," Captain Dean said. "We can't have this! You're frightened before you need to be! You're better off right now than if you were wrecked on a sand spit in the Indian Ocean. Here you've got good ice to keep you from getting thirsty. You can have it without stealing it, as you tried to do on shipboard. This is no time to be frightened."

Chips Bullock's hammer was fastened to his belt by a cord. Captain Dean took it from him. "I'm going to knock ice off the rocks so to have a path to the place where we struck. All those who can walk come with me. I'll need help with the things that have washed ashore. There must be something."

He was nearly wrong. No man would believe that a ship the size of the *Nottingham* could have vanished so completely and left so little behind, or that all that cheese and all that butter we had stowed so carefully, while we lay in the harbour of Killybegs, could have gone so completely to the bottom.

She must have struck at dead low water, around nine o'clock at night. Thus high tide would have been around four o'clock in the morning. Daylight probably broke about seven o'clock, so the tide should now be half out; and at the high-water mark there should have been heaps of material from the after cabin, from fo'c'sle and hold.

We found four lengths of deck plank, six timbers from the quarter-deck, a length of tarred rope, three pieces of canvas ripped from their fastenings, a bolt of Irish linen purchased by Captain Dean in Killybegs, a cutlass, the handle of a stewpan, a caulking mallet. Scattered among the shaggy masses of seaweed were fragments of cheese, small, like little sponges. And strangely—until I remembered Chips Bullock's work bag—there were as many spikes and nails in crevices beneath the seaweed as there were pieces of cheese.

Offshore, caught on something and held in one position, was a floating tangle of yards, sails and cordage that rose sluggishly to the top of each comber that rolled in to break on the fingers of black rock pointing out from every side of the island.

Captain Dean halted us just short of the seaweed and gave the hammer back to Chips. We could hardly hear him above the roar of the waves. "Langman, you and Mellen and Chips Bullock lay hold of the canvas, the planks and timbers and drag 'em back to the hole in the rocks. Take the tarred rope and set Cooky, Graystock and Saver to unravelling it. If they keep on being sick, drive 'em. We've got to get ourselves under shelter to-night."

He pulled at the waterlogged pieces of canvas, and with his pocket knife hacked off a small square.

"Yes," Langman said, "and while we're doing that, you'll eat the cheese."

"Mr. Langman," Captain Dean said, "I realise you're under something of a strain. Every scrap of cheese we find will be wrapped in this square of canvas and divided into equal portions. Make no mistake about that. On this island we'll all share alike."

Captain Dean motioned to us to come close to him. "Remember one thing above all else," he shouted. "It's better to crawl on hands and knees than to risk falling."

His hands had been concealed beneath his long vest. He held them out to us so that we could see them, front and back. Every finger had been cut almost to the bone by barnacles. Four of his fingernails were torn off. The finger ends were raw but, perhaps because of the cold, were not bloody.

"That's what a fall can do to you," the captain warned. "You can't afford to break an arm or a leg. Now spread out and hunt for those scraps of cheese."

He spoke heavily to Langman. "If you can't make Cooky and Saver and Graystock pick oakum, you and Mellen and White do it yourselves. There's just a chance that we can get fire out of it somehow—if it'll ever dry." For the benefit of the rest of us he said, "I've got a pistol and some wet powder. They're no good till the powder's dry."

We crawled over that slippery brown seaweed like animals nosing around a midden. We found fragments of cheese forced into and under the brown wet weed. Every piece of weed had to be lifted up to expose the rock hollows beneath. The coldness that went with handling that weed was unbearable. After two minutes of it, the pain in my hands forced me to hug myself until the sharp agony subsided. Tears ran down my cheeks, but there was nothing I could do about it.

Acting on the captain's orders, Neal went from one to another, with his square of canvas, collecting the fragments of cheese we pressed together in apple-sized pellets as boys make snowballs. After a search that seemed endless, we had picked up about as much as would have made three whole cheeses.

Neal, making a final round, passed us the captain's orders. "He says to go back to the hole and rest," he told us. "We'll hunt again at dead low tide."

On hands and knees we dragged ourselves back to the hollow in the rock. Perhaps something about the salt water in the wet seaweed had added to the pain in our feet, but so intense was that pain that our faces were contorted to the semblance of gargoyles—something not human.

At the hollow, we found that Langman, Mellen and Chips

had fixed two short planks over the ledges on either side, folded the ragged piece of sail across them, and weighted both sail and planks with boulders.

There was room to lie flat beneath it, packed close together. Flimsy as it was, it partly screened us from the pelting snow and rain. It wasn't much of a shelter, but it *was* a shelter; and we crawled beneath it to lie inert. My brain, as numb as my hands, moved slowly.

Captain Dean's voice was calm and full. "We've got to find some way to reach the canvas that's afloat. We must have that cordage for making oakum." To Langman he said, "What did you do about oakum?"

"Nothing," Langman admitted. "By the time we rigged the shelter, we were so close to frozen we crawled under it."

"Now look," Captain Dean urged, "we've got to have oakum. We can lie on it. We can braid it into something to pull over our heads and faces. Maybe we can dry it so a flint and steel will work on it."

"Where's that cheese?" Langman asked.

"All right," the captain said. "We picked up twenty-six balls of it. I'll cut 'em in even parts. We'll eat half to-day and half to-morrow."

"Why should *you* cut 'em?" Langman asked. "Why should *you* say how much we can have? Since you ran us on this rock, I don't trust you to do anything right. Anyway, you promised we could take a vote to-day on who'd be captain. You shouldn't be captain, now there's no ship."

Captain Dean was long silent. When he did speak, his voice was placid. "How long do you think it'll take you to decide?"

"Not long," Langman said, "especially if you go outside. It won't be a fair vote if you don't."

Captain Dean seemed unruffled. "I suppose you'd like my brother Henry to go outside, too."

"Yes," Langman said, "if it's going to be really fair, your brother should go. So should Whitworth. They're all on your side." There seemed to be no end to his effrontery.

Swede spoke up. "That doesn't sound reasonable, Langman. Why don't *you* go out? You're voting for yourself, aren't you?"

"I haven't made up my mind yet," Langman said.

Swede laughed, but without humour. "I've heard that before! When anybody says that, it means he's made up his mind to vote for the wrong man."

"We're wasting time," Captain Dean said. "I'll go out, but my brother won't. Neither will Miles Whitworth. They're entitled to vote on who they'll obey. I'll stay out long enough to cut seaweed for us to eat with the cheese. Seaweed can't hurt us, and it'll make the cheese go further."

He backed out into the snow and the rain, leaving the canvas-wrapped balls of cheese in my hands.

"Now," Langman said, "we want to do this all fair and honest. I don't care who's made captain, but I know Cooky Sipper wants me to be. He said so just after we got the canvas up. So did Graystock and Saver. All three of 'em voted for me." His voice sounded painfully virtuous.

"Cooky hasn't said a word since the captain helped him into this hole," Swede said. "If you know what Cooky wants you must have read his mind."

"I tell you I heard him," Langman cried. "Mellen heard him, too. Didn't you, Mellen?"

Mellen agreed promptly. "Yes, I certainly did. I heard him say, ' I want Mr. Langman.'"

"Well, I didn't," Chips Bullock said. "I didn't even see Langman talk to Cooky. When we were stretching the canvas, Langman said people as sick as Cooky and Graystock and Saver ought to have a separate hole in the rock, all to themselves. If I get sick, I don't want to be put off in a

hole in a rock with somebody that can't talk to me. I vote
for Captain Dean."

"You're an awful fool, Chips," Langman said. "You know
as well as I do he's been trying to get us in trouble ever since
we left the Nore. First it was privateers and then there was
this insurance money he was bound to get."

"Well, Mr. Langman," Swede said, "you've seen the size
of this island. We didn't pile up on it because of anything
Captain Dean did. We had bad luck. If Captain Dean had
been aiming for it, only a miracle would have brought us
within a mile of it on a night like last night."

"Neal is youngest," I said. "He ought to have first say
in this voting."

"I vote for Captain Dean," Neal answered quickly.

Langman sat up straight, bumped his head against one of
the crosspieces that supported the canvas and fell back again
between his fellow conspirators, Mellen and White. "Neal
says that because he's the captain's favourite," he said in a
shaking voice. "If a captain gets you into trouble, anybody
ought to have sense enough to know he'll never get you
out of it. Probably the captain threatened young Neal with
punishment unless he voted for him. I say his vote ought
to be disallowed."

"What's the matter with you, Langman?" Henry Dean
asked. "Why are you so dead set on discrediting my brother?
What do you hope to gain by it?"

"I don't expect to gain anything by it," Langman snapped.
"I've got a great respect for the truth, that's all. If any
British sea captain does the things your brother has done,
he ought to be exposed so he can't make a nuisance of
himself on the high seas."

"Langman," Swede said, "you're a hard man to argue
with. Everything you say is wrong. You make a liar out
of any person who tries to set you right. I vote for Captain
Dean."

"I vote for Captain Dean," I said. "That's five. Why doesn't somebody try to get a word out of Saver, or Graystock, or Cooky?"

"I'm ranking officer of this ship's company until this vote is settled," Langman said. "I refuse to let men as sick as Cooky and Graystock and Saver be interfered with! I told you they've settled on me. I know Mellen and White are for me, and so I'll vote for myself, and that makes six."

"Well," I said, "that accounts for all but Christopher Gray and Harry Hallion. Gray's a gunner and he scaled the guns with Swede. He must know Swede wouldn't be for Captain Dean if Mr. Langman's charges are true. I know they aren't true, and so does Swede.

"There's another thing to be considered. We have no way of knowing where this island is, but it can't be far from Portsmouth, and Captain Dean has friends in Portsmouth. If anybody's ever going to need friends, we are, when we get ashore. I can't imagine anything more unwise than cutting away from Captain Dean at a time like this.

"And bear this in mind, too. He was willing to leave this shelter so we could vote, but Mr. Langman wasn't. Doesn't that prove something to you? It does to me! It proves the captain plays fair, but Mr. Langman doesn't. I'm going to ask both Hallion and Gray to vote for Captain Dean."

Captain Dean's boots clattered on the rocks outside, and he came crawling back among us with an armful of dripping rockweed clutched to his chest. "The wind's dropping," he said. "Inside half an hour the tide will be as low as it'll go with this wind."

"You got no right coming in here like this," Langman shouted. "We haven't finished voting."

"I vote for Captain Dean," Gray said.

"Me too," Hallion said.

I told the captain that there had been seven for him and six against.

"I'm surprised," Captain Dean said. "I only expected three against me."

"Mr. Langman voted Cooky Sipper, Graystock and Saver against you," I said.

The captain stared contemplatively at Langman: then got his knife from his pocket and started cutting the rockweed into foot-long sections. The weed was brown and slippery, with little oval bulbs at intervals.

"Here," he said to Neal, "pass these around and I'll cut the cheese. Take a bite of the cheese and right away bite off a piece of rockweed and chew them up together."

"You got no right to tell these people what to eat," Langman said. "You never know what's poison and what isn't."

"You don't have to eat it if you don't want to," Captain Dean said. "It's just a way of making the cheese go further." He pressed the balls of cheese together to form a single cake, halved it and rewrapped one half in the piece of canvas. The other half he carefully divided into fourteen cubes while all of us rose on our elbows to watch him. He passed a cube to each of us who could stretch out his hand. Cooky Sipper, Graystock and Saver didn't move.

"I'll keep their portions till they ask for 'em," Captain Dean said. Then he turned his head to look at Langman. "On second thoughts," he said, "I'll let Neal hold it for them."

The seaweed, slippery to the tongue, had something of the sea's freshness about it, and when chewed with cheese it wasn't bad. I could have eaten all the cheese that the captain had wrapped in his square of canvas. By itself, though, the weed wasn't good, and when my little square of cheese was gone, I ate no more weed.

On our second journey to the northern shore of the island, the captain, by the grace of God, found a coil of cordage wound around a boulder that could just be reached when a receding breaker went hissing and rattling back over the black seaweed. Twice the captain lowered himself toward that precious rope, only to come scrambling back among us as another breaker churned toward us.

We tried forming a living chain extending from the unseaweeded rocks down across the seaweed, but that was no good. While the captain tried to untangle the rope from the boulder, a wave surged in; and before we could pull him up over that damnable seaweed, he was soaked to his armpits.

He shivered, slapped himself and stamped his feet. "Think of something," the captain urged. "We've got to have that cordage and canvas! We've got to reach it somehow. The next high tide may rip it loose; it may go out on to-morrow's low tide, when it'll be too dark to see. If we wait twenty-four hours these breakers are sure to wash it away!"

Chips stepped forward to the captain's side. "If we could get a running bowline on the cordage beyond the rock," he said, "it might hold until we caught it."

"Running bowline!" the captain said. He turned to stare speculatively at the rock around which the cordage was twined. A wave roared in to cover it; then hissed away.

The boulder was set in a patch of crushed shells and pebbles, on which there was no weed. The cordage was jammed between the gravelly stuff and the boulder's base.

The captain motioned for Swede to come and stand beside him. I knew what they discussed, though I couldn't hear a word they spoke because of the roaring of the breakers.

In the end Swede nodded his head, and the captain sent Langman hurrying off. In no time he was back with the piece of rope out of which the oakum was to have been made. Five minutes later Swede and the captain, with Neal between them, were showing Neal the working of a running bowline.

When Neal stood there on the edge of the rock, with that

fearful background of foam and roaring waves beyond him, I couldn't bear to look at him: yet I couldn't bear not to. I knew we had to have that cordage: knew that somebody had to go for it, and I knew, too, that the captain was right in picking Neal. He was the lightest: in all likelihood he was the quickest.

At a signal from the captain he slid down the weed in the wake of the receding wave. He put me in mind of an otter. He threw the rope before him and over the boulder as a boy throws a skipping rope: fell on his stomach over the boulder-top; slipped the loose end of the rope under the cordage and through the noose. Just as a towering breaker curled before breaking, he darted back, the rope-end in his hand, no wetter than when he had jumped down.

Swede, stretched far forward, grasped one of his wrists, the captain the other, and the two of them snapped Neal up over the face of the ledge.

Whether that running bowline would grip the cordage tightly enough to let us haul in the floating yards and sails to which it was attached, we couldn't know. The captain pulled it tight, then drew it gently toward him. The cordage rose up to the level of the top of the boulder around which it was snagged. Chips Bullock joined the captain in his pulling. When the bowline held, we all pulled, but still the cordage didn't come loose.

Twice more Neal went down into that foaming hole to move the bowline higher on the cordage—and at last we had our hands on the tangled wet rope.

The rest of that day was horrible beyond words. We hauled at that dripping cordage, fearful each moment that it would part from the floating timbers and sails to which it was attached. When we'd taken in all the slack we could, we strained and struggled to bring the tangled mass closer to shore.

The labour of hauling in that raft of junk seemed greater than mere men could undertake. The raft was attached to something—perhaps to a part of the sunken hull: perhaps to an anchor cable: perhaps to the stump of a mast, so that I had the feeling that we were trying to draw up a part of the ocean floor.

Worse than that, it was dripping wet, and the handling of wet cordage in a December north-easter becomes insupportable because of the violent aching in the hands. One can pull at it for a minute or two, but then he must stop and clutch his hands between his thighs in order to be free of that terrible aching.

Equally bad was our dubious footing on the surface of that rock. As we gained ground on the cordage, we staggered, slipped, fell on the icy ledges, and still contrived to move more and more of the cordage inshore: to find boulders around which to belay it, lest our gains be snatched from us by the voracious seas.

For the first time, that day, we saw the flood tide march up to the high-water mark, to leave our poor island shrunk to a mere nothing, barely rising above the tops of the combers that swept at us and past us—though in the sweeping it helped us in our efforts to draw the sails and spars closer.

In my pain and weariness and terror—and in that terror I was not alone—I had thoughts that helped and thoughts that hindered. If at flood tide the breakers crowded up so close to us, where would they be when December's full moon and spring tide were upon us—and every shore has its spring tide twice a month, at new moon and full moon—tides far higher than ordinary tides: so high that they seem bent on submerging land that cannot be submerged at any other time.

And how could my tutors and professors at Oxford have pretended to find truth and beauty in the adventures of

Ulysses? Ulysses, confronted by such tribulations as those that surrounded us, couldn't have helped himself—could only have turned to and been succoured by a god or a goddess in the shape of somebody or other—perhaps by Minerva in the form of an eagle. If he had been in our dire straits, ever-dependable Mercury would have built for him a stout ship from newly cut lumber—yes, and seasoned it for him, too. Mercury would even have done it for him on Boon Island, where no tree grew!

In a vision Minerva would have told him how to discover a great store of cheese. In the depths of his distress, Minerva would have appeared to comfort and encourage him—to restore to him the beauty of his youth; Jupiter would have thundered from heaven, ordering the seas to subside!

But the unhappy truth was that nothing like the *Odyssey* has ever been or ever will be. The troubles of Ulysses were brought upon him by his own stupidity and not, as Homer would have us believe, by the vindictiveness of Poseidon, that green-whiskered ruler of the vasty deep. The dreadful facts we faced on Boon Island taught me that Ulysses was a dilatory and philandering old fool; and if he had been with us on our rock, he'd have been exactly in our situation —despairing, helpless, hopeless, and perpetually on the verge of death.

December 13th, Wednesday

I HOPED that when the north-easter blew itself out, the sea would grow calm, but it didn't. When the wind swung, it backed into the north-west and west, meaning that bad weather had only temporarily abated. We were free of driving snow and rain, but breakers still roared deafeningly on the north and west. They pounded less on the south and east, but still they pounded, throwing off manes of white foam. The wind seemed colder than on the night we were wrecked.

With the break of day I heard Captain Dean calling Neal to come outside. I went out, too, to find the captain staring off to the north-west.

"Neal," the captain said, "see if you can remember those maps you drew in the little book."

Neal said he remembered.

"Can you recall the chief places you lettered on the maps, starting with Cape Porpoise?" the captain asked.

"Cape Porpoise," Neal said, "Cape Arundel, Bald Head Cliff, Cape Neddick——"

"That's it," the captain cried. "Bald Head Cliff! That's where the waves shoot up, yonder, and this is Boon Island! The last time I sailed east from Portsmouth, I sailed between Boon Island and Cape Neddick! Boon Island was to starboard and Bald Head Cliff to larboard!"

As the eastern sky grew brighter we could see the high

dark red rock face of Bald Head Cliff. Spouts of spray rose high against it.

If we'd gone ashore on Bald Head Cliff in a north-easter, instead of on Boon Island, the ship and every last one of us would have been battered to a pulp in a minute's time.

Captain Dean, cheered by the sight of the mainland, lay flat to crawl beneath the shelter and shout the good news to those within.

"Listen," he said. "I know where we are! We're on Boon Island! Just south of us are the Isles of Shoals, where the Pepperrells and other Portsmouth people have fish stages. All winter there's fishing off the Isles of Shoals. There'll be fishing shallops passing us from every direction—Portsmouth, Kittery, York. If we set up something they can see, they'll find us. They'll take us off. But unless all of you get out and go to work, we won't be able to set up anything. Your blood won't circulate. You'll die. You've got to come out and drag cordage and junk."

Nobody said a word.

"Another thing," Captain Dean said. "There's seals off the south side of this island. I saw their heads in the water, following me and watching me, just after dawn, the way they always do. There's ducks, thousands of 'em, swimming in big flocks off the south shore.

"Seals have to rest somewhere. If I can catch one of 'em asleep around midnight, we'll have enough to eat for a month. He'll have fat that maybe we can set fire to."

"Where's the rest of that cheese?" Langman asked.

"Right here with Neal Butler," Captain Dean said. "Those who want it must come out and get it."

He backed out himself, and behind him crawled the remnants of our wretched company, with the exception of Cooky Sipper. Even Graystock and Saver came out, looking like corpses.

The captain took the canvas-wrapped cheese from Neal.

"Go for seaweed to eat with it," he told Neal. "I'll cut and pass out the cheese myself."

He gave each of us a little cube of cheese. When he came to Graystock and Saver, he went upwind of them and eyed them contemptuously.

"You didn't eat your cheese yesterday," the captain said. "It's been saved for you, and I'm giving you yesterday's and to-day's too. You don't deserve either. You've been letting the rest of us work for you, and by rights your rations ought to go to those who've been doing the work."

"We were sick, and couldn't work," Graystock said.

"You're a liar," Captain Dean said. "Cooky Sipper's sick and can't stand up, but you're no sicker than the rest of us. You're scared, that's all! If you weren't, you'd get up and move off to do what has to be done, same as the rest of us. You've got to stay human, not be like helpless babies, or pigs that can be smelled a mile down-wind!" The captain was furious, no doubt about it, but he held himself under control, which isn't easy when dealing with people like Graystock and Saver—or Langman.

He gave them their little ration of cheese; then turned back to the rest of us. "Up to now," he told us harshly, "I haven't said anything about Saver and Graystock, but now I know where we are—now I'm able to see the things God gives us, so we can help ourselves and help each other—I'm going to say something. Yes, and about anyone who thinks he can do like Saver and Graystock."

"It's your duty as captain," Langman said, "to encourage your men: not to discourage 'em."

Captain Dean rounded on him. "What do you think I *am* doing? You ought to be called Wrong-end Langman! I want Graystock and Saver to go to work and help save themselves, instead of refusing to work. They're doing nothing but setting the rest of us an example in discouragement and despair. Nobody ever accomplished anything in this world without working day and night; but most people are such damned fools that they don't want to work at all, not at anything, just like Saver and Graystock. Give 'em a free hand and they won't even work to save their lives! You know the most discouraging thing in the world, Langman? It's for a lot of hard-working people to have to look at and listen to those who'd like to keep on living without doing anything at all."

"I suppose," Langman said, "I was Wrong-end Langman when I said you wanted to run us ashore."

Captain Dean looked at him long and hard. "Mr. Langman," he said, "don't forget that you were No-lookout Langman before we struck. Just what is it that you'd do, right now, if you had the say?"

"I'd build a boat," Langman said promptly.

"With nothing but a hammer, a cutlass, a caulking mallet and our pocket knives?" Captain Dean asked.

Langman glowered at him.

"I'll tell you exactly what we must do first of all," Captain Dean said. "We have to locate the highest point on this rock able to hold a mast that won't blow down. A mast that people on shore may be able to see if they ever come to the water's edge to look for driftwood or seaweed, or if they ever put out for fish or lobsters. Then we have to build a tent around it.

"Even before we do that we need oakum to lie on: oakum to protect our faces and hands and feet: oakum for caps and mittens and bellybands: oakum to keep the wind from blowing the tent to pieces: oakum to keep the rain from driving through the canvas. What's more, we can't build a boat until we have oakum. The sort of boat we build will need all the oakum we can pick between dawn and dark for a year!

"So right now we'll start to separate all the junk we pulled ashore yesterday.

"While we do that, I want Chips Bullock and Swede Butler to pick the highest spot they can find—preferably a smooth piece of ledge that has a crack in it that will let us step a mast with a canvas flag on top—a big one, that can be seen six miles away.

"I'm putting Neal Butler in charge of making white oakum from the tangled cordage and black oakum from the tarred shrouds. He's to take Hallion with him and Saver and Graystock and George White.

"I want Mr. Langman with me—also Mr. Whitworth and Gray—Mellen and my brother Henry. We'll free the yards of whatever junk is fastened to them, and save all the cordage that can be used to lash down the tent.

"When the mast for the new tent is stepped, all usable things are to be brought close to the mast.

"In addition to all these things, we'll have to patrol this island at dawn each day, and at sundown, and again at high tide and low tide. I'll take the first patrol with George White. Miles Whitworth will take the second patrol with Neal Butler. Mr. Langman'll take the third patrol with Nicholas Mellen. Swede Butler will take the fourth patrol with Henry Dean. Chips Bullock will take the fifth patrol with Christopher Gray."

For the first time Langman seemed to have no objection to Captain Dean's plans. "What about this shelter we've been living in for the past three nights?"

"You mean last night," Captain Dean said. "I'll tell you what about it. We'll floor it with oakum, and if any one of us falls so low that he can't relieve himself as he's supposed to do—by going to the place I select as a head and taking his breeches down and otherwise behaving in a civilised and Christian manner—he'll stay nights in this shelter until he's fit to live with other humans. For that matter, we may all have to stay here one more night, until the oakum's picked, the canvas separated from that pile of junk, and the cordage straightened so it can be used.

"Meanwhile the cutlass and Chips's hammer and the caulking mallet are to be used by those who do the separating. And I'll be responsible for them.

"Those who pick oakum will have to do it with their own pocket knives—and before the oakum-picking starts, I want Neal Butler to take Saver and Graystock to a pool of water on the south side of this island and see that they clean their breeches as well as they can be cleaned. Let it be a lesson to you—that I have to put a boy in charge of grown men to make sure they keep clean."

The ruin a furious ocean can wreak on a stout ship in an hour's time is beyond the comprehension of those who haven't seen it. It wrenches spikes from wet wood. It knots cordage into such intricacies as hangman's knots, six-strand Matthew Walkers, double cat's-paws, three-bight Turk's-heads. It smashes a main yard in the slings, strips a stern post from an inner post as readily as a child twists off a doll's foot.

The first thing we freed from the mass of junk was the foretopsail yard for Chips and Swede to use as the centre post of the tent. It was lodged in a frozen hoorah's-nest of canvas, rigging and ratlins that defied our knives almost as though it had been made of iron.

Captain Dean constantly urged us to cut the tarred rope in eight-inch lengths. "If ever we're able to make a fire," he said, "we'll probably have the tarred rope to thank for it; and the lengths'll have to be short or they won't dry."

The foretopsail yard was only half-freed when Neal came stumbling to us.

"Cooky's dead," he told the captain.

The captain snapped his pocket knife shut, stared hard at

Neal: then straightened up to look at the breakers, dirty green-white in the watery morning sunlight.

"How do you know?" he asked heavily.

"I took him the first oakum we made," Neal said. "I thought it might make him easier. His mouth was filled with phlegm. I tried to get it out, but couldn't." He stared at his hands and added, "His face was black. He must have choked to death."

"I see," Captain Dean said. He examined his damaged fingers, stooped for a stone with which to pry open his knife again; peered at the blade as though he found it strange: then caught up a rope-end and haggled off a fifteen-foot length.

"Well," he said slowly, "go back to your oakum pickers. Send White to the shelter. He and I'll take care of Cooky. We'll have to take him to the south shore and put him in the water. There's just a possibility he might float to York and start someone looking for us."

To me he said, "Keep right on as you are. See the others do, too."

He gave me the hammer.

"Couldn't you take his coat for yourself?" Neal asked.

"Why yes," Captain Dean said, "I think it would be all right to take his coat."

They stumbled off together across the icy rocks, and we went on freeing the foretopsail yard of its twisted accumulation of junk.

I was sorry to see them go, because there were a few things that I should have said to Captain Dean.

I wanted to speak about eating. This morning and yesterday morning each one of us had eaten as much seaweed as could be packed into a pint mug, and less than half that amount of cheese. Already my stomach felt gassy and abraded, as though I had been kicked there.

Now the cheese was gone. The captain had spoken about

going out at midnight in the hope of finding a seal asleep on the rocks, but I knew a little something about seals from watching them come up the Thames after whitebait.

Neither Captain Dean nor anybody else was going to find a seal sleeping on ledges in this kind of weather, when a single wave could crush a seal against a rock as readily as it could crush a cheese. They slept while floating where waves only rocked them like a cradle.

There was a thought hidden in all this, but it eluded me. My brain, like all the rest of me, was numb from cold and wet clothes, which felt as though nothing, not even heat, could ever dry them.

Seals, I thought confusedly, ate anything. They'd certainly eat cheese, and I'd heard that somewhere on the lower Thames a seal had killed a woman and eaten her. If that was so, then a seal would be quick to bite at Cooky Sipper's body, whether it floated or sank—whether it was clothed or unclothed. Therefore there was no reason why Captain Dean shouldn't take Cooky's coat for himself, and the rest of his clothes for those who needed them—and there wasn't one of us who didn't need more clothes.

I looked over my shoulder toward the patch of canvas under which we'd sheltered. Captain Dean and George White were dragging Cooky's body over the icy rocks and ledges. The rope was fastened around Cooky's neck, and I was glad to see that the body was unclothed, so there apparently was no need for me to mention those confused thoughts of mine to the captain.

There were some other things, though, that I hadn't said, and it was hard for me to remember what they were. With our cheese gone, we would have nothing to eat, so if the captain wanted Cooky's body to float ashore, it seemed to me, he'd do better to leave the body on a rock, where it would freeze. If it were frozen, it would float, maybe, as a cake of ice floats.

D

I wondered whether I was right. Only a little of an iceberg shows above water.

"What happens to a frozen body?" I asked Langman.

"What do you mean?" Langman demanded.

"I mean, would Cooky Sipper float if he were frozen?"

"Of course he wouldn't," Langman said.

"How do you know?" I asked. "Did you ever see a frozen man in the water?"

"No," Langman said, "but he'd sink."

I felt fairly sure that Langman was wrong about this, as about everything else. An iceberg never sank, did it?

The captain and George White made hard work of getting Cooky to the seaweedy rock-fingers of the south shore. They would pull Cooky's body forward until his head was almost at their ankles, then they'd get themselves across another ten feet of ledges, flat on their stomachs like two frogs; then rise and cautiously pull Cooky to them again.

If I hurried, I told myself, I could reach them even now, before they put the body in the water.

I felt Langman looking at me, a mocking twist on his thin, sallow face. That was a bad habit of his—staring fixedly at those he disliked, apparently under the impression that the person at whom he stared wasn't conscious of his stare—which of course wasn't the case. That was like Langman. He was about as perceptive and sensitive as a pig.

"What you got on your mind?" Langman asked.

"Why, nothing," I said. "I've got nothing on my mind."

He looked over his shoulder at the captain and White pulling and hauling at Cooky's body.

"Well," I said, "this isn't clearing that foretopsail yard."

We had it cleared by midafternoon, soon after Swede and Chips came for it and for a square of canvas to use as a flag. They had, they said, found a ledge with a deep crack in it

—one into which a spar could be pushed and shimmed into place with wedge-shaped rocks.

"Once we get that spar in place," Swede said to Langman, "it'll outlast you."

Langman looked scornful. "If we don't build a boat, it'll outlast all of us."

Chips swung his head from side to side. "I wish I had my axe," he said irrelevantly. "When we were cleaning that slot for the spar, we found slivers of rock. They're shaped like splitting wedges. We can use 'em for chisels if they don't splinter when pounded."

He and Swede carried away the foretopsail yard and the square of canvas; but dark came down on us before we were able to unsnarl the sails that were wrapped with rigging as a fly is wrapped in a spider web.

So we spent that night in the shelter in which Cooky had sobbed and moaned night after night.

Night after night?

Had we been three nights in that shelter? Why no! It was only *two* nights. I found it difficult to keep track. The first night we'd spent in a crevice, without covering. The next two nights we'd had a strip of canvas above us.

Things were different with Cooky gone. Not better, perhaps, but quieter. Cooky had always groaned and sobbed; and lying somewhere near him was another who moaned and groaned. It may have been Graystock. It may have been Saver. It could, God knows, have been almost any one of us. Now, with Cooky gone, there was a lot less sobbing.

December 14th, Thursday

I THINK our labours of the day before, and our depression because of the death of Cooky Sipper, would have kept us from even thinking of continuing our work on the tent on Thursday. The bitter north-west wind was more biting than that of the north-easter. I thought wryly of the winter chill of the Bodleian, often so penetrating that students insisted they couldn't read. This was a different cold, and its effect upon us forced us to do things we couldn't otherwise have done.

And that's another thing my sojourn on Boon Island did for me: it made me impatient of a person who, because of fancied ill-health or discomfort, fails to execute a task or complete an undertaking. No man is worth his salt if, by such a failure, he inconveniences others.

A man can't, I know, stay awake indefinitely, though I think he somehow contrives to sleep or to lose consciousness in spite of pain or mental trouble. Yet I'd have sworn I never slept on the night of the thirteenth. All night long my feet and legs either throbbed or burned or itched. Each one of those three ills seemed unendurable by itself, and certainly there was no respite from the constant movement of the men around me—an uneasy thrashing, as dogs thrash when wounded and in distress.

When daylight came I could see as well as feel the reason for my ailing legs and feet. My legs had swelled until they filled my sea boots, and a discolouring ridge of flesh puffed out above the boot tops.

Captain Dean, examining his own legs, said there was no help for it: the boots would have to go.

"It's the wet," he said, "and the cold that comes with this north-west wind. The only good thing about a north-west wind is that there's a calm after it stops blowing—if it ever does."

He raised his voice to make it heard above the rumble and smashing of the breakers.

"Sharpen your knives, everyone," he said. "You'll find whetstones under you. That'll remind you there's always something good to be said about anything or anyone. There'll never be any shortage of rocks on this island; none of ice, either.

"Here's what you'll have to do—and save the stitching. We'll need it to tie bandages." He severed the top stitch of the seam that runs down the inner part of the leg, then picked out the remaining thread as far down as the ankle. From the ankle he cut straight down through the leather to the edge of the sole. From that cut he slid his knife blade around the heel, pressing the blade against the sole. He did the same to the forward part; then folded the whole boot outward from his leg and foot.

When he rolled up his long underwear, both foot and leg were shocking sights. The leg, puffed and blistered, had open sores where his underwear and wet breeches had rubbed. The toes were pallid. Some of the toenails came away when the boot was folded over; but the toes didn't bleed: they just stayed that queer greyish white.

The captain drew a sharp breath. "You'll have to expect a little pain at first," he said, "but that's only the blood coming back into your legs."

The captain studied those nailless toes.

Then he said slowly, "Before any of the rest of you start

cutting off your boots, you'd better go out for canvas. We'll
have to make something to put on our feet so we can walk."

"Walk with feet like that one yours!" Langman cried.

"I don't have to answer that, do I?" Captain Dean asked.
"We've *got* to walk. More cheese might come ashore. We
must have more oakum. We must move out from this wet
shelter into a tent. We must have a place where we can pick
oakum under cover. We can't make oakum or raise a tent
unless we go outside. To do that we'll have to wash our
legs in something warm that'll clean 'em."

Langman groaned. "Something warm! Where'll you find
anything warm around here? Even if you found something,
what would you put in it?"

"I've watched everyone urinating about ten times a day,
haven't I?" Captain Dean asked. "I hated to see it wasted,
but I couldn't give up my powder horn if there was a chance
of getting a fire from the powder. Well, the powder's as
wet to-day as it was when we were wrecked, and I've carried
it next to my skin day and night. So now I'll put the powder
in a canvas bag. We'll use the horn for the warm stuff you
think we haven't got. Now take White and Miles with you
and go for that oakum. And remember: don't urinate till
I tell you to."

He sawed delicately with his knife-blade at the stitches
in his other boot top, and picked out the thread as carefully
as though his life depended upon it—and perhaps it did.

I was shocked and frightened by that glimpse of the
captain's leg and foot, and by the stench that had come from
it. I was sure my own feet and legs were no different; and
while it seemed impossible to walk at all on feet so painful,
I not only knew that I could do it, but I was filled with a
frenzy to pick the oakum necessary to protect our legs
and feet.

Those who have never picked oakum—and few people do

it except sailors when there's nothing else to be done on shipboard, or those who live in prisons or poorhouses—find it tedious, hard on the hands and on the nerves, to separate those stiff strands of fibre that make up a rope: then, with finger-twistings and knife-points, to fluff out each strand so that it becomes again a flattened mat of hemp.

But when oakum is needed to keep legs and feet from rotting, almost anyone works hard and quickly learns the knack of reducing a cable or a hawser to its original state of untwisted strands.

At the captain's direction we practised first on him, cutting two six-foot lengths of linen from the bolt, and a short length to use as a sponge. Each six-foot strip was a bandage, down one side of the leg, across the foot, and up the other side of the leg.

I don't know what we'd have done without that bolt of linen. For years I woke screaming from a dream of what would have happened to me if we'd had no linen to bind our legs.

Each side of the bandage lapped twice around the leg; but before the lapping was done, a poultice of oakum was set in place on the upper and lower part of the foot, from ankle to knee. Then the protruding linen was folded over the oakum, and narrow bands of linen held the whole in place. Over the outer linen was wrapped a square of canvas. Thus our feet and legs were cased in a quadruple bandage—a single layer of linen, a layer of oakum, a quadruple layer of linen, and a canvas leggin.

The captain had us slit the long legs of his underwear, and the legs of his breeches as well, and these were tied in place with the thread taken from his boots.

Since all these bandages were so bulky as to make the boots useless, he cut off the boot tops and made each top into a sort of knee boot, or knee pad, bound around his knee by strands of tarred rope.

We tried to economise on urine, but couldn't. The powder horn, its thick end removed and its stopper pounded tight, held about a pint, and we had to have one and a half hornfuls for each two legs and feet. In this we were fortunate, for the entire company, fearful of losing feet or legs, was consumed with the need to urinate, and calls for the powder horn were constant.

When we had finished with Captain Dean, he helped Neal and me to cut off our own boots and bandage our legs and feet. Before he turned back my first boot, he put his hand on my knee. "Don't look at them," he said. "They aren't as bad as they look, and you'll gain nothing by seeing them." There was no doubt in my mind that he was right, and I think that, by obeying him, both Neal and I saved ourselves from self-pity or despondency—states of mind that never bettered anyone.

With Neal and me to help him, Captain Dean sat the rest of the crew on the two ledges that had formed the wall of our shelter, and over their knees he laid the canvas beneath which we had slept. While we worked on them, they picked oakum, using the canvas as a table. Below the canvas the captain, Neal and I, on our padded knees, washed all those legs and feet with the warm contents of the powder horn. This washing was painful beyond belief, and the sailors howled and cursed as their legs and feet were sopped with urine. Nor could I blame them, for the toes of some of them broke off in our hands, and their blisters and abscesses, in some cases, were so deep that the bone showed through.

December 15th, Friday

SIX OF us were able—perhaps "willing" is a better word—
to crawl from beneath the canvas on the morning after we
had bandaged our legs. All thirteen of us should have come
out, for the tide, high at daybreak, might have deposited
something edible on shore, and our craving for something
to put in our stomachs was almost overpowering.

Those beside myself who dragged themselves into that
cold dawn were Captain Dean, Neal Butler, Swede Butler,
Langman and White—and God knows I probably couldn't
have done it if the captain hadn't crawled out first, with
Neal close behind him, and Swede close on Neal's heels. What
Neal could do, I told myself, I must do. Langman only came
with us, I think, because of his overwhelming fear that one
of us might find a scrap to eat and conceal it from him.
White, I thought, came because he was a bos'n, and bos'ns
regard themselves as being hardier than other seamen, and
averse to being outdone by anyone.

As we made our painful patrol of the high-water mark,
we saw two seals playfully nosing at a floating object, and
simultaneously Captain Dean came across a slender stick of
wood that might have been a broom handle.

The seals swam around and under the thing with which
they played, and whisked at it with their hind flippers, until
the water shoaled. Then they abandoned it, and lay offshore,
rising high in the water, puffing out their whiskers and

watching us from staring round eyes. I would have given anything I ever hoped to own if I could have got my hands on one of those seals, though I well knew I could never have held him.

When a breaker thrust their plaything against the rock, we found it to be two bones from salted beef, held together by the muscles of the joint. To add to this bit of good fortune, Captain Dean came across a lump of cheese the size of a child's head, and Langman found a mussel from which grew scores of long streamers of thin kelp, which Langman insisted were good to eat. The mussel he discarded with an expression of distaste, before the captain could stop him.

"A mussel is full of meat," the captain protested. "Well, one mussel wouldn't have gone far among thirteen men, but there's more where that one came from."

When we returned to the canvas shelter with this treasure trove, the others came out, dreadful haggard objects. Each was given a streamer of kelp; and all of them, as intent as an audience at a play, watched us smash those beef bones with rocks, and, with knife blades, extract a dab of marrow for each man.

"We'll eat all the cheese right now," Captain Dean said. "We'll lash that saucepan handle to the end of this broomstick with spun yarn. Maybe, when the tide is right, we'll find enough mussels to give us a real meal—and can pry 'em off the rocks without losing our hands.

"Then," he went on, "we'll all go to the flag mast and build the tent and pick more oakum for it. We can't spend another night in this rotten shelter."

The men, haggard, bearded, misshapen, just stared at him. I think they were only a quarter conscious, partly paralysed by the biting cold of the night just past. Three of them—Saver, Graystock and Mellen—crawled silently back beneath the canvas.

Captain Dean stooped to peer after them. Then he gave up. After all, there's no use driving those who have passed the limit of endurance.

The size of the tent was determined by the area of the rounded ledge that held the centre pole.

The ledge was shaped roughly like a humped-up triangle, sliced from the side of an enormous hogshead. This triangle rose from a welter of boulders. It was narrow: then widened as a wedge of orange peel widens, to descend, still widening, and vanish among more boulders. Thus the tent of necessity was three-sided, like a pyramid. Its height was regulated by the distance between the rock and the lowest lashing of the canvas flag.

Captain Dean helped us pick the corner posts for the tent. When they were set in place, Swede, Langman and Harry Hallion formed a living step-ladder on which the captain mounted to lash the posts to the mast. The rest of us dragged pieces of sail across the rocks, arranging them so they could be fastened to the corner posts with spun yarn.

The canvas at the base of each of the three sides was anchored by broken pieces of deck-planking. The planks were held down by boulders.

The placing of the boulders was a source of great concern to Captain Dean. "If those timbers aren't properly secured," he said, "the canvas is sure to blow down on us. Such things always happen on the coldest night, when you won't be able to see your hand in front of your face."

So outside the single row of boulders atop each plank, he made us lay another row of boulders. Then he insisted we lay a third row on top of this double row—big boulders, too large to be handled by one man. How, with my half-frozen hands, I could have been of any help in the handling of them, I cannot recall. All I remember is that in order to do so, I had to take a firm grip with my feet, and when I did, they felt as thought I stood in nettles.

Langman worked as hard as anyone, but he never stopped talking about the boat. As in the matter of privateers, he couldn't drop a subject for a minute, once he was embarked on it.

"If the full-moon spring tide rises above the top of this rock," he said, "what good's a tent going to do us? Nothing will help us then but a boat."

"Look," Captain Dean said, "I've measured this rock. Right here where we're standing, as near as I can figure, it's fourteen feet above normal high-water mark. According to my reckoning, the tide rise here is seven feet. I don't believe any spring tide could be three times as high as a normal tide."

"It *can* be," Langman said. "There's some places only a little north of here where the tide rises and falls twenty-eight feet. I've heard Woodes Rogers say so when he was sailing to Newfoundland."

"I know those places," Captain Dean said, "but that's 'way north of here. The same thing's true in England. You get some terrible high tides in the Severn estuary, but you never get any such tides on the Isle of Wight, which isn't far away, as the crow flies. And I'll tell you another thing, Langman. This is the fifteenth of December, and according to my lights——"

"It's the sixteenth," Langman interrupted. "To-morrow's Sunday."

"No," the captain said, "this is the fifteenth. Sunday isn't until day after to-morrow."

"I figured it out," Langman said. "To-morrow's Sunday."

"We've got to get this tent finished," Captain Dean said, "and there's no sense arguing over which day's Sunday. The thing I want to impress on you is that my reckoning shows full moon to be due December 27th, a Wednesday. We must have had one spring tide already, because there should have been a new moon day before yesterday."

"The twenty-seventh would be a Thursday," Langman said.

"Well, whichever day of the week it is," Captain Dean said, "it's twelve days to spring tide, and if we don't get this shelter done, and the tide *does* rise that extra fourteen feet, and we *do* have another onshore blow, and we *do* have to have a boat to save our lives, we can't *have* a boat unless we shelter ourselves during those twelve days between now and spring tide. The tent has to come first."

* * *

Those of us who worked on the tent were the captain, Swede Butler, Langman, Neal, Harry Hallion and George White.

All the rest—Henry Dean, Christopher Gray, Nicholas Mellen, Saver, Graystock and Bullock—as soon as the sides were up took shelter within it, and three of them—Chips Bullock, Saver and Graystock—looked as though nothing on earth could ever induce them to come out again.

The others, under the urgings of Henry Dean, did their best to pick oakum; but when they wouldn't work, and just lay or sat there, their eyes opaque like those of a fish, holding their hands to the pits of their stomach and crouching over them as if to send a little warmth into those numb extremities, there seemed to be nothing to be done about it.

We could hear Henry beg them to get on with their picking. That was one of the advantages of the new shelter. We couldn't sit up in the old shelter, and so had to go outdoors to pick oakum.

In the tent we could stand up, if only three or four stood at a time. The rest could sit up.

The day we finished the tent Henry Dean and Nicholas

Mellen, fumbling around a little pile of junk we hadn't yet untangled, came across the rawhide seizing of one of the yards. It was still fastened to a fragment of the yard, and when it was pried loose and unwound, it looked like a piece of soggy cowhide about eighteen inches wide and two feet long.

When Henry Dean brought it back to the tent, even the men who seemed half dead sat up to look at it, and there was an instant demand that it be distributed for food.

"Food!" Henry Dean exclaimed. "You can't . . ." Then he stopped and said, "I'll speak to my brother."

He came out to where we were rolling boulders against the bottom of the canvas. "The men inside," he told Captain Dean, "want this rawhide divided. They think they can eat it. I think it might hurt 'em instead of help 'em."

The captain felt it with speculative fingers. "No," he said slowly. "It wouldn't hurt 'em. Food is what you think it is. A lot of critters live on things that wouldn't be much help to other critters. So do a lot of men. Probably you wouldn't care much about eating a mouse, but Chinese do and think they're nice. They eat 'em, and like 'em. You divide this rawhide into thirteen pieces. Give one piece to each man, and make him chop his own into little pieces, just as fine as he can mince 'em."

Perhaps that rawhide did give everyone a little strength, for after each had eaten his share, those in the tent went back to picking oakum. When night came we not only had shelter over us, but we had a layer of oakum beneath us— a thin one, to be sure, but one that wasn't wet. It was damp, yes; but it wasn't wet, and up to now we had been wet every night—wet, and cold with a cold that beggars description. Those who live beneath roofs, or in dry caves, with dry clothes next to their skins, can't imagine what it's like to exist surrounded by a tumult of breakers, in wet clothes, on sharp wet rocks, and in cold so intense that every boulder in sight is covered with a thick armour of ice.

But we had a little more room than we'd heretofore had, though we still lay tight against each other, belly to buttocks so as to take advantage of the slight warmth that each of us, by the grace of God, contrived to hold within himself.

December 16th, Saturday

THE WORLD, I've found, is full of people who cannot realise that *everything* is hard work—everything. People turn to sailing, or to fishing, or to acting, or to painting, or to play writing—to any one of the thousand different occupations —with some sort of a vague idea that it's easy work. Sometimes work can be enthralling if it's done as an avocation instead of out of dire necessity, but it's hard work just the same.

So I question that the building of our boat on Boon Island was harder work than writing a play, or sheepherding, or chopping wood; but I suspect that no work has ever been done under such adverse circumstances.

The place we selected to build the boat was on the south side of the island, where ledge-fingers ran slopingly out toward the south. The ledges were less abrupt there than on the other three sides, and the surf less violent.

It was on the south side, always, that the seals thrust their bullet heads from the water to watch us, and it was aggravating to see twenty or thirty of those round heads examining us from popeyes, and puffing out their whiskers at us, as if amazed by our presence on their island.

Sometimes, surprisingly, even though the wind blew from the north, a huge swell would roll in toward that south side and there'd be the watery shadows of ten or more seal floating in it, seemingly higher than we.

Just before the wave broke, the seals would rise shoulder-high for a clearer look at us, then slip away, down the far side, while the wave curled over with a roar. I couldn't imagine Boon Island without breakers hurrying toward its shores from every direction, as if to a boisterous and senseless rendezvous.

The day had started inauspiciously because Langman, having determined that the day was Sunday instead of Saturday, had whispered sulkily with Mellen and White, during the night, and come to the conclusion that to work on Sunday was wrong. All of us, he told the captain, should observe Sunday with him and Mellen and White. I knew, as well as I knew my own name, that he was just being contrary.

Captain Dean shook his head wearily. "Mr. Langman," he said, "I have no intention of attempting to speak for God, but you evidently have a personal God that differs in some respects from mine. My God accepts those who worship Him, regardless of whether they worship on Greenwich time or on Cape Porpoise time."

"That's blasphemy," Langman said quickly.

"What's blasphemous about it?" Swede asked.

"Let him call it anything he likes," Captain Dean said. "In good weather we've always observed the Sabbath on my ships in a fitting manner, provided the weather made it possible for us to do so.

"But if a storm happened to hit us on Sunday, we did anything necessary for the welfare of the ship.

"You've insisted for days that our lives may depend on this boat because the full-moon tide may force us off.

"Very well, Mr. Langman. I think I can speak for God. I think I can say you'll be forgiven for working on Sunday, just as God would forgive you for eating a seal on Friday, if you were a Catholic—and if we were so fortunate as to kill a seal.

"So you'll take your turn hauling plank, Mr. Langman, and so will Mellen and White, just as if it were Saturday, which it is."

"That's more blasphemy, and it's still Sunday," Langman insisted.

Swede looked at him as if he wanted to kill him, and I wish he had.

A smooth piece of ledge, sprinkled with boulders, lay just above the seaweed fringe. This ledge sloped easily toward the seaweed fringe and ended between two rock fingers.

That rock was our shipyard, our launching stage, our naval storehouse.

Our only tools were our pocket knives, Chips's hammer, the caulking mallet and the cutlass.

Our only shipbuilding materials were the remnants of the *Nottingham*. With Chips's hammer we had strained our muscles to draw nails and spikes from the few wet planks we had recovered, but we had failed so lamentably that our chief reliance for putting the boat together were the nails and spikes salvaged from Chips's work bag.

While those of us able to walk dragged timbers, planks, canvas and cordage to the launching stage, the captain and Swede undertook to make the cutlass into a saw—a task that would never, I thought, be accomplished except by the direct intervention of Mercury, Minerva and another half-dozen Greek divinities like those who were forever getting Ulysses out of his difficulties.

Neither Mercury nor Minerva, however, had a helping hand in the transformation of the cutlass. Chips thought of the way it could be done, but was too weak to do anything except advise us in our labours.

He had come down with the same sort of sickness that had finished Cooky Sipper. Being a heavy man, the blisters and ulcers on his feet and legs were worse than ours, and he couldn't stand upright. So he stayed in the tent, while Captain Dean and Swede worked beside him on the cutlass. His voice was weak and choked with phlegm, as Cooky's had been, and he found difficulty in making himself heard above the everlasting slashing and crashing of the breakers.

The captain and Swede brought sharp-edged rocks into the tent. While Swede held the blade of the cutlass at an angle against the sharp edge of a rock as a man holds the blade of a razor at an angle against his cheek, the captain would smash at the blade with a similar rock. Thus a V-shaped nick would be broken out of the cutlass blade.

They started with a nick at the hilt end, a nick at the point and a nick halfway between each of the three nicks. Then they subdivided each space between the nicks until the blade became a series of jagged saw teeth.

Then Swede took one of those chisel-like rocks and Chips took another, and they rubbed and rubbed at each nick until both sides had bevelled edges and the teeth were sharp.

When they started I didn't believe they could do it. Since Boon Island, I believe the right sort of man can do anything.

Even less than I believed a saw could be made from the cutlass did I believe that a seaworthy boat would emerge from the materials at hand, but we *did* build it, even though we had less with which to work than strolling players would need to build a stage in a barn.

In spite of all our handicaps, we had something to hearten us, for on this day mussels in quantity—though little different from the one Langman had thrown away—were discovered in the western pools and indentations.

Early in the afternoon, at low tide, Captain Dean and George White left the shipyard to patrol the island for scraps of wreckage and our daily repast of seaweed and ice. The captain carried his broomstick with the saucepan handle wrapped to the end by rope yarn and strips of linen.

In cutting seaweed, they uncovered a pool in which a mussel was attached to the hard-packed mixture of shell and rock fragments that lay at the bottom of all such depressions.

It was one of the big mottled sea mussels, unlike the clean blue ones that grow in beds on gravel spits near the mouths of rivers. This one was an old, old mussel, survivor of countless storms such as those through which we had passed —survivor, too, of the crashing blows of countless millions of breakers, exactly like those that had thundered in our ears for six long days and nights—or was it five—or was it seven, as Langman said?

*   *   *

Even in the writing I am constantly uncertain of dates when I trust to memory.

The days seemed endless: the nights were a torment of aching cold, of fear, of trepidation—ah, those nights, with the breakers thundering at our very shoulders! Always, in the night, I had thoughts of eternity: of death, and of never ending punishment that might continue forever, forever, forever, forever . . . No wonder our companions cried aloud to God so frequently! No wonder Langman thought Saturday was Sunday! No wonder I must so often go back to the calendar I reconstructed with the help of Captain Dean and Neal Butler. Sometimes even the captain couldn't remember, and both of us had to rely on Neal's proficiency as a "quick study."

*   *   *

Old as the mussel looked, however, it was unquestionably a mussel, and a mussel is food, no matter how overgrown and thickened it is with pink and grey encrustations, with sprigs of seaweed.

Captain Dean prodded at it with the stick to which the saucepan handle had been lashed, and when the shell was free of the trash in which it grew, White snatched it from the water. So Captain Dean and White, crawling to other pools, raked the weed back from the edges. In the end they uncovered thirty-nine. A few were young and blue: mostly they were ugly, encrusted, ancient.

The captain said he and White could have got more if their hands could have stood it; but the pain that results from repeatedly immersing hands in icy water, even when the immersion is momentary, is such as to agonise the most hardened sailorman. It can't be borne.

When White and the captain returned, the captain held his hands behind his back, White doled the mussels into them one by one, and the captain passed them around, picking us at random, so that there was no way of telling who would get which mussel.

There were three apiece, repulsive-looking, lumpy, with hard, mottled fungus growths upon them, and with a sort of beard attached to one end. We opened them by forcing a knife-point between the tight shells, then sliding the blade around through the hinge. In spite of their looks, they seemed savoury enough to us—once we had learned how to rid them of the infinitesimal pearls with which they were infested. The pearls could only be removed by squeezing them out; by rubbing the meat between the tongue and the roof of the mouth.

Certainly I have never wanted another mussel since those days, but they gave our seaweed a fishy juiciness wholly lacking when the seaweed was eaten alone.

Langman, protesting that in all likelihood they were poisonous, for a time refused to eat them; but when he saw Mellen and White swallowing them avidly, he ate them too, sneering at all of us.

I think they must have given us a little strength, for after

I had choked them down I returned more hopefully to my labours on that hopeless boat.

For the bottom of the boat we stretched an oblong of canvas flat on the sloping rock, weighting each corner with a boulder so it couldn't blow. On the canvas we laid three planks side by side, fastened together, but fastened in a way that would have sickened a savage from the heart of Africa.

The ends of those planks were jagged. We had no way of rounding them off except by smashing them with a hammer, since the saw was too precious to waste on anything trivial; so all that day was spent in getting ready to build rather than in building, and—seemingly most important of all—in endless discussions as to who should go in the boat if ever it was finished.

December 17th, Sunday

EVEN SAVER and Graystock, those lumps of men who
wouldn't pick oakum unless they felt like it, and Chips
Bullock, who was willing to work but couldn't, wanted to
be in that boat when she was launched, if she ever *was*
launched.

Probably this was because to-day, our first Sunday, the
captain discovered, on the snow-covered fields of the mainland, moving specks that must have been people—church-
goers, in all likelihood.

I think by that time we were all of us half-demented, for
we shouted and waved our arms, hoping to catch the
attention of those far-off specks—and surely there wasn't a
one of us who didn't know that we, all brown and grey,
with grizzled beards and wrappings of oakum, could be
no more apparent to those on shore than a seal would
have been.

But the sight of those moving specks upon that distant
slope made each of us conscious of how near we were to
bread and meat, to warmth and drink and other people, to
houses and soft beds and dry clothes, to salves for our
festering feet and the sores on our knees and hands; so even
before the floor of the boat was completed, all but a few
were urging that they be allowed to go ashore in her.

Two exceptions were Swede and Neal. Swede didn't say
it openly, but he was determined Neal must be saved, if

anyone was. And equally apparent was Neal's determination not to leave his father.

I sympathised with Swede.

If I had the say as to who should go in the boat, I'd have picked Captain Dean first and Neal second: the captain because he was strongest and would have influence on shore: Neal because he was youngest and with the greatest possibilities. But I never would have picked Swede. His feet were so crippled that I considered him useless—which eventually taught me never to under-rate a determined man, no matter how helpless he may seem.

Even poor Chips Bullock argued his case to the captain in a faintly raucous voice, pleading that without his hammer and his nails and spikes, the boat would have been impossible.

The captain said, "Yes, Chips. We'll do the best we can."

Graystock and Saver, useless as they were, united in saying they deserved a place in the boat because of their physical condition, which was bad.

Strangest of all the arguments was that of Harry Hallion, who said he thought he ought to go because he spoke Indian.

"Indian?" Captain Dean asked. "What kind of Indian?"

"Nova Scotia Indian," Hallion said. "I lived with an Indian woman all one winter."

"Nova Scotia Indians are Micmacs," Captain Dean protested. "The Indians around here are a different breed. In the winter they live in the woods—and that's one place we're not going when we get ashore." He never said "if we get ashore." He always said "when we get ashore."

Becoming suddenly angry at all this pretence, the captain ordered all those not working on the boat to return to the tent and pick more oakum—more oakum—more oakum.

"There'll be *nobody* go in this boat," he shouted, "unless we can plug every hole with oakum. Right now she looks as though she'd have more holes in her than she'll have wood."

Repeatedly, that day, we stopped working on the boat and went to the tent to help in the picking of oakum—not only because of the intense cold, but to consult with Chips Bullock as to the best way to erect a stanchion at each corner of the floorboards.

The glimpse we'd had of those people on shore must have made each one of us, even the captain, worse than desperate; for he took out a piece of black oakum from next to his skin. He let us feel the oakum. "Is it dry?" he asked us. "Feel it!" He passed it around. Swede and Neal and I said that to us it still felt damp; but all the others, Langman included, pretended to find it dry. Langman was always wrong, and the captain knew it, but this time he wanted to take Langman's opinion.

So he took a pinch of gunpowder from the canvas pouch, produced his useless pistol and cocked it; then did what he'd already done a thousand times—put powder in the pan, wrapped the lock and the pan with the oakum, snapped the flint . . . snapped it: snapped it: snapped it: over and over.

We could see the spark inside the oakum: smell a delicious, tantalising odour of tarry scorching. There was even a faint hint of smoke. He kept on pulling the hammer back and snapping it; pulling it back and snapping it.

Then he passed it to Langman, who did the same. Then Langman passed it to me, and I tried and tried.

All we got was a faint wisp of tarry-smelling smoke.

Another thing I learned to dislike on Boon Island were the wiseacres who are forever saying, "Where there's smoke there's fire." At Oxford I often heard Latin-speaking dons —the worst kind—throw that remark at each other. *Flamma fumo est proxima.* Where there's smoke there's fire.

It's not so; but there's no more use arguing with people who quote that saying than there would be in wrangling with the old Roman who is credited with first uttering it. The old Roman is dead: the others nearly so. "Where there's smoke, there's fire," indeed! I'd have liked to hear them talk like that on Boon Island!

Since this was Sunday, we held services in the tent. Captain Dean led us in a prayer that thanked God for His mercy in letting us stay alive; that thanked Him for granting us ice to chew and mussels to eat; that implored God to let us be seen from the mainland; that begged Him to send a ship near this dreadful rock.

All of us repeated his words in a hoarse and shivering chorus—all except Langman and White and Mellen, who, having decided the day wasn't Sunday, refused to pray with us.

I think, though, Langman was somehow helped by those Sunday services, in spite of being so certain that our Sunday was the wrong one: because when Neal and I made our last patrol of the day at dead low tide, around three o'clock in the afternoon, Langman came with us, and so did George White. They helped us in our daily search for mussels, so that we were able to bring back eight for each man.

December 18th, Monday

I KNOW how a condemned man must feel when he is about to die for no sin of his own: then is half promised a reprieve that never arrives.

Seven oars for seven men we'd planned for the boat, and a longer steering oar. In order to make them we had to saw planks to the proper length: then split the planks with the sharpened rocks Chips Bullock had discovered.

That was a labour undertaken by Neal and Swede and me while the captain and Langman planned the fastening of the boat's sides.

The cutlass-saw was the instrument we used to saw those planks; and for incarnate devilishness that saw was perfectly designed to plague persons already plagued to the limit of endurance.

The handle was too small to allow the use of both hands; and the starting of a cut with those jagged teeth was a trial. All the wood was wet, and there seemed to be no way of holding the planks firm. We succeeded at last, after a fashion, by wedging one end of the plank beneath a boulder and forcing the opposite end upward.

Then the wielder of the saw, stretching himself under the plank, would haggle at it, always drawing the saw toward himself, until enough wood had been gnawed away to allow the plank to be broken.

We called the different days of the week by the names of occurrences, and I thought for a time that this day would

be called Oar Day—the day before having been our first
Sunday, and the day before that Boat Day, and the day
before that Tent Day, and the day before that The Day We
Cut Off Our Boots, and the day before that Cooky Sipper's
Day.

But our labours on the oars were dwarfed by a discovery
made by the captain.

At dead high tide, around ten o'clock, the captain raised
a hoarse shout and pointed off to the south with his oakum-
wrapped hand.

Beyond the breakers, beyond the round seal heads that
watched us and watched us, were the sails of three vessels.

They might have been fishermen or coasting schooners,
but at least they were vessels—the first sign of a sail we had
seen; and to me, who had felt sure that no fishermen would
venture out of port at this season of the year, they were a
sight that sent through me a choking surge of hope.

They were moving straight out from shore, to the eastward, probably out of Portsmouth, the captain said: taking
provisions to the Isles of Shoals, perhaps, or going for
cargoes of salt cod.

Again everyone crawled from the tent to see those three
wonderful sails, and to wave their arms and halloo hoarsely.
The three vessels looked to us to be about nine miles from
us, but still we hallooed. No shout can be heard at a distance
of nine miles. All of us knew that. Perhaps our shouts were
a form of prayer.

When the sails, sliding gradually to the eastward, became
dim specks on the horizon, the oakum pickers crawled back
to the tent. They looked like sick bears, and felt, if I could
judge by my own feelings, even sicker than they looked.

Neal and Swede and I went back to making oars. The
task before us seemed insurmountable—as impossible,
almost, as drilling a hole through a block of granite with
a needle.

December 19th, Tuesday

THOSE OARS, I thought, were the most troublesome thing about the boat—though I suppose that each part of every enterprise always seems most difficult and most important to the one to whom it's entrusted.

Nonetheless, the oars seemed vital, for unless the wind was in the east, we couldn't depend on our sail to carry us to the nearest land, which, if Captain Dean's reckoning was correct, was six miles away. Even under favourable circumstances—better circumstances than the bitter ones we had so far encountered—we would be three hours, at least, rowing that clumsy boat to shore.

And row we must, not only to get the boat across that turbulent stretch of water, but to keep ourselves moving so we wouldn't freeze.

Yet the oars, split with rock-wedges from boards, were the same width from end to end. They had to be narrowed at one end, and smoothed, so that men could use them effectively. The saw was useless to smooth those sharp edges. Our knives made no impression upon them, for the wet boards only roughened when we tried to bevel the corners.

The best we could do, in the end, was to knock the ice from a ledge and rub each oar against the rock, working the oar around and around, rasping at it until we brought it to some faint semblance of smoothness. I couldn't let

myself think what such oars would do to the hands of those
who paddled with them, even when the hands were padded
with oakum.

Tide was high at eleven; so at daybreak, before we went
to work on those devilish oars, Neal and I patrolled the
island.

The wind, for a change, was in the south and the seals
had moved around to the north side.

For a change, too, there were four gulls at high-water
mark, wailing dolorously. One was eyeing something, first
from one side, then from the other, as gulls do; and as we
made our way toward it, the gull picked up the something,
flew straight up with it: then dropped it on the rocks, so
that we knew it was a mussel.

When we shouted and waved our arms, the gulls flew
away, mewing. Neal picked up the mussel, broken by its
fall, and divided it with me.

As he chewed at that orange-coloured meat, spitting out
seed pearls as he did so, he moved from me to stare off to
the westward, where low, shelving ledges made an easy
descent to the rising waves.

I followed the direction of his gaze, and my eyes caught
what his had caught—a short stick, a trifle bent, standing
up straight from those shelving ledges.

There was something about the curve of that stick that
filled me with an almost insupportable excitement. I knew
it couldn't be what it vaguely resembled! It couldn't be!
Such things happen only in the *Odyssey*, and through the
direct intervention of Minerva.

The surf swirled around the stick as we hurried toward
it as rapidly as our bandaged and aching feet would let us.

Neal crawled out on the seaweed. I held his arm while he
reached for the stick.

It was exactly what it had looked like the moment we
saw it. It was an axe helve, and on the end of it, yellowed

with salt-water rust, was the axe head, with the hone-marks still showing on the still sharp blade!

It's amazing how small a thing can make such a difference to so many people! Without that axe we were almost helpless, though I think we were never wholly hopeless.

With the axe, our spirits rose, our work no longer stood like an impenetrable wall before us.

We shouted the news of the axe to Captain Dean and Langman: showed it to those in the tent, to raise their spirits. They passed it from hand to hand.

"That's mine," Chips said. "The nails are mine, too. I ought to be allowed to go in the boat."

Nobody answered him. He was the only one who didn't know how sick he was.

"We'll need that oakum to-morrow," I reminded them. "If we have the right wind but shouldn't have enough oakum, we wouldn't dare to put her in the water."

Everyone, even Saver and Graystock, struggled to soften pieces of cordage, to separate the strands, to pick the hemp apart.

We went back to the oars.

With Neal holding each board upright, wedged between rocks, the axe chipped smooth slivers from the corners of the planks. The portions to be gripped by the hands of the rowers became round. Neal and I exchanged places at intervals, for the sake of warmth; but I think the thing that kept us warmest was the feeling of miraculous accomplishment.

December 20th, Wednesday

THE BOAT was shaped like a punt, with square ends and square sides, and we spent all day putting the final touches on her—if anything about that boat could be called final. She was a marvel of incompleteness.

We had no way of judging how high she'd ride in the water when seven men were in her; nor was there any way of knowing how our caulking would hold.

All day long we drove oakum between the stern board and the sides: the bow boards and the sides.

The floor boards had been laid on canvas; and when they had been caulked as well as we could do it, the canvas was drawn up around the sides and ends like a shroud.

We stretched canvas over her bow and stern, binding the canvas with cordage. "It might be," Captain Dean said, "that if waves start slapping us, that canvas may help to keep out some of the spray."

Her height was a little increased by running a long strip of canvas around her, fastened to the stanchions; but it was too low. It had to be, so that the men who knelt in the boat could use the oars as paddles.

Remembering now how that boat looked, I can't believe that so many of us were eager to trust ourselves to her. To-day I wouldn't trust such a travesty of a craft to get me across the Isis at Oxford, but it's easy to forget what a man will do when he's faced on the one hand with certain death, and on the other hand with a chance to live.

The easiest thing to say is that we were insane because of the things we'd endured. Surely I was insane, because I was eager to go. I was even sorry for Swede and Chips, who weren't strong enough to do so, and for all the others who couldn't for lack of space.

Yet we weren't wholly demented, because we made half a dozen bailing scoops—a simple matter now that we had the axe, though without the axe it would have been beyond our powers.

And we spent the last hours, right up to dark, in clearing seaweed-covered boulders from the narrow passageway down which the boat would have to be pushed in order to reach the sea. So we were sane enough to know that if a wave let this strange boat down on such a boulder, we'd have small chance of saving ourselves.

We spent those hours, too, in cutting seaweed to floor the ledge on which the boat rested, and to cover all the interval down to the growing seaweed. Without that protection, the canvas shroud on which the floor boards had been laid would have been cut to ribbons on barnacles by the time we got her to the water.

As we cut the seaweed, we ate as much of it as we could stomach; for the tide, high at noon, had shut us off from the mussel pools that were reachable only at low water.

In the tent, that night, I may have slept a little, but only a little, because of the excited discussions as to when the boat should be launched. Sometimes my hearing blurred, and there seemed to be breaks in the talk. This, I suppose, was sleep, for when my ears snapped open, someone, always, was talking.

The tide was low at seven in the morning, high an hour after noon, and low again at two hours after dark.

What, then, was it best to do?

To start at dawn, when the ocean might be stillest?

E

No: there was the great stretch of seaweed to be crossed at low tide, and the danger of falling!

Yes, but over against that was the hazard of arriving at our destination when the tide was high, concealing perilous ledges and possibly covering beaches that might, at low tide, be reached even though the boat were swamped.

To start at flood tide, then? That would mean that the tide would be falling when we reached our destination, and that offshore currents might push us away.

Ah yes, but beaches would be exposed—more safely approached. Offshore ledges would be revealed—more readily skirted.

Some argued for starting on the half-risen tide in the morning.

Langman in the beginning argued against all starting times that were proposed, and in the end argued for all of them. I think he wanted to take credit for anything good that happened, and dodge the responsibility for anything bad. The world is full of people like that, but most of them haven't Langman's malice.

December 21st, Thursday

THE DAY, to the amazement and delight of all, was better for our purpose than any we had so far seen, though bitter cold. The sun rose red but unclouded, and there was a glassy sheen to the sea. On the north shore there were breakers, though not bad ones. On the south shore the swells came in from both directions, to gurgle, hiss and sigh along the brown seaweed-covered fingers of ledge, but for the most part they surged in without breaking to spend themselves in foam.

The captain urged everyone from the tent at daybreak. "Tide's dead low," he shouted. "We've got a lot to do to-day, so try to get enough mussels to last you through to-morrow."

I knew what he had in mind. He hadn't liked the looks of that red sky in the east.

When we were back in the tent, hacking with our knives at those miserable mussels and chewing our hated seaweed, the captain said, almost diffidently, that he had been thinking about the boat and her launching.

"I know we made seven oars," he said, "but I've come to the conclusion that seven is too many to pack into a boat that size and shape, even when she's well built. It seems to me that two would be better than seven."

When he would have continued, his words were drowned by a roar of protest. The loudest roar came from Swede Butler, but Langman's was almost as loud.

"If only two go," Swede cried, "you wouldn't take Neal, and it was Neal found the axe! Without the axe you'd still be working on that boat! If anybody deserves to go, Neal does."

"It was my axe to begin with," Chips rasped. "I need medical help."

"It wasn't yours any more after you'd lost it," Swede said. "It belonged to all of us, same as a seagull would belong to all of us if we could catch one."

Langman shouted, "You needn't think I'm going to sit here like a bump on a log while the captain goes ashore all alone to spread the news about how he didn't wreck us on Boon Island on purpose! No, sir! I'm going in that boat if anyone does!"

Captain Dean looked sick. "I still think seven is too many. Would you be willing to try it with just me alone?"

"Oh no!" Langman said. "I haven't forgotten how you hit me with the loggerhead the night we went ashore! I wouldn't want anything like that to happen again."

The captain looked at him intently. "I hit you because you'd stolen supplies that rightly belonged to all of us. You were mutinous! You planned to take the ship for yourself and White and Mellen."

Langman's eye was sardonic. "Who'd believe such drivel! Just to make sure you don't slander innocent men without giving 'em a chance to answer, I insist on taking White and Mellen. They'll have fair play or I'll know the reason why."

"In that case, Captain," Swede said, "you'll have to take my boy, and you'll have to go yourself, because you're captain. You might as well take two more. You'll have to do a lot of rowing, and the best men we've got are none too strong."

"It's too many," the captain repeated. "But if that's the way you want it, Mr. Langman, I'll fill the boat. I'll take my brother because he *is* my brother, and I'll take Mr.

Whitworth because I promised his father I'd share and share alike with him."

A chorus of complaint went up from Saver and Graystock, that wholly worthless pair, from Chips Bullock, who was so weak from his lung trouble that he could hardly get to his feet, from Christopher Gray the gunner and Harry Hallion. We crawled from the tent as fast as we could, and for once were grateful for the ear-filling rumble of the breakers, which kept us from hearing the brainless clacking of those we left behind.

It was decided that when we slid the boat into the water at dead high tide, the captain and Neal Butler should be in her, while the rest of us waded in to hold her firm until she was free and clear. Then the captain was to pull in Langman, whereupon the two of them would hoist in the other four, with Neal steadying the boat with the steering oar.

Those we were leaving, barring Chips, who couldn't stand, came to the launching-ledge and crouched there, five unkempt specimens of humanity, all haggard and hairy. I suppose none of us, with the exception of Neal, looked better; but we could use our hands and feet, whereas those we were leaving either couldn't or pretended they couldn't. Thus we felt sorry for them, and those for whom one feels sorry seem sadly woeful.

"Well," the captain said, and his eyes wandered from man to man of those sorry five, "pray for courage, and don't stop moving. If we can reach shore, you'll have help and warmth and food and decent clothing."

He seemed to search his mind for something more to say, couldn't find it and so laid hold of the bow of the boat and started her down the seaweed-strewn ledge toward the water.

I imagined I knew how he felt—empty inside, wrung dry by cold, hunger and the prospect of that long row to the mainland in this cranky contraption of driftwood and old canvas.

"Where's the axe?" Langman asked. "Where's the hammer?"

Swede shook a fist at him. "You don't need the axe and the hammer!" he cried. "You've got to leave us something!"

White stumbled up with both tools and gave Langman the axe.

"Captain Dean," Swede shouted. "Don't let 'em take those tools!"

The captain spoke mildly to Langman. "You might as well leave them."

There was something snake-like about Langman's face, in spite of his black beard. He lowered his head and faced Dean defiantly. "They couldn't use 'em, even if we left 'em," he said. "Even if there was anything to use 'em on, their hands won't hold 'em. They've got the saw. When we reach land we may need those tools to build a better boat."

Nobody answered. We were too intent on the long swells rolling towards us—on waiting for the large one, the third wave, after which we might expect two rollers that would be less troublesome.

The captain raised his hand and shouted, "Now!"

"Push her in," Langman cried. He dropped the axe in the stern, bawled at the captain to get aboard, and signalled Neal to climb in as well. White tossed the hammer after the axe.

She slipped easily enough over the thick layer of seaweed we had spread beneath her. Her bow floated and rose up. With the canvas strip we had stretched above her sides, she had only eighteen inches freeboard.

We waded in with her, up to our knees, up to our middles. The shock of the water on my feet and legs was indescribable, because pain cannot be described.

Captain Dean, looking seaward, waved his arms wildly. "Hold her!" he screamed. "Back her!"

Ahead of the boat I saw a long swell moving in from the south. On its crest were the heads of a dozen seals, all staring down at me.

"Pull her back!" Captain Dean cried. "Pull!"

The boat was sluggish and immovable in my hands, and the icy water around my middle drove the wind from me. I had no strength to pull.

I felt her rising and rising. I caught her gunnel to rise with her. She turned sideways and loomed, tilted, like a slanted roof, before my face. I saw Captain Dean and Neal slide down against the gunnel, with oars tumbling all around them. I made a despairing, fruitless clutch at the axe, caught among the oars.

Then the wave broke, the boat turned over and above me, and I was buried in a choking smother of foam through which I struggled while icy thoughts darted like needles in my brain.

This was the end of it! Our precious axe was lost again; the hammer as well; all the oakum we had picked so endlessly; all the oars that had tortured us; all the planks and boards so painfully and hopefully pieced together; the stanchions, the canvas, the nails and spikes so arduously assembled! Everything was gone—everything but life itself.

December 22nd, Friday

OUR CLOTHES froze that night, though we lay close together.

Probably we had thoughts, in spite of the shudderings that racked all of us when we crawled back to the tent after getting ourselves from the water. If I *did* have thoughts, I can't recall them, though I remember cursing Langman for putting the axe in the boat.

Nor can I remember what I thought when Swede came in alone, after we were bedded in our nest of dank oakum.

"She's gone," Swede said. "Lock, stock and barrel. I tried to hold her, but the tide pulled her out and the waves broke her into a tangle. She floated off to the south."

He hunted for Neal and wedged himself down beside him.

"It's started to snow," Swede said. "Thick: from the south. You couldn't have made it!"

He said no more. In that frigid tent there was silence that was almost tangible, like a fog. Even Captain Dean lay there, staring up at the peak of the tent, above which hung the canvas flag that had failed us as utterly as had all our puny but excruciating efforts.

With the coming of daylight Swede pulled himself to the tent flap. "The snow's stopped," he said. "The whole world's plastered with it."

He looked helplessly from the tent, made an effort to get to his feet, fell to his hands and knees.

"It's got to be scraped off the tent," he said.

"Why has it?" Langman asked. "Don't Eskimos make houses out of snow? I say leave the snow on the tent. It'll protect us from wind."

Swede rolled over clumsily to look at Langman. "Langman," he said, "you're a whoreson, beetle-headed, flap-ear'd knave! You're against everyone and everything, and you keep right on telling lies to try to prove you're right. If we leave the snow on the tent and get more snow, the canvas will split, or it'll fall down on us. Snow's heavy! And you talk about Eskimos!"

"Eskimos *do* live under snow," Langman said defensively.

"Why don't you tell the truth?" Swede snapped. "They live in ice huts, and they have fur clothes and fire—yes, and tools. We've got none! It's thanks to you that we're without tools."

Captain Dean got heavily to his feet. "Now, now!" he said. "We've got to live together. And Swede's right. We'll have to scrape the snow off the tent. If we do, maybe those on shore will see the tent and the flag against the snow."

"I don't believe it," Swede said bitterly. "If those ashore had their eyes open, they'd have seen this tent and flagpole long before now. They're probably like most of the farmers where I come from—spend half their lives walking around with their heads hanging and their mouths open. Well, I'm going to *make* 'em see us!"

"I say with all this snow, we ought to stay in the tent," Langman said. "We're all half frozen. We'll slip in the snow and break our legs."

"No," Captain Dean said. "That's exactly why we can't stay in the tent. We're more than half frozen, and unless we keep moving, we *will* freeze."

"If they want to freeze," Swede said, "let 'em! They'd probably be more help to us dead than alive!" He crawled out into the snow, glittering white on the boulders and ledges, and bright blue in the shadows.

Neal went to the tent-flap to join his father. We heard them scratching at the snow to dislodge it from the sagging tent sides. Then they set off slowly toward the ledge where we had built the boat.

Since the tide was low at eight in the morning, the captain and George White and Langman and Christopher Gray went to the north side for mussels. We had nine apiece that day, with seaweed in place of bread and sauce and dessert.

I think the loss of the boat had shocked all of us: first into a state of horrified resignation, then into desperate activity—though Swede's openly contemptuous attack on Langman may have had something to do with waking us from our lethargy. Certainly there was rancour in the mind of everyone able to think—even in the minds of Langman's cronies, White and Mellen. In all their faces I saw sullen fury at Langman's folly in putting the axe and the hammer in the boat, and at his insolent insistence that he did so to let us build a better boat when we got to land.

We knew that wasn't so: knew that his seizure of the tools was unreasoning hoggishness on Langman's part, and there was hot resentment against Langman, and an irritation against everything. I think that was why there was a general outcry against the mussels on the ground that they were too cold, too tough, too bitter, impossible to swallow, too hard on the bowels.

There was even more unrest when Swede and Neal crawled back. Swede had found the tattered remains of two hammocks. Neal dragged in one. Swede dragged in the other and went to Captain Dean for his mussels.

"Look at these hammocks," Swede said proudly. "Just what we need for a raft!"

Captain Dean peered from Swede to Neal and back again. "Just eat your mussels, Swede," he said. "You worked hard to save that boat. There's plenty of time to discuss a raft."

"Oh no, there isn't," Swede said. "I've already lost the use of my feet, but I can still use my hands. I may lose them any minute. We'll have to build the raft before I lose my hands too."

A groan went up from the circle of scarecrows huddled in the tent.

"We'd work ourselves to death," White protested, "and have the same thing happen that happened to the boat."

"No," Swede said. "It wouldn't be anything like the boat, because it wouldn't be overloaded, and I wouldn't launch it till I had the wind with me."

"Swede," Captain Dean said, "let's talk this over some other time."

"Some other time—when my boy and all the rest of you are dead?" Swede said politely. "No! I'm building a raft while I've got my hands. If nobody else helps me, Neal will."

Harry Hallion spoke up. "He won't help you much when it comes to spiking her together. We used all our spikes on the boat. If there's any left in the junk, he'll never draw spikes without a hammer! What'll he use? His teeth?"

"We'll build it without spikes if we have to," Swede said. "We'll lace it together with cordage."

"On a raft," Captain Dean said, "a part of you would be in water most of the time—*all* the time, maybe. The nearest land is six miles away. How long would you last in water like this?"

"I don't know," Swede said, "but I prayed to God yesterday while I was trying to hold the boat. I prayed again this morning. I prayed to Langman's God, whose Sunday is Saturday, and to our God, whose Sunday is Sunday—to Langman's God, who wants us to observe Christmas the day before Christmas, and to our God, who doesn't care when we observe it, so long as we celebrate it with an understanding of what Christmas means. Both Gods told me what to do. They told me to build a raft."

I realised suddenly what Swede was saying. He was saying that God gave his only beloved son to save the world from itself. Now Swede, having communed with that God, was willing to give himself in order to save *his* only beloved son from a cruel and lingering death. He was not only willing to give himself: he had, in his mind, already done so.

December 23rd, Saturday

THIS WAS the day of the seagull—a Langman Sunday, the day before Langman's Christmas, and the day we started the raft.

In making the boat we had deliberately ignored the foremast yard, not only because of its awkward length—twenty-four feet, a veritable tree—but also because it was so tangled and cluttered with the innumerable confusing attachments of such a spar that by general agreement it had been spurned by all—passed over after one look at the tattered shreds of canvas still clinging to it, and its wrappings of frayed and frozen preventer stays, lanyards, bowlines, bridles, sheets, lifts, yard tackles.

Just that yard alone was enough to turn me against ships, and I wondered why three-masted square-rigged vessels were ever made in the first place.

I asked Captain Dean, as we dragged it to the spot chosen by Swede; but he didn't know.

"Probably," he said, "we build square-riggers because nations like France and England have to fight wars every few years. To fight wars you have to have warships; and warships have to carry a lot of men. If you put a lot of men aboard a big schooner or a big brig, both easy to sail, there wouldn't be anything for sailors to do between fights, so they'd make trouble like Langman—mutiny, probably, or die of boredom. To keep 'em busy you've got to have a hundred sails for 'em to set or take in every half-hour, and

five or ten thousand sheets and lifts and tackles for 'em to
haul on at five-minute intervals."

He cogitated: then added, "Maybe shipbuilders are like
Langman. Maybe they get a foolish idea in their heads, and
can't recognise a better one when it's presented to 'em."

Swede and Neal had been at that spar since dawn, pounding
the ice and snow from it and its attached junk.

"I've got it all figured out," Swede told Captain Dean.
"First we'll sharpen up our knives and cut through each
piece of cordage on the top side. Then we'll roll the spar
over, knock the ice off the other side, and pull the cordage
free. All that cordage is slushed with tar, so the short pieces
can be burned later, when you get fire."

When we got fire! Ah, would that day ever come!

Captain Dean nodded. "If we start at the centre when we
strip the junk, two of us can start knifing a groove around
the middle. We'll hammer our knife-blades with rocks.
Maybe we can cut an inch-deep groove all the way around.
That'll leave only a ten-inch cut to be made with the
saw."

I suspected irony and glanced at him quickly, but he was
serious enough.

A ten-inch cut through that tree trunk of a spar! And
with a saw made by pounding a cutlass into jaggedness
against the sharp edge of a ledge! I tried to figure the
amount of sawing we'd have to do in order to make that
yard into a pair of logs.

If Langman hadn't lost the axe, two men whose hands
weren't frost-nipped might, by spelling each other, do the
cutting in half an hour.

But without the axe—with the saw alone: that miserable
saw which would only cut when pulled backward—that was
different!

Would two men make half an inch an hour?

Not through the thick part of the yard, they wouldn't.

Perhaps when they were nearly finished, and the yard could be balanced on a boulder, so the blade wouldn't bind in the cut, they might make half an inch in an hour. *Perhaps* they might.

In any event, half an inch an hour was the best we could expect—and with ten inches to go, we'd be twenty hours making the cut. But there were only nine hours of daylight in each day, provided there was no snow or rain: provided the wind wasn't so piercing that working in it was impossible.

And how many of us, afflicted with gurry sores and partly frozen hands and feet, were capable of using that saw at all?

"Clear away the junk in the centre," Swede told Captain Dean, and his voice was jubilant. "Then I'll start the groove. Neal can hold the knife. I'll do the hammering."

In the face of Swede's excitement, I banished my doubts about our ability to sever that detested spar. If Swede's faith was so unconquerable, I could have faith too.

I went to work on the twisted cordage. It resisted my knife-blade like strands of metal.

"Take it a strand at a time," the captain said. "Wriggle your knife-blade under a single strand: then drag the blade toward your stomach."

There were eight of us working at that spar, and we must have looked like hairy bears, nosing at a log in hungry curiosity.

Langman came from the tent to watch us. In his hand he held the saucepan handle we had salvaged in the distant past.

"Get your knife and go to work," Captain Dean said.

"It's Sunday," Langman said. "Remember the Sabbath day to keep it holy."

"It's Saturday," Captain Dean said. "What excuse will you have to-morrow for not working?"

"To-morrow's Christmas," Langman said, almost indulgently.

He seemed disappointed when the men on both sides of the spar made no reply. He had to have attention, Langman did; and he didn't care how he got it.

He left us, slipping and sliding across the wet seaweed toward the mussel pools on the south shore.

The tide was low. I hoped Langman's respect for his private Sunday wouldn't prevent him from hunting food for the rest of us—though the mere thought of mussels almost made me retch.

Gradually we gained on the cordage and junk, half-numbed by the clack, clack, clack of Swede's rock as he rapped it against the back of the knife-blade that Neal clutched.

Into that monotonous clacking, suddenly, intruded an uproar as startling as it was unexpected. Shrill through the noise of the breakers came a raucous screaming that brought us up all standing. Against the dark background of the seaweed-covered ledges we saw a preposterous mixture of man and wings that gyrated and flapped and rolled about.

"It's Langman," Captain Dean said. "He's caught a seagull!"

He had indeed, or the seagull had caught him, for the big bird was screaming, squalling, flapping its wings, beating Langman's head with giant pinions. I thought for a moment that the gull had lifted him from the rock. But the gull fell at last and Langman leaped upon it, and we saw he was beating it with the saucepan handle. At last the gull ceased to flap and flop, and lay still.

The air above the man and the struggling bird had been alive with gulls, wheeling, squealing, and wailing; but when the bird was quiet, every last one of those gulls fell silent and winged off toward the mainland as if terror-stricken.

Not one remained behind. There was something oppressive about the sudden departure of all those noisy creatures whose screams had shrilled through the roaring of breakers from dawn to dark each day.

Langman came slowly back to us, dragging that huge bird across the icy ledges, and threw it down beside the spar.

"There!" Langman said. "There's some food that's better than mussels!" He was proud of himself, and with good reason.

We crowded around that enormous gull, fondling it, burying our fingers in its beautiful warm white breast, and sniffing its dusty clean smell. It was a black-back—snowy white on belly, head, neck and tail, but with black wings and a black saddle: largest of all gulls; almost twice the size of ordinary large gulls with pale blue backs: nearly three times that of young grey ones.

"I'll skin him," Langman said importantly, "and we'll eat him. I wish you could have seen how I got him. I cut enough seaweed to cover me, and then I raked up a mussel and put it on a flat place, right near the hole I'd picked to squat in. Then I hung the seaweed all over me, so I looked like a boulder. When that old gull came overhead, twisting his neck and squinting at that mussel from all sides, he looked as big as a goose! Yes, sir! Then he stuck out his feet and came down all sprawling, a regular ostrich, and I just put out my hand and grabbed him. That was the surprisedest gull that ever landed on *this* island!"

For a moment I almost liked Langman—almost forgot his effort to oust Captain Dean; his almost certain plot to seize the *Nottingham*; his insistence that Captain Dean had purposely wrecked the ship; his stubborn refusal to admit the well-established fact of Sir Isaac Newton's reflecting telescope; his willingness—eagerness, even—to blacken Captain Dean's reputation and by implication to damage the reputation of all who sided with the captain; his persistence in observing the wrong Sunday. Yes, for a moment, but only for a moment, I forgot that persistence in wrong-headedness is the most dangerous of all human failings.

Langman skinned that gull with loving care, making an incision at the top of the head and running the cut all the way down the centre of the back to the tail.

"We can make ear muffs with this," he said as he worked. "We can fasten feather pads inside spun-yarn caps, so that those who go out on patrol can have better protection for their ears and noses. We can make a pair of feather-lined gauntlets and take turns wearing 'em."

I was amazed to hear such helpful thoughts from Langman. Sometimes it's hard to remember that the leopard never changes his spots: that the most hardened criminal has endeared himself to someone, but is no less dangerous.

Langman peeled the wings back to the first joint, leaving all the wing-feathers attached to the skin. When the skinning was finished, he had a rude square of feathers almost three feet long and three feet wide.

"How'll we dry it?" he asked Captain Dean.

"Tie it around Neal before it freezes," Captain Dean said. "His skin's smoother, and chances are he isn't as lousy as the rest of us."

So that was what was done. Swede took the big black and white skin and went with Neal to the tent, to be out of the wind.

The division of that bird's body among thirteen men wasn't easy, and I was glad Langman turned over the task to Captain Dean.

First the captain gutted it, finding two six-inch tommy cod in its gullet. The intestines and the small fish he placed on a board to freeze, along with the thigh joints, the wing joints, the thick neck, the feet, and the skull.

"We can chew 'em later," he said.

Then he laid off the breasts, still warm, and cut them into

thirteen lengthwise strips, taking a little from the long, thick centre strips to add to the thin side strips.

The men watched the division with jealous eyes, each one certain, after the manner of hungry men, that his was the smallest portion.

Chips Bullock wouldn't come from the tent, even for meat, so the captain called for Neal to take Chips's portion to him.

"Make him eat it," the captain told Neal.

Langman was derisive. "I suppose," he said, "you don't trust any of the rest of us to take that to Chips."

"I don't even trust myself," the captain said.

When a man's hungry, he doesn't waste time thinking how meat tastes. There's blood in it, and a little hope and a little strength. He just chews at it until it dissolves and trickles down his throat. Then he's angry and desperate because there isn't more.

December 24th, Sunday

LANGMAN, inflamed by his success in capturing the seagull, was at us all Sunday to celebrate that day as Christmas.

Swede, equally determined to keep on with the raft while the weather was endurable, spoke to him sharply.

"What is you want to celebrate, Langman?" he demanded. "Don't you remember what Christmas was like in London? Remember how all the sluts and beggars and cripples gathered in front of church doors, all mealy-mouthed and pious, and their eyes rolled up, hoping they looked as if they were talking to God? Remember, Langman?"

Langman, his lip curled, eyed him sideways.

"Well, I remember," Swede said. "When the church doors were opened and the alms and doles were handed out, all their piety disappeared and they fought each other like cats and dogs, each trying to get the others' alms away from 'em. They'd go off down the street, cursing and fighting, and push their way into public houses and get roaring drunk on gin!"

"You're against Christmas!" Langman said angrily.

"There you go," Swede said, "twisting things around! I'm not going to have any first mate telling me how to celebrate the birth of Christ, or when to do it. You say to-day is Christmas, but you're wrong. When the proper time arrives, I'll celebrate Christmas in my own way."

Captain Dean turned to me. "Miles, you were in Christ

148

Church. You must have heard talk about the celebrating of Christmas."

"Yes, sir, and my father and I often talked about it. He said it should be a festival for children and for the poor— not a time for people to cripple themselves financially by exchanging expensive gifts that most givers can't afford and most recipients don't want. He said Christ would be the first one to pity those who can't decide which day to celebrate, and to laugh at those who, because of politics, say how it shall be celebrated."

"That's blasphemy again!" Langman cried.

"No, it's not," I said. "Every don in Christ Church knows that the Puritans by act of Parliament forbade merriment or religious services on Christmas. They said it was a heathen festival. Charles II revived feasting on Christmas. That's politics."

"Anyway, the date has always been the same," Langman insisted.

"That's not so," I told him. "I've heard professors lecture on it. Some of the ancients said Christ's birthday was May 20th: others said April 19th: still others put it on the seventeenth of November. One man held out for the twenty-eighth of March. Then January 6th was celebrated as his birthday for hundreds of years."

"I say this is Christmas," Langman persisted, "and the rest of my seagull should be divided for a feast."

"All right," Captain Dean agreed. "Go ahead and divide it up. You'd better give Swede at least half of the neck. He seems to be doing most of the work on the raft."

The junk was completely stripped from the spar that Sunday noon, and we took turns using the cutlass-saw. The saw didn't really cut the wood: it abraded it: chewed it: wore it away.

By noontime Langman had divided the body of the gull

and summoned us to the tent for what he persisted in calling our Christmas dinner.

"We can't distribute this by lot," he explained, "because some are better able to eat than others, and if I passed it out by lot, the wrong men might get the wrong thing and not be able to eat it. So I've taken Captain Dean at his word: I've gone ahead and divided it up.

"Now take Chips Bullock. He can't eat much, and he can't hardly chew at all, so I've given him the heart and the liver. Then there's Graystock and Saver. They claim they can't work or walk or do anything to help us, so I've given each of them one of the fish we found in the craw. The captain gets the two wings. There's not much meat on the wings, but there's some, especially when they're pounded on rocks. The same thing is true of the feet. You might not think there was much in seagulls' feet, but there is, especially when they're pounded to a pulp; and they last longer than plain meat when you suck at them, so I'm giving Christopher Gray the feet.

"I figure there's about as much in one of the thighs as there is in two wings, so I'm giving Henry Dean one of the thighs and Harry Hallion the other.

"Then there's the back: that hasn't got much on it, but the bone is thin and can easily be pounded; so I've divided it into two parts and White gets one part and Mellen gets the other.

"There's a good deal of nourishment in the skull and in the neck, so I've split the skull in two and cut the neck into three parts, one of them a little larger than the other two. I'm giving Swede half the skull and one of the small pieces of the neck.

"Whitworth gets the other half of the skull and the other small piece of neck. Neal gets the large piece of neck."

As he talked, he passed around these fragments of bone and gristle.

"That seems fair," Captain Dean admitted. "What's left for you?"

"Well," Langman said, "I may seem to have a little more than some of you, but I really haven't. I'm taking the windpipe and the intestines. They're frozen; and when they're pounded up together, they'll probably be about the same thing, in the long run, as a piece of neck—especially when they're mixed with seaweed."

By the grace of God, when that cutlass-saw had chewed its way half through the spar, we lifted it and banged it against the edge of a ledge.

To our triumphant amazement it cracked and split; so that when four of us took one end and four took the other, and we put our weight on it, it broke all the way across— jaggedly, it's true; but it broke.

So when we crawled into the tent for the last time on that false Christmas, the two pieces of spar lay side by side on the flat ledge, ready to be joined together in a raft— though my half-frozen brain was incapable of knowing how it could ever be done.

December 25th, Monday

CHRISTMAS ON Boon Island!

I write the words reluctantly because they deny each other. They're unreal and don't belong together. Christmas belongs with warmth, with love, with good cheer, with feasting, with happiness, with gratitude for years past and years to come, with an understanding of the meaning of Christmas. . . .

There were spittings of snow and a north-west wind that drove snow-dust beneath the tent and through every crevice, no matter how solidly we packed oakum along the tent-bottom.

Swede, when he went out at dawn to work on the raft, crawled back in again, baffled.

"The wind's so cold the whole sea's smoking," he said. "That wind cuts like a knife. Let's see that seagull's breast."

He fumbled out the oakum wrappings that Neal, like all the rest of us, wore inside his coat; and when he pulled out the beautiful black and white skin, it had lost its stickiness. It wasn't dry, but it was flexible, like parchment.

"If we could cut this apart," Swede told Captain Dean, "we might make protectors for our ears and noses. Then some of us could stand this wind."

The captain took the skin from him, stretched it over his knees and stroked it.

"It's a shame to cut that breast," Swede said. "We could make a whole helmet out of it."

"Only a helmet for one man," the captain reminded him.

"What would do us the most good," Swede said, "is to cut it into pieces to fasten inside our oakum mittens so our hands won't get numb. Of course, we ought to have some for our ears and noses."

Taking the skin from the captain, Neal pressed it tight over his head. He was the only one among us who didn't have a grizzled beard; and his face, beneath that soft, white gull breast, with the black wings hanging down on either side, reminded me poignantly of how he had looked on the stage at Greenwich, reciting Colley Cibber's epilogue to *The Walking Statue.*

He lifted the gull breast from his head and studied it. "If you take off the large parts of each wing," he said, "you could run spun yarn through them and tie one over each ear. They'd be big enough to protect your ears and your cheeks, too."

Langman took the skin from him and examined the wings. "What about the ends of the wings?" he asked.

"Well," Neal said, "you could cut off the stiff quills and weave the feathers in and out of our oakum ear muffs. You could weave 'em in on a slant. They'd cover your ears a little, and stick out over your eyes and nose and mouth."

In the end we used the black back-strips to thicken the backs of mittens. The beautiful white breast, after long discussion and the drawing of diagrams on the skin with the points of knives, we cut into strips long enough to pass from ear to ear across the nose.

At the base of the breast were the tail feathers. Captain Dean looked up at Langman. "This tail doesn't fit much of anywhere," he said. "How about giving it to Neal for a Christmas present?"

Langman sneered, but nodded his head in acquiescence.

All that Christmas morning we wove and patched our oakum headgear and mittens with those strips of seagull skin. There were enough to make five feather-lined helmets that would let five men work at one time in the teeth of that north-west wind.

The captain took the first helmet we finished. When he had clumsily tied it on with spun yarn, he said abruptly, "Low tide's about now. We've got to eat something! That something's going to be seaweed, and we can't stay alive unless we eat it."

He went out after the seaweed, and when he returned, four more helmets were finished.

We choked down the seaweed. Then Swede crawled on his hands and knees to the captain, to Langman, to George White, to me. All he did was take us by the shoulders and look into our faces; but that was enough to shame the four of us into following him out into that searing wind.

We had no hammer: no spikes: no nails. We had to build that raft out of four lengths of plank that Swede and Neal had somehow worried from the junk the day before.

All we had to fasten the planks to the spars was rope that could be cut into desired lengths and slapped against ledges until, freed of ice, they were flexible.

We must, the captain explained, do everything with cordage, so he showed us how to haul cordage into place, thread it beneath the two pieces of spar in such a way that the pieces were four feet apart; then bring the ends of each piece of cordage together and splice them. Thus the spars were joined loosely by a series of rope loops.

Into these loops we thrust the four lengths of planks. Spun yarn was knotted from side to side of the loop and between the planks to prevent the planks from folding against each other. Then each loop was tightened as is a tourniquet. With one man on each end of a loop, a stick was thrust through the slack and twisted and twisted, until the loop was as tight as it could be made.

When any one of us reached the limit of his endurance,

which was often, he told Swede, who went back to the tent with him, helped him relinquish his feathered headgear to another, who crawled reluctantly into that whistling, spume-laden blast. Swede was the only one who had faith in what we were doing. The rest of us were helping him rather than ourselves.

By dark of that Christmas Day the planks were laced in place: the tourniquets that held the lacing were fastened so they couldn't slip or come loose. When even Swede was willing to stop, and went from one of us to the other, patting our backs and thanking us for the work we'd done, I had a momentary thought that Christmas was truly Christmas, even on Boon Island.

December 26th, Tuesday

OUR LIVES depended on the weather, and if that north-west wind had blown another day, if for another twenty-four hours the combers, each one whitecapped, had raced at us and all around us, steaming and smoking, as the sea always does in frigid spells, I think our work would have been wasted and our hopes dashed.

But on the day after our true Christmas, the weather moderated.

I may seem to speak overmuch about the weather—about the hours of high tides and low tides; about the spring tides that threatened our lives and the neap tides that let us go farther out on the seaweed-covered rock fingers in our search for mussels; about the snow or sleet that might crush our tent; about the offshore winds that bit into our bones, and the south winds that could, if Providence so ordained, float evidences of our existence to the distant beaches that we sometimes saw, always fogged by mist from breakers.

Yet weather *was* our life, and so must be explained to those who see weather with different eyes, and to one who has been exposed to the ocean and its winter furies, the words "the weather moderated" bring inexpressible relief—a surcease from agony, from despair, from dark depression. . . .

Londoners—city dwellers—who despise sailors and countrymen, can never in their ignorance know the beauty of those words, just as they can never know, in their restricted world, the marvels that exist in the worlds of others, or appreciate the magic qualities of all the things they look upon as commonplace: the wonders of fire, of sweet water, of shelter.

In Greenwich we listened in amazement to those Londoners who longed for and acclaimed cloudless skies at times when countrymen were praying for rain and losing their crops and even their farms from drought; who were perpetually being caught in thunderstorms because they turned resolutely from the west and put their faith in a narrow strip of blue sky in the east; to whom a tree was merely a tree, and they unable to distinguish between a pine, a fir, a spruce or a larch; to whom a bird smaller than a pheasant was merely a bird, without a name, without a song. . . .

Ah! Fortunate, fortunate city dwellers: fortunate that so many countrymen and seamen are inarticulate, unable to express their thoughts concerning those who dwell in cities and are so profoundly lacking in knowledge!

And so, to our joy, the weather moderated!

The wind, what there was of it, couldn't make up its mind what to do. It blew gently from the east: then came fitfully from the west.

Swede, working at the pile of junk for materials to strengthen his raft, nosed at those breezes like a weathervane. He was afraid, and so were the rest of us, that the wind would back up—move to the west and south without first going to the eastward and the south-east. When, after a storm or a blow, the wind backs up, unpleasant weather will soon return, just as some sort of evil follows the appearance of a ring around the sun or around the moon.

We stepped a fence post of a mast on the raft and hung the two hammocks on it, to serve as a sort of double lugsail. We fastened three pieces of wood—oars, we called them, and were too weak to laugh at ourselves—to the spars. Then, because Swede insisted we must, we lashed bridles to both ends of the spars, with long rope-ends trailing from them.

At noon the tide was lower than ever before, because of the full moon, and we brought in a treasure trove of mussels. We left half of them unopened. There was something about that raft that sickened those who worked on it.

Only Swede grew constantly more cheerful.

"There's got to be two little pulpits built up at each end," he told Captain Dean. "We can lay two piles of cordage, bow and stern: then lace the piles in position. That'll keep us out of the water. They ought to be big enough so we can kneel on them."

"Who's we?" Captain Dean asked. "You and who else?"

"I don't know," Swede said. "The Lord will provide."

The captain shook his head and let his eyes wander around the horizon as if in hopes of finding the something that the Lord would provide. He studied the tall rusty face of Bald Head Cliff, the long sands of York and so on to the open sea beyond. Then he straightened, as if incredulous.

"Why," he said, "there's a sail! There's *two* of 'em!"

He raised his voice shouting, "Sail! Sail!"

We dropped our armfuls of cordage. We got ourselves to the highest part of the rock and stared longingly at those two far-off sails. They seemed to be sloops, but they were so distant, we couldn't be sure which way they were heading: whether they were inbound or outbound. We could hardly see their hulls, but our unreasoning longing to be rescued was so strong within us that we shouted and waved, waved and shouted—all of us but Swede.

When we stopped our waving and our shouting and just followed the progress of those small pink sails, Swede laughed at us.

"You think I haven't got a chance to reach shore on this raft," he said, "yet you go shouting and waving at two sloops that are fifteen miles away if they're an inch. You'd never have seen 'em at all if the wind hadn't blown from the north-west all day yesterday. There isn't one of you that can see a man when he's over six miles away. There isn't one of you whose voice could be heard a mile away. If that's the way you feel, every last one of you ought to be fighting for the chance to go on this raft with me."

I had to admit that he was right, and that our behaviour in shouting and waving at those two far-off sail showed we were close to panic. Yet the sight of those sail, and our shouting and our waving, had done something to our spirits so that when we had finished Swede's cordage pulpits, and went to the tent to eat our seaweed and ice, we were more hopeful about Swede's venture than we had hitherto been.

When he stayed behind us, brooding over his raft and talking endlessly to Neal, he put me in mind of a bridegroom, garrulous over the inescapable fate awaiting him on the morrow.

December 27th, Wednesday

LOVE, true love, is, I suppose, always intemperate, whether it's the love of a man for a woman, a woman for a child, or a father for a son. Certainly Swede's love for Neal was a consuming passion, and equally certainly Neal's comprehension of that love was unusual and beautiful.

Even before sunrise Swede had left the tent, and Neal with him. I couldn't hear what Swede said to Neal, but there was a buoyant quality to his voice. When I went outside, I found the wind, wambling and uncertain the day before, had dropped to a dead calm—and when I say calm, I'm speaking only of the wind. The canvas on the tent pole hung flat against it; but the sea—ah, that damnable sea! There may be such a thing as a dead calm around Boon Island, but it must be in the summer. When we were on the island, the sea was perpetually heaving, surging, on every side, as if afflicted with waves of nausea.

If the breakers came at us from the west, the island seemed to catch them and pull them around, billowing, on either side, as a woman, battered by wind, draws a cape around herself.

But the air, at least, was still and frost-laden. There was frost on the seaweed: ice on the naked boulders—spume-ice left by the north-west wind.

I went over to the raft on which Swede and Neal were sitting, lashing two oars to the sides with spun yarn.

"I know the signs," Swede said cheerfully. "That wind's

coming around. When the tide's low at one o'clock, she'll move in from the south. No doubt about it."

"How're your feet?" I asked.

"Gone," Swede said lightly.

"Wouldn't you feel better if we cleaned them?" I asked.

Swede shook his head. "I don't want to see 'em," he said. "I don't want anybody else to see 'em. They don't hurt, and if you did something to 'em, they might start hurting again."

The captain and George White crawled from the tent just as the sun came up. Against its rising disk the rollers on the horizon were like the teeth of our cutlass-saw.

"Well, Captain," Swede said triumphantly, "this is the day! Full moon! Onshore wind!"

The captain shook his head and with his oakum-swathed hands dragged at the spar that formed one side of this spider-web of a raft, laced together with cordage. The spar pulled free of the ice beneath it. It was too frail a support for my taste. The two hammocks, rigged as sails on its stump of a mast, hung limp and ineffective, like the folded wings of a sleeping bat.

"I've made up my mind to one thing," Captain Dean said. "If this raft sets off, I won't be on it."

"That's your privilege," Swede said.

"I won't be on it," Captain Dean said, "because I've weighed the chances, and the chances of getting ashore alive with this raft aren't as good as staying alive on this rock. I ought to forbid you to go. Yesterday we saw two sail heading east. They must have come out of the Piscataqua River, making toward the Isles of Shoals. I'd say they're probably running out of salt fish in Portsmouth. Either that, or they need fresh fish. If they run out of fish in Portsmouth, they're bound to run out in York, too, or Cape Porpoise, or some such place. Boats'll put out of those ports, just as they put out of Portsmouth."

F

Swede put his arm around Neal's shoulders and spoke to Captain Dean. "Captain, I'm leaving here at low tide. You'll help me put her in over yonder, where those ledges point out to the west, won't you?"

I was watching Neal. His eyes seemed to be examining the lashings of that strange raft. They lifted suddenly, met mine and instantly dropped again. They looked hurt, like the eyes of a dog whose master is deserting him.

"Help me get seaweed, Neal," I said.

He climbed obediently from the raft, and as he went, his father's fist rapped him affectionately on the shoulder.

We skirted the tent and started that hated circuit of the island, hunting for any useful thing that might have been sent to us by the sea's grace.

"Neal," I asked, "has your father ever told you he'd like you to go with him on the raft?"

Neal shook his head. "He wouldn't let me. I said I'd go, but he almost snapped my ears off."

"He'll never make it," I said. "Have you asked him not to go?"

"No," Neal admitted. "He *wants* to go. He's *determined* to go."

"Yes," I said, "I can see that."

"He *might* make it," Neal said, "if he had an onshore wind and a strong man to use the paddle. Anyway, nothing can stop him." He hesitated; then added, " I don't want to stop him."

When I was silent, Neal added, "When he was in the Naval Hospital, he thought he was as good as dead. He said he wasn't pulling his weight, and he was ashamed to be seen in the hospital uniform. On the *Nottingham* he pulled his weight. He was happy again. He was even happy on this island—until his feet froze. Then he couldn't pull his weight any more. He thinks this raft'll let him pull his weight."

"Not if he doesn't get ashore," I reminded him.

"He doesn't look at it that way," Neal said. "He says everything's in his favour. He says somebody may see him if he gets half-way to land. He says if he gets almost to land, somebody's *sure* to see him. He says if he doesn't get to land and the raft does, they'll find the raft—and then they'll find us."

"You wouldn't stop him if you could, would you?" I asked.

"No, I wouldn't," Neal said. "If he let me or anybody or anything stop him, he'd never forgive himself. He knows he's going to die, and so do I. I don't want him to die unhappy. Once he's on that raft, headed for shore, his mind will be at ease, no matter what happens."

There wasn't anything I could say to that. Neal, when I'd first encountered him in Greenwich, was a fine boy— the sort of boy anyone would be proud to have as a son or a brother; but the things that had happened to him in five months had changed him from a boy into a man—a man who would be a credit to any society, to any country, no matter along what lines his life might be cast.

Swede was right about the wind. At noon it moved in faintly, a little east of south, and the captain gave the word to drag the raft to the spot Swede had chosen. The dragging wasn't easy, and we did it by inches. Swede counted for us as he probably once had counted in the St. George's Light Dragoons—"One, two, three, hup,"—and at the "hup" we'd all lift together. By "all" I mean the captain and Neal on one side with Langman and me; on the other side Gray, Hallion, Mellen and White.

The others couldn't lift, they said, but they had crawled from the tent to watch, all but poor Chips Bullock.

Between every few lifts we crawled forward to move rocks from our path, and came back to lift again, sliding the raft forward three inches, five inches. The hardest part was finding footholds sufficiently secure to make lifting possible.

At the water's edge the captain stepped back from the raft.

"Put her in," Swede shouted. "She's headed right for shore!"

"Yes, put her in," George White said. "I'm going with him. With this breeze I think we can make it."

Langman, I thought, as well as could be seen on a face so covered with whiskers, had a smug look. If one of his own men hadn't been going with Swede, I was sure he would have protested bitterly. He never would have gone himself, and he would have done everything possible to prevent Swede from going alone.

"If you're determined to go," the captain said, "I won't try to stop you, now that you've gone this far——"

"Push her in," Swede said.

"But I want to urge you to wait one more day, or two days."

"What for?" Swede demanded. "Get her in the water!"

There were murmurs from the oakum-draped figures sprawled on the rocks around us, their limbs at odd angles, like those of dead men.

The captain fumbled in his clothes and with difficulty produced coins, which he gave to Swede. "These are all I saved," he told Swede. "They may help you, one way or another. And there's just one thing, Swede. When you get to shore, have somebody light a fire on the beach. Have 'em light two fires. Have 'em do that before they do anything else."

"Two fires," Swede said. He crawled aboard the raft and swept us with a glance that made my heart contract. "I know you wish us well," he said. "I wish all of you well." He steadied himself by grasping the spar on either side, and we ran the raft into the water. George White climbed over the stern, and we pushed as hard as we could.

The raft moved heavily between two ledge-fingers, and her hammock-sail flapped. She almost stopped, settled down as a wave receded, then picked up way again. She moved out until she was parallel with the tips of the ledge-fingers: then sluggishly swung broadside to the distant coast line. A slow surge moved her forward. The bow rose a little. The surge slid back and left the side of the raft caught on an unseen ledge.

White struggled with the lashings of his oar. The free side of the raft slipped under water. The surge returned and the raft tilted sharply. Then another surge moved down from the north side of the island, pressed against the submerged side, and the raft rolled over. A crying rose around us like the squalling of seagulls above a school of fish.

The raft had spilled in deep water. I found myself on a ledge-finger near the wallowing contraption. Swede came to the surface, gasping, and swam easily to shore, holding a rope-end in his hand. Neal and Langman dragged him up on the seaweed.

I saw the captain, at the end of another rock finger, reaching and clutching for a piece of wood—White's rude oar. He caught it and pulled. White's head emerged from the water. I thought he was dead. The captain dragged him up on the ledge, hoisted him to his feet and held him by the waist, doubled over. I saw he couldn't be dead, because he still clung to the oar.

Swede, clutching his rope-end, seemed able to say nothing but "Help me! Help me!" in a voice that quavered so the words were hardly distinguishable.

Incapable of using his feet, he straddled a seaweed-covered boulder, pulling at the rope-end until others came to help.

Between us we got the overturned raft into the cove and ashore at the spot from which we had launched her.

"Help turn her over," Swede gasped. "Turn her right side up!"

"You can't make it, Swede," the captain said. "White's finished. He's full of sea water. He's sick!"

"I'll go alone," Swede said wildly. "Turn her over, Captain. I've got to go!"

"You can't go, you fool," Langman said. "It'll be dark before you get ashore. You'll freeze in those wet clothes. It's too late."

"It's not too late," Swede cried. "We'll never get a brighter night than to-night—full moon, no clouds, onshore breeze, high tide at seven! Make 'em turn it over, Captain!"

"Not if you're going alone," Captain Dean said.

Swede, on his knees, caught the captain's hand. "Don't do it for *me!*" he implored. "Do it for these others!" He swung an oakum-swathed hand in a semicircle to include all those stooped, bearded, wild-looking creatures. I was afraid to look among them for Neal.

Harry Hallion shuffled across the slippery seaweed to stand beside Swede and the captain. "I'll go with him," he told the captain. "I can swim. White couldn't. If Swede feels the way he does, I think we can make it."

The captain eyed him dubiously.

"Anything's better than this," Hallion said. "You're wasting time. Get her turned over for us."

Captain Dean motioned to us to help him drag the raft from the water and turn her right side up. Swede, half-sobbing and half-laughing, scuttled among our legs like a shaggy dog, wanting to help, trying to help, but only succeeding in getting in our way.

She slid up easily on the seaweed, and we turned her gently for fear of smashing her. The mast and the hammock-sails were gone, but the pulpits hadn't been dislodged.

"Push her in!" Swede shouted, and there was a terrible urgency in his voice. "We don't need a sail! Get her in before the tide turns!"

He rolled himself on to the raft, rose to his knees, unknotted the lashings of the oar still fastened to her side, and shook the oar at us like a spear.

We slid her into the water, and as she left the ledge Hallion crawled in with White's oar.

A swell from the south raised her. Miraculously she slipped down it, toward the mouth of the little cove. A cross-swell from the north pushed her to the west and she cleared the mouth of the cove, Swede and Hallion thrashing the water with their makeshift oars.

Behind me someone prayed, the same incoherent prayer that had risen so often to my own lips—Oh God Oh God Oh God Oh God . . .

I felt sick all over at the smallness of that miserable raft, the cold immensity of that heaving ocean, the far far frosty distance over which the raft must float, the seeming pitifulness of those two human specks—yet who was to feel sick when those two specks were in truth, and unknown to themselves, great in spirit, and therefore happy!

There was distance and haziness between the raft and Boon Island when Swede turned, raised his oar and waved it. I looked at Neal. He wasn't among those who knelt on ledges or clung to boulders, following the slow movement of the raft with straining eyes, urging it on, urging it on. Neal would, I knew, have felt that same empty sickness I had felt.

I got myself back to the tent. Neal was sitting beside Chips Bullock, holding one of Chips's hands in both of his.

"He was alive when I came in," Neal said. "He held out his hand to me and I took it. He didn't say anything, but his eyes asked. I told him about the raft. I think it made him feel better."

Chips's eyes were closed. His face was peaceful, and I was glad he was gone. He hadn't died alone in a hole on the rock, with someone who couldn't speak to him, as he had feared he might if Langman, on Election Day, had become our captain.

There was coming and going in the tent. At dusk, th
captain said, the raft seemed to be half-way to land. Some
times it would go from sight: then rise again on a wave
Nobody talked about it. We were exhausted. Also aroun
high tide time, the wind rose and howled around the ten
and through its many chinks, and the surf made speech nex
to impossible for exhausted men.

December 28th, Thursday

God only knows why so many of us are unable to tell the truth about occurrences. A man is said to blench at a distressing sight, when in reality his colour changes not at all. A lady, supposedly, swoons or blushes at a word she has heard her father and her brothers use a thousand times, whereas the swoon or the blush occurs only in the imagination of the lady herself, or in that of the narrator of the incident. If a writer dislikes wine, all drinkers are drunkards, staggering and revolting. Those of whom we approve have smiling countenances and warm hearts: those of whom we disapprove are hyenas in appearance and behaviour. If two nations are engaged in a war, the one we dislike is a land of beasts, brutes and matricides; whereas we, to them, are bullies, murderers and patricides. Each nation is fighting a righteous war, brought about by the intolerable knavery of the other. Too many of us write of men and affairs as we think readers would have us write. Perhaps most of us are not only incapable of seeing things truly, but never do.

I think that when Captain Dean called me from the tent at dawn on the day after Swede and Harry Hallion had gone floating off on the raft, and Chips Bullock had died, he knew what that day would bring forth, and I think he was struggling desperately to find the inner strength to face it.

Captain Dean was what is known as civilised. He recognised and detested the bad days that selfish and greedy men, civil war, French influences, gambling, bad laws and worse law enforcement had brought upon England. On Boon Island he had willingly done physical things that those beneath him hadn't the moral strength to do. He had endured without anger the cowardice of Saver and Graystock: the helplessness of his own brother; the malicious opposition of Langman, White and Mellen. He had ventured out into the black cold of midnight in the hope of catching a seal unaware. He had washed our ulcerated legs and feet with urine: persuaded his unwilling crew to pick oakum for their own protection: almost paralysed his hands to dredge up mussels for us; and now I think he foresaw that a worse trial was upon him—one that would require him to ignore standards that civilisation builds up within a decent man.

As I crawled from the tent, Captain Dean stopped to speak to the men. "We'll make the full circuit of the island," he said. "Tide's high at eight. When it starts to fall, I want Chips's body on the ledge nearest the tent. White, that salt water you swallowed yesterday hasn't hurt you. You're still the strongest—you and Langman. Drag out Chips's body. Put it on the ledge. When Mr. Whitworth and I come back, we'll say a prayer over it and roll it in the water."

He followed me out. The tide was higher than we had ever seen it. The breakers, pounding and bellowing, were close and enormous.

"There's no doubt about it," Captain Dean said. "There *have* been spring tides that washed right over this island. There *must* have been."

He looked back at the tent. There was no sign of movement within its sagging sides.

We made our slow circuit of the island, watching for floating objects or anything usable cast up by the sea. There was nothing in sight—nothing except the seals that reared head and shoulders from waves to follow our every movement with insatiable curiosity: little black and white sea-swallows, skittering from wave to wave with limp feet trailing, and everywhere an infinity of sea ducks, swimming in vast shoals; chunky round black ones with white cheeks: little slender brown ones with bristly combs, diligently raising pointed beaks to heaven and genuflecting to each other—and all complacently ignoring us.

Our rounds completed, the captain peered intently toward the distant mainland, then glanced disconsolately toward the tent.

"They haven't done as I told 'em," he said. "They haven't taken him out."

When I didn't answer, he said, "Go in yourself, Miles. I can't allow them to disobey orders like this."

I went to the hut and pulled aside the flap. Earlier, when I had crawled out, they were lying down, huddled together, as motionless as Chips Bullock.

Now only Chips lay there. The others, even Saver and Graystock, were sitting up. I sensed a feverish excitement.

"Why didn't you take Chips out?" I asked. "The captain said to put him on the ledge."

"We haven't the strength," Langman said. "We're weak from lack of food."

I looked from one to another. Neal crawled out from among them and stood beside me. "They want to eat him," he said. "They're afraid to ask the captain. They want you to do it."

"I never said any such thing!" Langman said. "I'd never eat a fellow creature."

"We'll get mussels for you at low tide," I reminded them.

"Mussels!" Henry Dean exclaimed. "I gag whenever I try to swallow one!"

"Look, Whitworth," Graystock said, "those mussels make every last one of us sick! The captain'll do whatever you ask him to do. Ask him to let us have Chips. There's no use wasting him, the way we wasted Cooky!"

Well, there was no use lying to myself. When the captain rolled Cooky into the sea, I'd almost protested—almost, but I hadn't quite dared. I hadn't let myself formulate clearly in my mind that there was no good reason why we shouldn't have eaten him.

I stood looking from them to the body of Chips Bullock. I had no feeling at all except pity for Captain Dean.

When he came in among us I said, "Captain, these people want to eat Chips Bullock."

"Not me!" Langman said.

"Captain," I said, "we ate a seagull last week. Mr. Langman killed it, and Mr. Langman ate a mouthful of it, like the rest of us. He was glad to get it and so were we."

"What's that got to do with it?" Langman asked sharply.

"It's got this to do with it," I said. "Gulls are scavengers. They eat anything dead. The one we ate might have eaten part of Cooky Sipper."

"Everyone in England eats eels," Christopher Gray said. "Eels eat anything that's dead."

"You'll never catch me eating the body of a fellow human," Langman said. "My conscience would never let me rest."

"You've already got more on your conscience than any one man should be called on to endure," Captain Dean said.

"Eating a man would be a sin," Langman protested. "If I agreed to it, I'd be forever damned."

"It's a terrible thing," Captain Dean agreed, "but in my opinion it's not as much of sin as swearing to a lie that robs a man of his good name. You've lied about the insurance my brother and I carried on the *Nottingham*. You lied when you said I purposely ran the *Nottingham* ashore. I think you're damned already."

Langman eyed the captain sourly.

"Captain," Christopher Gray said, "Hallion lived with Indians in Nova Scotia, and Hallion said that when one

Indian killed another in battle, he ate the dead Indian's heart. Hallion said Indians thought it gave 'em courage."

"We could use a few Indians' hearts on Boon Island," Captain Dean said. "I think all of us could! We've lost the only one who didn't need to eat an Indian's heart . . . Swede Butler."

"Are you accusing us of cowardice?" Langman asked.

"Mr. Langman," the captain said, "I ordered you and George White to drag Chips Bullock's body to the ledge nearest the sea. Why didn't you do it?"

"I told Mr. Whitworth," Langman said. "We're too weak."

"If you're too weak to do that, you're weak from hunger. And if you're hungry enough, you'll eat anything. I know. Yesterday I tried, like a dog, to eat my own frozen excrement. I think you didn't move Chips because you secretly wanted to eat him but lacked the courage to say so."

"I'll never eat a fellow human," Langman repeated.

"We'll vote," Captain Dean said. "We'll vote whether or not we'll eat this body. Neal, you're youngest, but you won't vote until after all the others."

"I want to vote," Neal said. "My father would have voted Yes, and that's how I vote."

"Mr. Langman?" asked the captain.

"Never shall it be——"

"All right," the captain said. "You vote No. Christopher Gray?"

"I vote Yes," Gray said. "Captain, we're almost dead from lack of meat."

"Henry Dean?" the captain asked.

"Yes," his brother said.

"Charles Graystock?" the captain asked. "I'm in no doubt about you or Saver."

"Yes!" Graystock shouted.

"And Saver?"

Saver said Yes in strong, firm tones. Nobody could have guessed, from the quality of their voices, that from the moment we dropped from the *Nottingham's* foremast on to the seaweed of Boon Island, those two had been the malingerers, resented by all, perpetual thorns in the captain's flesh, refusing to work; sullen, even, when fed with mussels gathered by others.

"Now let's see," the captain said, "that's five in favour of eating. That only leaves three to vote—Whitworth, George White, Nicholas Mellen. So there's no need to vote further. We'll eat him."

"What about *you*?" Langman asked.

The captain ignored him, and I knew why. The captain didn't want to vote Yes; but if he had, Langman, at the first opportunity, would have taken oath that the eating of Chips Bullock had been done at the captain's suggestion. He might even have implied that the captain killed Chips in order to eat him. That was the sort of person Langman was. Unfortunately there'll always be Langmans in this world, to set people and nations against each other—to condemn the good and extol the bad—to spread sly rumours and spit on the truth.

There was something horrible about the open excitement of Saver and Graystock when the captain agreed to the eating of Chips, but ironically I was not horrified by the inner relief I felt myself.

I was even puzzled by the steadfast refusal, on the part of those who had most feverishly urged the eating, to help carry the body from the tent.

When Neal and I offered to help the captain, he waved us sharply aside. He wanted the others, the responsible ones, to do it; but when he gave the necessary orders, they lay in their places like dogs that, even though whipped, refuse to carry out their masters' orders. Their eyes rolled up at him, exactly like those of cowering dogs, and it was plain that no orders, no prayers, no punishment, would persuade them to take part in the act they'd begged the captain to permit.

In the end, Neal and I helped him drag out the body. He had tried to do it alone, but it was too much for him. Even with our help it was almost too much for all three of us, so that when the body lay on the cold ledge, we were numb mentally and physically, and the captain took us back to the tent, where he lay with eyes closed, until the men again wailingly asked for meat.

At half-tide he roused himself, and instantly the men were silent, watching him, their eyes stubborn. They wouldn't help. They just wouldn't help.

We had the saw, made so laboriously from the cutlass, and we had our knives. We had nothing else except spun yarn, taken from the tent, and two squares of canvas, cut from the boulder-weighted slack we had left when the tent was built.

"First," the captain said, "I'll make a bag of the clothes and put 'em in that rock crevice yonder. Then I'll wrap the head in the clothes, and the feet and the hands and the skin —and the other things. And the bones. We'll have to bone out the meat, so we can wrap it and cut it into equal pieces. We'll put the clothes in a crevice with boulders piled over it. We'll make a cross out of two pieces of wood and wedge it in the boulders."

His mention of the cross made us feel better.

He hefted the cutlass-saw.

"Now," he said, "I want the two of you to go to the north side of the island. See whether anything's come ashore. Look at the mainland for signs of boats. I've got things to do, and I'm reconciled to doing them. To me, this is meat."

He touched Chips's body with the tip of the saw; then continued, "Eventually it will be meat to both of you:

something over which to say grace. Nothing more. Until then I'll do what has to be done, but I'll do it alone. You aren't reconciled yet; and what I'm doing, I'm doing for your father's sake as well as for your own."

When Neal and I hesitated, he impatiently waved us away. "I'll need help in skinning and boning out," he said. "When I'm ready, I'll wave and you can come back."

The labour of skinning a human body is beyond belief. Perhaps a surgeon would make nothing of it. It might seem simple to a butcher. To us, with our scarred and half-frozen fingers and hands, it was next to impossible.

When in exasperation I cursed my helplessness, Captain Dean urged me on. "We can't stop," he said. "If we stop now and wait till to-morrow to finish, it may freeze so solid we can't do anything with it."

The skin wasn't like a rabbit pelt or a deerskin, that can be raised a little at the neck and then pulled off cleanly from the whole body. This skin had adhesions, so that when it was raised at the neck, it had to be pared away from the flesh beneath by continuous slicing and slashing. Also, unlike an animal's skin, it was tender in spots, so that it was forever ripping or being pierced by our knives.

I thanked God we were no longer hampered by the gulls. If they had been about us, as they had been before Langman killed that progenitor of all gulls, they would have swooped upon us to snatch the flesh from our very hands and soar away, yelling in triumph.

The tide was on the make before the meat had been stripped from the leg bones and arm bones, and laid off from the ribs and back. All these were rolled by Neal in tight cylinders and tied with rope yarn.

We wedged the bones into the crevice in such a way that no seal or gull could dislodge the boulders above them.

Even then we weren't finished, for the rolls, the slabs of

meat from belly and buttocks, the liver, the heart and the fat-encased kidneys had to be sunk in an even deeper crevice nearer the tent, covered with three feet of seaweed to guard against freezing, and the seaweed in turn topped by a double layer of boulders.

We worked in silence, except when Neal brought the kidneys back to the captain, after washing them in salt water.

"Keep those on top of everything," the captain said. "That fat is just as good as mutton tallow. Maybe we can use it for poultices."

When we returned exhausted and depressed to the tent to feed those comrades who had lain there, sunk in helplessness because of some frightened quirk of their disgusting brains, Langman, White and Mellen, as able-bodied as any of us, refused to eat.

"An insult," Langman mumbled, "to the spirit of a friend."

"Langman," Captain Dean said, "my duty by you is done. Eat or don't eat, as you please. But my duty to the rest of us is *not* done, and if I hear any more talk out of you about this meat being anybody's spirit, you'll rue the day!"

"Are you threatening me?" Langman asked.

"Yes, I'm threatening you," Captain Dean said. "If you pour out your spleen on these others, I'll protect them by stopping your mouth. This meat I'm offering is nobody's spirit. It's beef. It was animated once by a soul and a spirit, but the soul and the spirit have gone from this island, leaving only beef behind."

He threw up his hands in disgust at Langman's mutterings, drew his knife and carefully divided the rolled meat into slices.

"Listen carefully," he said, before he handed out the slices. "We have enough beef for a week, if we're careful. If Langman, White and Mellen don't eat, we'll have enough for a longer time. But this you must do: you must scrape the beef to a pulp, and with each piece of pulp you must chew seaweed. You mustn't gulp it down. You must *not* gulp it down."

He handed around the meat, and the tent was filled with the soft sound of scraping and chewing, audible above the angry roaring of the breakers.

I tried to remember what Captain Dean had said about being reconciled. I expected to be revolted by the meat and the seaweed, but I wasn't. It wasn't offensive. It wasn't nauseating. It had no more taste than raw beef or raw venison.

All I could think of was Langman, meatless, staring out from the darkness with hard and hating eyes, and once I thought I felt Chips Bullock behind me, a little stooped, his head lowered, laughing that silent, belly-shaking laugh of his at Langman, Mellen and White.

December 29th, Friday

Boon Island taught me the danger of trusting those who
at any time have lied about their reasons for doing things.
It taught me, too, that no man should ever say, "I'll never
do this," or "I'll never do that," or should ever affirm,
"Nothing could persuade me to do this; nothing could
make me do that."

Never, Langman had sworn, would he eat human flesh.
It was sinful, it was unlawful, it was repugnant to all the
dictates of his conscience. He had implied that the eating
of *any* human flesh was heinous, but that to eat the flesh of
a friend was worse: was obscene, infamous, abominable—
and somehow he had persuaded White and Mellen that such
a specious argument was worthy of consideration.

The wind had threatened us by backing up on Thursday.
On Friday that threat materialised. Shortly after midnight
a mixture of snow and rain from the south-west slatted
against the tent; driblets of water trickled down upon us,
first from one spot and then from another.

Even before daybreak the men, restless, were demanding
meat. The snow and the rain, they said, might damage it,
freeze it, ruin it. It should be brought out and distributed.

"You'll get your meat," Captain Dean assured them, "but
I made up my mind to something yesterday, when able-
bodied men lay here and wouldn't lift a hand to do the
necessary work to provide the meat because they pretended
to be too weak: then ate with the strength of wolves. This

179

is what I decided. If they've got the strength to eat meat, they had the strength, yesterday, to help me cut it up. They wouldn't do it! I'm sick of people who won't help themselves."

Nobody said anything.

"So," Captain Dean said, "let's see where we stand. Swede is gone and Harry Hallion with him. Cooky Sipper is gone. Chips Bullock is gone. Mr. Langman's conscience won't let him eat human flesh. Neither will White's nor Mellen's.

"That leaves seven of us. All seven will draw a reasonable ration of meat this morning, but each one of us must do something in return, and that's pick enough oakum to thatch this tent.

"That means Saver and Graystock will pick oakum or get no meat. It means my brother will pick oakum, even though he *does* have epileptic fits once in a while. It means I'll pick oakum, Mr. Whitworth will pick oakum. So will Neal Butler and Christopher Gray. Is that understood?"

"Just give us the meat," Graystock said.

"That's not enough," Captain Dean said. "I want your promises, made in the hearing of all in this tent. Each one of you must swear that if he eats meat, he'll pick oakum as long as he can move his hands. Saver, do you solemnly swear you'll pick oakum with the rest of us?"

Saver said he did, as did Graystock and the other four of us.

"All right," Captain Dean said. " I expect every one of you to live up to your promises. If you don't, I'll take steps."

He went to the tent-flap, hit it with his fist to clear it of snow and ice and peered out into the storm.

Langman got to his feet and moved close to the captain. "Captain," he said, "we've changed our minds about the beef."

The Captain looked at him incredulously. "You mean to say you and White and Mellen changed your minds? It's not a sin to eat this beef?"

"No," Langman said. "It's not a sin to eat beef. When we understood it was beef, we saw we'd made a mistake."

Captain Dean shook his head. "But only last night your consciences were bothering you! How did you persuade your consciences to accept this as beef?"

"Why," Langman said, "we just told our consciences it was beef. For a while our consciences wouldn't listen, but in the end they did. I almost woke you up in the middle of the night to tell you our consciences had stopped bothering us."

"Well, I'm glad to hear it," Captain Dean said, "but there are two or three other little things that your consciences will have to consider before we admit you to our society. In the first place, you have to give us your word that you'll pick oakum for thatching the tent."

"You have my word," Langman said.

"Now I'll have to have White's word," the captain said, "and Mellen's."

Both White and Mellen spoke up quickly. They'd pick oakum.

Captain Dean seemed pleased. "There are two other things," he said. "One is the matter of Sunday. It's of small moment to me what day of the week a man worships his God, but if he arbitrarily picks a Sunday that differs from the one we celebrate, he creates unrest, and we have all the unrest we need without creating more. Your Sunday, Langman, is an irritation. If you eat meat with the rest of us in spite of your yesterday's conscience, you can persuade your conscience to accept our Sunday, too."

"All right," Langman said. "But to-morrow's Sunday just the same."

"Then you won't want any meat," Captain Dean said.

"Just a minute," Langman said. "I didn't say I wouldn't worship on the day you do."

"For God's sake," Saver said. "Stop talking. Give us our meat!"

The captain looked as genial as a dirty, tired, whiskered man could look. "Now you know how we felt, Saver," he said, "when you and Graystock just lay there and let the rest of us do your work for you."

He turned back to Langman. "You had your chance yesterday. You were offered a fair share of all we had, and with no strings attached. But you made a show of yourself by refusing to take what we offered. You weren't honest about it. So if we give you meat now, you'll have to pay a penalty for past dishonesty: you'll have to be honest with us—if you can regard that as a penalty, which I don't."

Langman was indignant. "I've always been honest! Didn't I divide that seagull with you?"

"That's physical honesty," Captain Dean said. "Almost everyone is physically honest. I'm talking about mental honesty. Most of the men in this tent are both physically and mentally honest. I think even Mellen and White are mentally honest. They're just indebted to you, and so they accept the things you tell 'em as being true, which they aren't."

"I don't know what you're talking about," Langman said.

"If you don't, you're weak-minded," Captain Dean said, "and that's the last thing I'd accuse you of. You said repeatedly I ran the ship ashore purposely, and that's the stupidest, silliest piece of mental dishonesty I ever heard."

Langman widened his eyes at the captain. "If that's all that's bothering you," he said, "I'll trade my opinion for the same amount of meat that everyone else gets."

"That is to say," Captain Dean said, "you give me your word you won't repeat that outrageous lie, ever again."

"Why, of course," Langman said, all mealy-mouthed.

The captain pulled aside the tent-flap and went into out the snow.

Langman looked around at the rest of us with his lip lifted in that sardonic smile of his. I thought I knew the meaning of that offensive smile.

Unless I misjudged Langman, no promise of his was worth anything at all. No matter what he promised, he'd make a mental reservation that would free his twisted mind of the need to carry out his promise.

Even if he were somehow prevented from making a mental reservation, that devious brain would invent a loophole that would release him from his obligation.

Statesmen, often, are like that, and so are men of business —which may explain why the English guard themselves so carefully against men of business as well as against some statesmen—usually the wrong ones.

I think the captain, having brought Langman around to his way of thinking by a sort of justified blackmail, tried to make sure of his conquest by being kinder to him and Mellen and White than to the rest of us. He gave them slivers of liver, whereas the rest of us got along with slices of muscle, full of tendons from which the meat separated reluctantly. The best I could say for it was that it was better than the rawhide we had chopped and swallowed so avidly.

Tough as the meat was, there wasn't one of us who couldn't have eaten three times our allotment, and Langman even demanded more as a reward for picking oakum all day.

"Look here, Langman," Captain Dean said. "You undertook to pick oakum for the same amount of meat that the rest of us have. If I give you more, I'll have to give more to everyone else. Then, before we know it, there won't be any for anyone."

Langman argued senselessly that he and Mellen and White

were entitled to more because they had refused to eat the day before, when all the rest of us had eaten.

"Whose fault was that?" Captain Dean asked.

"It was yours," Langman said, "because you didn't tell us the meat was beef until we'd made up our minds it was something else."

The captain, however, was adamant. "All right," he said, "but you're asking for too much, and it's bad for you to eat too much. Not wicked: not sinful. No more sinful than eating seaweed. But you refused your ration yesterday and you've had your ration for to-day. Now you can keep right on working."

He only left the tent to drag in more cordage for us to pick apart and make into oakum; and while we made it, he wove it. By dark that Friday he had woven a thatch of oakum that covered the top of the tent and extended two-thirds down the south-eastern side.

So thanks to Chips Bullock and to Langman's slippery conscience, we were not only fed, but were free, all night long, of the rivulets of icy water that had trickled down upon us all through that snowy, rainy day.

December 30th, Saturday

"HAVE SOMEBODY light a fire—two fires—on the beach," Captain Dean had told Swede before he set off on the raft; and for days our minds, if they could indeed have been called minds, were centred on hunting for smoke on the mainland.

Because of Friday's rain and snow, we couldn't see Cape Neddick or the beaches; but on Saturday the snow and rain stopped, and land was once more visible—a land of dark pines, long sands, forbidding cliffs, with no trace of smoke discernible anywhere.

Neal was out of the tent at dawn, studying that shore line.

We did what we could to buoy up his hopes—and ours, too.

"Yesterday was so rainy," Captain Dean said, "that there wouldn't have been dry wood on the beach."

Neal glanced at him, and the captain looked away.

"They might have had to go far before they found a house," I said. "Two or three days might pass before fires could be lit."

Neal didn't reply. He just crept back into the tent and went to picking oakum.

I don't know what happens to the minds of prisoners or of men in circumstances such as ours; but I suspect they move more slowly, always—more and more slowly, until they scarcely move at all. If that weren't so—if their minds worked actively on their situations, their lives would be unendurable and they'd die.

While there was a possibility of seeing smoke, we seemed content to sit and pick oakum: to wait until the captain had finished carving more beef for us: to wait until the next time someone went to the tent-flap to scan the land for a wisp of smoke.

We were like sleepers half-awake, who mutter disjointed sentences, utter words that seem to a dreamer to be intelligible. Like those aroused from dreams, we resented attempts to make sense from our mumblings.

Altercations broke out unexpectedly. When Langman gabbled something about "This day our daily bread," Christopher Gray, the gunner, flew at him.

"What you want to talk that way for?" Gray demanded.

"What way?" Langman asked.

"You said ' This day,'" Gray said. "That means that this day's Sunday, but you know it ain't. It's Saturday. You promised the captain you'd have the same Sunday as us."

"I never said to-day was Sunday," Langman said.

"You said, ' This day,'" Gray repeated, "and ' This day ' means Sunday."

"I never did," Langman said, "and if I did, ' This day ' doesn't mean anything except *this* day. This day can be *any* day."

Gray, enraged, lunged at him, and they thrashed ineffectually around our odoriferous oakum floor.

We caught Gray and set him upright. Forgetting Langman, he picked numbly at the hemp before him.

The captain came in among us and gave us our slices of beef.

"Any smoke?" Henry Dean asked.

"None that I could see," the captain said. He looked apologetically at Neal.

Langman sneered. "You wouldn't have seen it, even if

you had one of Newton's reflecting telescopes. Any fool would know they never got ashore."

"Keep your mouth shut," Captain Dean said.

"That's not part of our bargain," Langman said. "First thing I know, you'll tell me I can't have meat unless I stop hearing and seeing and smelling."

The captain groaned in disgust and collapsed heavily beside his coil of cordage, only to rise again when Mellen and White, without warning, belaboured each other.

The captain pulled them apart and sat between them. "What's all this?" he said. "Why waste your strength on each other?"

"Nobody can call me a liar," Mellen said, "just because I recall one or two things that happened when I was with Woodes Rogers."

"I was there," White protested. "He talked about how a beautiful woman cooked for him when we stopped in Brazil to give the ship a pair of boot tops."

"Well, she was!" Mellen insisted. "Shaped like a fairy queen."

"Fairy queen hell," White said. "I saw 'em. They looked like cows and smelled like pigs, all of 'em!"

White and Mellen cursed each other.

The thought came to me that their dispositions had changed, and their voices, too. Their voices were breathless, squealing, like pigs struggling at a trough. I wondered whether the meat had done it, or the salty ice we chewed to quench our thirst, or the unending cold, or our inner fears of the eternity that had drawn so close.

I pulled at Neal's sleeve, and we went out on the rock. We looked all along the coast for smoke. Like the captain, we saw nothing.

"Neal," I said, "it might help these men if you recited parts of plays to them."

Neal shook his head.

"Why not?" I said. "It might keep them quiet."

"No, it wouldn't," Neal said. "Nothing would keep them quiet. They'd laugh at any part of any play, because plays aren't worth believing. Nothing's true except this." He swept his arm from the tent toward the ocean and the mainland.

There wasn't much I could say.

"Anyway," Neal said, "I've forgotten everything. I don't want to remember, and I never will. I'll only remember that my father hated the stage and wanted to keep me from it. I want to forget my name, even. I want it to be what it should be—Moses. That's what my father and my mother named me.

"If I'd never gone near the theatre—if I hadn't done what my father didn't want me to do—the *Nottingham* wouldn't have sailed when she did. She wouldn't have gone to Killybegs to take on butter and cheese. She'd never have struck this island. It's all my fault."

"Look, Neal," I said, "if you want to start thinking that way, you can trace every bad thing in the world back to some little incident that nobody was to blame for. Instead of blaming yourself, blame the circumstances that brought that nasty little fop to Greenwich. Blame the thing that made him a fop in the first place."

Neal's eyes had a hunted look. I think if there'd been a hole on that barren rock into which he could have crawled, he'd have crept there to get away from me, from Captain Dean, from his memories, from the eternal thundering of the breakers all around us.

"I know how you feel," I said, "and I'm glad you do. My father was right, too, and I wish I could tell him so. I can hear him now—' pint-sized clowns in tatters and tarnished gold lace, making faces and laughing like hyenas at their damned dull witlessness.'"

Singularly, I thought of Sir Isaac Newton and his discovery of the reflecting telescope: of Langman, who said there could be no such thing—who laughed at the truth. And ironically it came to me that there would be people like Langman who would say that there was no truth to this island or to the tribulations we'd endured upon it: that our labours were nonsense. It came to me suddenly that when I left this island, if I ever did leave it, I wanted nothing to do with the Langmans of this world—nothing to do with those who derided the truth, and defiled it.

We went back to the tent. The captain, carving pieces of fat from Chips Bullock's kidneys, looked up at us sharply. "Any smoke?"

When we shook our heads, he sliced off a piece of the fat, laid it on a board and pounded it with the handle of his knife, spreading it into a thin sheet.

"There," he said. "That's pretty near the same as the mutton tallow my grandmother used to make. Each one of you can have an equal amount. You'll have to make it go as far as possible.

"We'll flatten it out, flatten it out, and when it's as thin as we can make it, we'll take off these oakum bindings and wash our feet and legs again, same as we did before. The fat ought to be good for deep sores. It's bound to help those who've lost toes."

December 31st, Sunday

IF A man, on the last day of any year, chooses honestly to consider his shortcomings, he must always be depressed; and if any people anywhere ever had occasion to be downcast on the last day of that year, it was we on Boon Island.

The sight of our legs and feet on the day before, when we applied the poultices of kidney fat to them, had frightened us. They were worse—much worse—than they had been in the dim and dreadful past, when we cut off our boots and first swathed ourselves in oakum. The sores were deeper: the toes broke off more easily, though without pain.

Then Henry Dean screamed that horrible epileptic's scream of his in the deep dark, and flung himself around the tent as though he had eight legs and eight arms, all made of steel. When we finally pinned him down, he twisted and turned in our hands with almost unbelievable violence, and on top of that he groaned horribly, and there's something catching—something poisonous—about groans.

The whole night was a bad one and after Henry Dean had stopped thrashing and writhing, and had fallen into an epileptic's heavy sleep, I lay staring upward, afraid of the dark, afraid of what must happen to my feet and legs if this cold continued—if we went on and on, being drenched daily by the salty spit from the breakers—if I lost the use of my hands and could no longer occupy myself in the brain-deadening task of picking oakum.

In my thinking I groaned, realised too late what I was

doing, tried to turn it into a cough, and produced a sort of squawk, like a crow with a beakful of food.

I felt a hand fumbling at my shoulder and heard Neal say, "Are you all right, Miles?"

"Of course," I said. "Of course I'm all right. Are you all right?"

"We're *all* all right," Captain Dean said. "Even my brother's all right—or will be when he wakes. All of you felt how much strength he has. Just remember you're all as strong as Henry if only you make up your minds to be."

He hesitated: then added, "I've been thinking. I don't believe we've been praying right. We've been praying as if we didn't know God at all—as if he was some sort of distant image, away up above the stars somewhere—an image with whiskers, like ours.

"Well, he isn't an image. He's real. And since we expect him to answer our prayers, he can't be far away. We believe he'll help us if we deserve to be helped, but we don't ask him for that help in the same way we'd ask our own fathers for help."

He hesitated again. "Would anyone like to speak to God? If you can't find the words, I'll speak for you, but I think you might feel better if you did your own speaking."

"I'd like to speak to God," Neal said. "I'd like to speak about my father. God, I'd like to have my father told that I know what he did for us. You must know what he did, God, and I hope you won't let it be wasted."

"What do you mean by that, Neal?" the captain asked.

"God knows," Neal said.

After a time the captain spoke again, conversationally, as if God were in the tent with us. "God," he said, "you've been kind to us, though some might think you haven't been. By giving us ice to eat, you've saved us from the most horrible of all deaths: you've given us work to do, so that we've preserved our sanity: you saved us from disaster when you overturned the boat: you let the sea wash up the cordage from which we made clothing and shelter: you gave us seaweed to eat: you gave us Swede Butler to strengthen our courage . . ."

Langman spoke up. "Don't forget the seagull."

"Yes, God; the seagull," Captain Dean said. "The seagull helped us. All things considered, God, we've done as well with these blessings as any equal number of men could be expected to do, and all we ask, God, is that you don't withdraw your favour from us."

"Aren't you going to ask for a ship to take us off?" Langman demanded. "Why don't you ask him to send the seagulls back? There hasn't been one sighted since I killed mine!"

"Ask for fire!" White demanded.

The captain shook his head. "Ask for them yourselves if you think it'll do any good," he said. "If God feels we should be helped, I think he ought to be allowed to work it out in his own way. I don't feel qualified to tell God what to do or how to do it. I wouldn't feel justified in asking him for more seagulls. He probably had a good reason for sending 'em away from the island."

I couldn't improve on what the captain had said, and the others were silent as well; but I think we all felt better because of Neal's and the captain's talks with God.

For the first time I felt about God as I'd so often felt about my father: felt that he'd do anything reasonable I asked him to do, and that if he should refuse, he'd only do so for my own good.

There were lines of light showing around the edges of the tent-flap, so I went out with the captain to help him with the meat.

Neal followed me. He didn't even look toward Cape Neddick or York.

"Neal," the captain said, "I want you to find another hole in the rock where we can store part of this meat. I want you to attend to moving half of it, and I don't want to know where you put it. I don't want anyone to know: not even Miles."

Neal nodded and moved away.

Captain Dean watched him go, then turned to me. "Was it three days ago, Miles," he asked, "or four days ago that Swede and Hallion put off? I forget. Every day seems a year long."

"It was Wednesday," I said.

"Miles," he said slowly, "I think Neal knows his father's gone."

"I know he does," I said. "I know it, too, and so do you."

"Yes," Captain Dean said, "but he knows more than we do."

"Yes," I said, "I know that he *thinks* he knows, but that doesn't necessarily mean he's right. I hope he isn't."

When the captain didn't answer, I asked him what he meant by asking Neal to find another hole in the rock.

"I don't quite know," the captain said. "I think this meat has made some of the men a little crazy. Have you noticed Saver's and Graystock's eyes when I pass around the meat?"

I said I hadn't.

"Well," Captain Dean said, "I had a ferret when I was a boy. I'd turn him loose in the stables, and he'd kill rats. When he jumped on a rat, his eyes looked red. I don't think they *were* red, but that's how they looked. That's how Saver's and Graystock's eyes look when they get their meat. If that's how they feel about it, they might crawl out of the tent any night. Being the sort of people they are, they wouldn't hesitate to steal what rightly belongs to all the rest of us, and they haven't enough brains between them to exercise restraint or common sense in their eating. They'd eat until they dropped dead."

G

He watched Neal coming slowly back to us, picking his way over the icy ledges.

The captain drew four large bundles of meat from beneath the seaweed and piled them in Neal's arms. "Be sure they're covered with three feet of seaweed," he told Neal.

When Neal was out of hearing, the captain asked, with seeming carelessness, "What is it Neal thinks happened to his father?"

"Well," I said, "you know how I feel about Neal. From the moment I saw him, I've thought of him as a brother—a younger brother. I wouldn't want you to think that there's anything odd about him—that he has hallucinations, or anything of that sort."

The captain sniffed. "I know hallucinations when I see 'em, Miles. The night the *Nottingham* was wrecked, I was sure none of us would last until morning. Then when morning came, I had a feeling. Not an hallucination. I don't know how you get feelings, or where they come from; but I had the feeling we were going to come safely out of this. I still have it, and I still think I'm right. That's no hallucination. Now what is it that Neal feels about his father?"

"Well," I said, "he thinks he saw his father in a dream, or something like that. His father told him the raft hadn't a chance of getting to shore with two men on it. He told Neal that since he was a good swimmer, he was going to get into the water and swim and push. He thought that if he did that, the raft might get to shore, so he was going to try it."

The captain nodded. "I see."

"Well, that's what Neal thinks, Captain. He thinks his father swam as long as he could, and then just slipped off."

"I can think of worse ways to go," the captain said.

January 1st, Monday

THIS WAS the day we saw the smoke.

Neal saw it first and was less affected by it than the rest of us. He left the tent early, no doubt to make sure that nothing or nobody had disturbed the place where he'd hidden the beef.

When he came back he said, almost idly, "There's smoke on the mainland. It's blowing to the eastward."

We jostled each other to crawl from the tent to see this sign—the first hopeful one we'd seen in three long weeks. There it was—a plume of smoke from a fire that must have been newly kindled, for the plume, a mere smudge to begin with, grew constantly longer and longer, drifting ever farther to the eastward as we watched. What it meant, we couldn't know, but Captain Dean insisted that it must be a signal—a signal to let us know our plight had been discovered.

As near as we could tell, the smoke was rising to the south of west, probably, the captain thought, from somewhere between York and Portsmouth.

Langman insisted it couldn't be a signal, because the fire was so far south of the direction in which the raft had been heading when it put out from Boon Island; but the captain said this didn't necessarily follow.

"Why would anyone bother with a signal?" Langman asked. "There's an offshore breeze, and only six or eight miles to go. Any sloop or schooner could sail that distance in less time than it took somebody to start that fire."

"I don't know," Captain Dean admitted, "but I know that raft got ashore. If it got ashore, somebody saw it. Anybody who saw it would recognise it as the work of seamen who had next to nothing to work with. That raft was laced and knotted with everything from bos'n's knots to granny knots. Where else but on Boon Island would a lot of wrecked seamen have nothing to work with?"

All day long we argued the matter. Only Neal refused to discuss it; but the arguments of the rest of us rose and fell like waves. At one moment we were elated in a firm belief that the smoke was a signal: in the next moment we decided it couldn't be a signal: that it must be an accident; a hay barn afire; a farmer clearing land.

One thing was apparent. Before we saw the smoke, my companions were images of Death itself: horrible, haggard, slow-moving creatures, tangled of hair and beard, stooped with hunger, swathed about the head and hands and legs with clumsy bands of oakum.

After they'd seen the smoke, they stood straighter: their voices were stronger: their eyes less wild and staring.

What was worse, they were hungrier than ever, and quick to demand more meat from the captain.

"If you're so sure that smoke's a signal," Langman said, "you must be equally sure that they'll send a ship for us. Why shouldn't we divide half of the meat that's left?"

The captain shook his head. "When they say they want more," he said, "they want three times what they've been getting. That's too much for half-starved men to have.

"There's another thing: we've none of us ever had meat like this. There's no telling what it may do to us. You must know what happens to half-starved men when they eat too much. They get sick. Sometimes they die."

He lifted the seaweed covering from the store of meat,

drew out a generous chunk and sliced it quickly into ten parts, each part almost twice the size of those we'd hitherto received. With each slice went a handful of seaweed from the pile that had covered our little stock.

They crawled off in two groups: Langman, Mellen and White in one group: Graystock, Saver and Gray in another. All of them scraped diligently at their meat, and chewed at their seaweed; and from time to time they turned their heads to gaze covertly at the captain, Neal, Henry Dean and me.

There was no doubt about it: each group was plotting something.

Captain Dean shuffled his feet on the icy rock. "I don't like it," he said. "We'll have to put a guard over this meat. I said I was sure the smoke was a signal, but I'm not sure at all. I'm not sure of anything but this: if they steal this meat and eat it all, they won't hesitate to kill someone in order to have more."

The rest of that day was a nightmare. The wind cut cruelly, but all day long we were in and out of the tent, not only to scan the far-off coast line in the hope of seeing a sail outlined against it, but to keep watch on the spot where our beef was stored.

By midafternoon, while the smoke continued to drift from west to east, the tide was half out and it was apparent to all of us that no vessel would venture out in the short time remaining.

That night the captain lay across the tent-flap. Neal lay between the two of us, and in the early dark I could feel Neal shaking, feel him swallow, as people do when their minds are not at rest. His shaking may have come from the cold, but I somehow knew he was thinking about his father. Remembering how Neal had shrunk from me when, on that long-gone summer day in Greenwich, I had inadvertently touched him, I did nothing; but the captain said, "Neal, roll over on top of me and keep me warm. And Miles: come closer, Miles."

We huddled together.

I could feel rather than hear the soft patting of the captain's hand against Neal's shoulder. Neal's shudderings and swallowings lessened. I suppose we slept.

January 2nd, Tuesday

When, because of bad weather, there was little or nothing to do on Boon Island except pick at that loathsome oakum, or stumble around the island on our eternal patrols, the days sometimes seemed endless because of their monotony and the biting cold.

Probably the very monotony was so deadening that the time passed more rapidly than we thought.

There was no monotony, God knows, to that second day of January; and the endlessness of that one day, by comparison with other memorable days of my life, went on and on until, at nightfall, I felt as though I had lived years.

The captain, as usual, was first out of the tent, and the tent-flap had no sooner fallen behind him than sounds came from him, a sort of hiccuping and gasping, broken by quavering hootings, such as come from a loon.

Thinking he might have caught epilepsy from his brother, I crawled out to help him. He was on all fours, pawing feebly at the rocks, as if trying to return to the tent.

I thought of broken bones: of a captain made helpless at the hour of our greatest need, and my heart sank.

"What's the matter?" I asked, frightened sick by his apparent weakness.

I got him by the arm and tried to help him up.

He caught me by the shoulders and leaned against me. I

couldn't tell whether if falling he had knocked the breath from himself, or was in such excruciating agony that his face was contorted by it into a twisted travesty of a grin.

"Sail," he gasped. "Boat!" Tears ran down his cheeks: snuffling like a child, he swung an arm to the westward, turning me in that direction.

There, half-way between us and the shore, a scant three miles away, was a little sloop, bobbing and bowing, curtsying and rocking over the heavy lead-coloured swells, heading straight for the centre of the island's western shore on a cold and sharp north-west wind.

I couldn't believe my eyes. I rubbed them, looked all around the horizon: then looked back at the sloop. I wasn't dreaming! I wasn't imagining things! She yawed a little as she slipped down the face of a following sea. A man holding to her mast flapped an arm at his helmsman. She was a real vessel with a patch at the foot of her jib. She had people aboard—living human beings. My throat constricted: my breath caught convulsively at my chest. I couldn't speak: I couldn't draw air into my lungs.

I pulled at the tent-flap and croaked, "Neal!"

He crawled out, white-faced, saw the sloop and made a whimpering sound. The others came out, too. They just stood there, staring at the beautiful little vessel, while tears of which they were unconscious trickled from their eyes and clung in silvery drops to their matted beards.

We spread out along the western side of the island, trying to convey by gestures, to that man who stood before the sloop's mast, a part of our joy, our gratitude. . . .

Captain Dean waved and waved, pointing to the south-east, where the sloop could run close to the island—close enough down-wind to hear our voices; but the sloop brought to at the north end of the island, came into the wind, and dropped her anchor and jib. She was as far offshore as the island was long.

"Wave her off," Captain Dean told us. "She'll drag her anchor—pile up on a ledge!"

There were three men aboard her—smoothly shaved men with rosy faces, warm clothes, fur hats. Well-fed men, quick-moving, firm on their feet, unlike us: strong men, pillars of strength: symbols of life and salvation.

Captain Dean pointed out to sea, flapped his hands to warn them off. With his arms he made slow circles. To us his meaning was apparent. He wanted them to pull off shore: to sail in circles until high tide. He pointed again and again to the south-east, where they could safely come into the wind and speak to us.

Certainly their anchor was dragging, or their roding too short, for she was constantly drawing nearer, pushed by those damnable swells out of the north.

We groaned with relief when she hoisted her jib and fell off a mile to the eastward, headed north, tacked into the west, and then stood off and on, lively as a duck, waiting for flood tide.

Under the best of circumstances, waiting can be one of the worst curses that man is called upon to endure—waiting for a loved one, while the mind conjures up visions of injury, disaster, death: waiting tensely, despairingly, for a reply to a letter: waiting fearfully for a battle to begin: waiting for a ship to sail: waiting for a guest to arrive or to go: waiting sleeplessly through the watches of the night for the day that seems determined not to come: waiting, all a-sweat, for the cessation of pain, or for the doctor who may relieve it: waiting apprehensively for a storm to strike or, when it has struck, to abate. Never, I thought, as I waited for that sloop to return—as all of us waited, torn by our fears, our nerves a-jangle—would I wittingly add to man's burdens by keeping anyone waiting.

With that sloop in the offing, waiting became a poison, so that voices all around us broke, arms and legs jerked uncontrollably, minds and thinking were disarranged. Some laughed like women: fell into black depressions, trembled, cursed, groaned, stammered, yawned cavernously.

Captain Dean, once more calm and composed, carved our meat and passed around the seaweed—and after an eternity the little sloop slipped in to coast back and forth across the southern tip of the island. With each pass she drew closer. We could see she carried no boat; only a bark canoe lashed alongside her cabin.

The behaviour of the three men who sailed her filled me with anxiety. They eyed us warily: glanced at each other, as if in doubt. They didn't like what they saw, and I couldn't blame them.

"You've got six feet at flood tide," Captain Dean shouted. "Fifteen feet offshore you've got six feet."

The sloop's master waved his hand, brought the sloop into the wind, dropped his jib and spilled the anchor over the bow. The three men ducked under the sloop's boom and studied us again. They looked worried.

"Ship *Nottingham*," the captain shouted. A wave curled over and fell noisily. He waited for the roaring to subside: then tried again. "Ship *Nottingham*. London to Portsmouth."

We couldn't tell whether or not the three men could hear.

Captain Dean turned to the rest of us and spoke sharply. "I don't dare tell 'em how much we need food. They might not come ashore."

To the sloop he shouted again. "Fire! We need fire! Cold! Frozen!" He held his ears: bent over, he hugged himself.

The three men conferred.

Captain Dean knelt and went through the motions of

using a tinderbox. He pretended to blow on a fire and then to warm his hands before it.

Two of the men unlashed the canoe, lowered it over the side and held it while the third man stepped down into it, knelt in the middle, and took two paddles that were handed to him. One he stowed beneath the thwarts. With the other he pushed off from the sloop and, still kneeling, headed for the cleft in the rock where we were gathered.

"Remember," Captain Dean warned us, "don't say a word about our meat."

The man in the canoe held his paddle steady, looked behind him, waited for a swell to come near his stern: then dug in his paddle and came rushing toward us on the slope of a roller. Captain Dean and George White braced themselves at the head of the cleft, caught the canoe by the bow and held it where it was while the wave slipped back. The canoeman, still clutching his paddle, climbed out over the bow and helped White and Captain Dean carry the canoe up higher, out of harm's way.

"We knew somebody had been cast away, and probably here," he said. He spoke slowly, and with assurance, a little like those who came up to Oxford from Warwick or Hereford —from places like Stratford-on-Avon or Broadway, where people have had the benefit of schooling.

"I'm John Dean," the captain said, "master of the *Nottingham* Galley. We went ashore——"

He broke off, looked from the canoeman to Langman and back again: then asked, "What day is this—sir?"

"This is January 2nd, a Tuesday," the man said. "I'm Nason. Richard Nason. Kittery. Part owner of the sloop *Head of Tide*."

"It can't be Tuesday," Langman said. "It must be Wednesday."

Nason looked at him oddly. "Why must it?"

"Because I kept count," Langman said.

Nason turned back to Captain Dean. "Yesterday was Monday—New Year's Day."

Captain Dean nodded. "We went ashore Monday, December 11th. There was a north-easter blowing."

"You've been on this pile of rocks since the eleventh of December?" Nason asked incredulously. His eyes swept over us, examining us from head to foot—from our oakum hats, with bits of seagull feathers and seagull skin woven into them, the oakum mittens on our hands, the oakum wrappings fastened to our shoulders, chests and legs, the clumsy oakum sheathings of our feet. He shook his head as if he found us incredible.

"Kittery?" Captain Dean asked. "Isn't that across the river from Portsmouth?"

"Yes," Nason said, "and I better not waste time. We'll have to take word to Portsmouth about you. You need help as much as anyone *I* ever saw!"

"Yes," Captain Dean said. "We need help. When you send word to Portsmouth, see that Captain Long and Captain Furber are told. They're old friends. You tell 'em I'm John Dean of Twickenham, Jasper Dean's brother."

"Wait a minute," Nason said. "I'll write it down." He fished in his clothes and produced a small account book: then stared at Captain Dean again: at me: at Neal Butler.

"No fire all that time?" he asked. "How could you live!"

Christopher Gray broke into a sort of snuffling, such as a dog makes when he whuffles for the scent of an animal behind the wainscoting.

"It seemed like a long time," Captain Dean said apologetically. "We built a boat and lost it. Then we built a raft. This boy's father built it." He put his hand on Neal's shoulder.

Nason cleared his throat. "Oh, yes," he said. "The raft! We figured there'd been two men on it. We figured a lot of men worked to make it, on account of the knots. We found it at high-water mark. Under a tree beyond high-water mark there was a man. One man. With a piece of wood tied to his wrist. He'd used it for a paddle. His hands were all raw, with the bones showing. He got as far as the tree and then I guess he lay down and froze· to death."

He shook his head, put his account book back in his pocket, and became suddenly busy. "I'll start a fire for you. Got any wood?"

"One or two pieces," Captain Dean said.

"You've probably got knives," Nason said. "Slice up wood slivers for kindling." He moved toward the tent.

"What colour was the man's hair—the one under the tree?" Captain Dean asked.

"Black," Nason said, "with white streaks."

He looked at Neal. "Was this boy's father—the one who built the raft—was he on the raft too?"

"Yes," Captain Dean said, "but he had yellow hair."

"That's too bad," Nason said. "That's a shame."

He took a tinderbox from his shirt, a tin one, with a candle ring on the top—then went into the tent ahead of the rest of us, being more active and quicker on his feet; but came out more quickly than he went in. His cheeks had lost their rosy, clean-shaven look, and were grey and mottled. He held to the canvas of the tent.

"The men are pretty weak," Captain Dean explained. "When it snows or the wind's bad, they don't make the effort to go outside. I've stopped trying to make 'em. You get used to it."

Nason swallowed. "You go in and make a fire hole," he said. "Clear away the oakum in the centre. Lay up a circle of rocks. Cut your shavings and put 'em in the circle; then I'll light the tinder and a candle. I'll leave the tinderbox with you."

When Neal and I came past him with rocks to make the

circle, Nason put out his hand and took Neal's rock from him.

"I'm sorry about your father," he said.

Neal just nodded, his shoulders back and held high—a fine-looking boy, in spite of his oakum helmet and his outlandish swathings.

"That was quite a thing," Nason said. "Paddling a raft ashore in the dead of winter."

"He wanted to do it," Neal said.

Nason examined him attentively. "We hunted everywhere," he said, "up and down the beaches."

"I saw him in a dream," Neal said. "He got off the raft so it would be sure to get to shore."

Nason turned to look at the sloop: then at the sky in the south-east. Some of the colour came back to his cheeks. "Yes," he said slowly. "That would explain it."

"Could I find the place where the raft came ashore?" Neal asked. "I've got to go there."

"I'll take you there myself," Nason said heartily. "You can stay with us. I've got five brothers and four sisters. There's so many Nasons in Kittery that we've worn grooves in the river, sailing up and down it. You come and stay with us: you'll fit right in between Benjamin and William."

Neal looked at him, then at me. For the first time since I had known him, he was on the verge of tears.

Nason seemed embarrassed. He gave the rock back to Neal, took a deep breath and entered the tent again.

The circle of rocks was almost finished. The slivers of wood were stacked in the centre.

Nason fell to his knees, pried the cover from his tinder-box, took out the flint and steel and placed a small piece of charred linen on the slivers. He struck the flint with the steel rod; the spark ignited the linen; but when he gently held the point of a sliver to the flame, it wavered and died.

"Here," he said to the silent, kneeling figures around him, "slice the ends of those slivers so they're shredded." He pulled a sheath knife from his belt and feathered the end of one of the slivers. Captain Dean, Langman, George White, Neal and I did the same.

"Now I'll do what I should have done first," Nason said. "The sight of you people started me off on the wrong foot. I'll try to light the candle."

He stood the stub of a candle in the candle ring on the top of the tinderbox, rested a piece of tinder against the wick, and again struck sparks from the flint. The tinder ignited: flickered; went out.

"Damn it," Nason said, suddenly exasperated, "don't crowd up so close to me! If you can't move back, stop breathing! How can I start a fire with you blowing your breaths all over me!"

He looked at Neal and was suddenly contrite. "Hear me talk," he said disgustedly, "and you without fire for more than three weeks!"

He produced another piece of tinder, placed it on the candle wick struck the flint with the steel—and the tinder caught: the wick smoked—and a yellow flame stood up from it!

Nason turned his head away and whooshed with relief. He stacked up the feathered bits of wood like a little tent, lit one of them from the candle. The flame spread from one stick to another.

Captain Dean leaned down and caught one of Nason's hands in his.

The odour of smoke must have affected my eyes, because I couldn't see for the wetness in them.

Fire! Warmth! Cooked food! Who knows what it's like to be without them?

Only animals! I had the thought that some of us had truly become animals.

For the second time Nason took out his little account book and a stub of pencil, and in the book he wrote down the facts that Captain Dean had given him.

"I'll go to Portsmouth to-night if I can," he said. "If I can't, I'll go first thing in the morning. I'll see Governor Wentworth. I know Captain Furber and Captain Long. They'll send proper-sized vessels for you, and proper boats to take you off—and food."

He looked at the emaciated, bearded faces, accentuated by the flickering light of the fire. "What have you lived on? What have you had to eat?"

"We saved some things from the ship," Captain Dean said. "Some cheese and meat. Then we had mussels and a seagull and seaweed."

"My God!" Nason said. "Seaweed!" He made another note in his account book, thrust it in his pocket and scrambled from the tent.

"The wind's moving into the south-east," he said. "I don't like it."

The tide was half out, and the breakers were pounding on the uncovered ledges.

"I can't run the risk of launching that canoe where I ran in," Nason said.

Captain Dean agreed. "I thing the safest place is around to the north-west. There's a deep cove we can show you."

Nason studied that rim of surf. It was pounding the island from every side, but certainly the waves were less frequent, the sudsy area larger to the north, showing that the drift was toward the mainland. Everywhere else the drift was onshore.

"All right," Nason said, "I'll send the sloop around to the north." He looked at us uncertainly. "Can any of you people help me get my canoe across the island?"

"We'll all help you," Captain Dean said. "Four men'll have to stay here and tend that fire. Miles, you stay. And

Langman. Keep Graystock and Saver here, too. Watch that
fire! Whatever you do, don't choke it! Nurse it! And put
the tinderbox and candle out of harm's way."

He went into the tent and looked at the brisk little fire
while Nason set off in the direction of the sloop, gesticulating
to his shipmates—sweeping his arm around to the north:
pointing insistently to the north-west.

The others followed along behind him, the captain and
Neal, Christopher Gray, George White and Charles Mellen
—all but Henry Dean, who lay near the fire, twitching
dangerously. If Henry should have an attack of epilepsy
now, there was no telling what might happen to the fire.

The sloop's jib rose: her anchor came up and was catted,
and she went dipping off to the north, over the long surges;
then bore around to the westward, so that we knew Nason
had been understood.

The little fire burned brightly, and we stood damp pieces
of wood around the circle of rocks, hoping that the burning
shavings would dry them out. While we cut more shavings,
Graystock and Saver pleaded for meat—for just one slice
of meat. "We're wasting this fire," Saver said. "We could
be roasting meat over it."

"Keep on cutting shavings," I told them. "Under the
circumstances, I think the captain'll let us have more to-
night, when there's no danger of losing the fire."

To watch the progress of that bark canoe across the island
was harrowing. Nason and the captain carried the front
end: White and Mellen the stern, while Neal stumbled
alongside Nason showing him where to put his feet, and
Christopher Gray did the same for Captain Dean.

They had overturned it on the two paddles, using the
paddles as carrying poles, and because the four men slipped
constantly, the canoe's progress was erratic and fumbling
like that of a beetle on a rough field.

The little cove for which they were headed was one we

all knew well, because into it, after the wreck, we had pulled all the cordage and most of the junk from which we'd built the boat and raft. It had a smooth gravelly bottom; and when the four men righted the canoe and lowered it at the head of that little cove, I drew a deep breath of relief. That, I thought, was all there was to it: news of our whereabouts, of our hunger and our miserable condition, was already as good as in Portsmouth.

Langman, evidently angry because Nason had disagreed with him as to the day of the week, watched the proceedings with a jaundiced eye.

"What's going on down there?" he suddenly demanded. "By God, that fool Nason is going to run the captain out to that sloop! He can't do that! He can't let the captain get to Portsmouth ahead of the rest of us!"

He shouted, "Here! Here! No! No!" and ran from the tent.

Nason slid the canoe into the water. Captain Dean, holding a paddle, knelt in the bow.

Before Langman reached them, Nason stepped into the stern, and pushed hard with his paddle. Both men took a few quick strokes. The canoe veered sideways, as if twisted by a current. Her starboard side dipped sharply. When Captain Dean abruptly leaned to larboard to preserve her balance, she dipped even more sharply beneath him. A cataract of green water poured over her gunnel, the canoe slid out from under them, and both Nason and the captain went overboard in a surge of foam. Everybody, it seemed to me, was shouting, running and falling down.

Nason came up gasping, caught the canoe and pushed it ashore. The captain staggered to a seaweed-covered ledge, looking half-drowned.

Hands grasped the canoe, emptied water from it, and swung it gently to the water again to let Nason hoist himself aboard. This time Nason, kneeling alone in the middle, stroked his little craft out of the cove, surmounted the green surges, and went safely aboard the sloop.

The western sky was a dingy grey, and the little sloop weewawing toward that greyness, was too small and fragile for my peace of mind.

"I thought I was gone," the captain told us when he dragged himself to the tent. "I must have swallowed a tubful. The sloop looked so close to shore, I thought maybe we could all get away this afternoon, but the currents suck around that north side like a millrace! There's something dirty blowing up from the south-east."

He stopped outside the tent to hang over a boulder and rid himself of the salt water he had swallowed. I went on in to see Langman draw from beneath the edges of the tent an armful of tarry rope-ends, hidden away for just this purpose.

"Now that we've got the fire to cook it," Langman said, "there'll be an extra meat ration to-night."

He ignited the end of one of those pieces of tarred rope, laid it carefully on the flickering shavings: then criss-crossed a dozen other rope-ends above it.

The rope burned with a sound of sizzling. Up from it came a cloud of yellowish-green smoke that on the instant thickened the air within the tent to a sort of dry, strangling soup.

All in a moment's time our eyes, our chests, our stomachs were choked. We couldn't breathe: we couldn't think: we could hardly make the effort to get ourselves past the tent-flap and into the open air.

When we had clean air in our lungs again, we hoisted Neal on our shoulders until, clinging to the flagpole, he could cut away the cap of oakum around the apex of the tent and slash holes in the canvas. Through them a spurt of discoloured smoke went drifting out to sea.

That night, when we had recovered from our sickness and the fire was burning with a clear flame, the captain was generous with the store of beef; and we, taking turns in charring it over the bright fire, found it delicious . . . heartening . . . and gave no thought to its origin.

January 3rd, Wednesday

If WE hadn't been racked by disappointment, exhausted from over-exertion, befuddled from hunger and dazed by the smoke within that tent, I doubt that Graystock and Saver would ever have been put on watch that night. They had been spared most of the labours that had drugged the rest of us and so they were assigned to stand fire-watch—the last watch before daybreak.

Perhaps this had come about because of their constant malingering—because of their repeated insistence that they were too weak to work; because of the filth in which they lay in spite of our freely expressed disgust. Perhaps, because of all this, we had come to feel that they were too weak to be harmful, too helpless to be dangerous. I know now, of course, that those who seem weakest and most harmless are the greatest threat to any society, and the most to be feared.

Richard Nason and Captain Dean had been right in looking askance at that south-east wind, for its gusts grew stronger and stronger: then snow came whirling in at the top of the tent. Sometimes the wind pulled the smoke up with it and set the fire to glowing. At other times it beat at the blaze with icy fingers, flattening the smoke around us.

God only knows how Saver and Graystock had discovered where Neal had hidden our reserves of meat entrusted to him by Captain Dean. Perhaps they had loosened the foot of the tent and watched him when he first hid it, or when he went back to thicken the protecting seaweed above it. But discovered it had been.

Thanks to the warmth of that ineffable fire, I had truly slept that night, instead of shivering in a sort of intermittent nightmare; but before dawn on that tempestuous Wednesday morning, I came to my senses to find Neal prodding me. The captain, too, was awake, because I saw the glimmer of his eyes in the light of the fire.

Beside the fire sat Graystock, feeding it with bits of tarred rope, and inching forward the end of a board, drying it above the flame. I could see the surface of the board boiling and sizzling in the heat before it reluctantly caught fire.

Neal put his lips close to my ear, so that I could hear his whisper. He could have shouted without being heard by Graystock, because of the pounding of the breakers.

"Saver went out," Neal said. "I heard him talking to Graystock. He went to get meat."

"He couldn't do it," I whispered back. "He couldn't find his way. His feet wouldn't let him."

"He knew where it was," Neal said, "and he couldn't wait."

So we lay motionless; and out of the snowy darkness came Saver, that complaining, querulous, inert, filth-smeared lout: that weak-willed laggard, incapable—according to his own whining protests—of standing on his feet. For three long weeks he had battened on our sympathies—and now, coated with snow, he stood on those supposedly useless feet, grinning as he readjusted the tent-flap, and drew from beneath the oakum coat that others had woven for him a roll of the meat from the carcass we had dragged from the tent for him—and skinned for him, and dismembered for him, and boned out for him, and rolled and tied for him—because he was too weak to do any of those things himself.

Too weak, indeed! His determination to live on others was as the strength of ten!

They were delighted with themselves, Graystock and Saver

were! They grinned and tittered as they crouched over the fire, carving little chunks from that roll of meat, impaling them on the points of their knives, and placing them carefully on the glowing coals.

The odour of the roasting meat filled the tent, piercing and mouth-watering.

Captain Dean got carefully to his knees. When Saver and Graystock speared the roasted chunks with their knife points and popped them into their mouths, he reached out with those long arms of his, seized each one by a shoulder and pulled both of them flat on their backs.

"Get up, all!" Captain Dean shouted to the rest of us. "Wake up! Look at these two, caught red-handed, their mouths crammed with the meat they should have defended with their lives. Animals steal food that belong to others— unless they're trained. Then they can't be made to steal their master's food! Look well at these two! Not men! Untrained animals!"

He picked up the roll of meat and gave it to Neal to hold.

"You, Saver! You, Graystock! What do you have to say for yourselves?"

"I heard a seagull," Saver quavered. "I was afraid the seagulls might get it. I was going to divide it as soon as daylight came."

Langman snorted. "There hasn't been a seagull near this island since I killed the one we ate."

"There's nothing on this earth worse than an ingrate," Captain Dean said slowly. "You're an ingrate, Saver! Graystock, you're an ingrate! Ingrates never change, no matter how much they're coddled and babied! They want more and more! If they don't get more, they steal the belongings or the good name of those that coddle 'em!"

Graystock pointed at Saver. "He was the one! He knew where it was! I didn't do anything."

The captain laughed. "You've both bitten the hands that

fed you. How do you say, those of you who've been bitten?
How should these ingrates be punished?"

"I've wanted 'em out of the tent," Langman said, "ever
since they started fouling themselves. I say put 'em out!
Let 'em get along the best they can!"

"Make 'em wash their clothes in salt water," Henry Dean
said. "Make 'em strip to the skin and wash, starting now."

"Why waste time on 'em?" White said. "Let's kill 'em!
Let's kill 'em quick!"

"We'd be justified in doing so," Captain Dean said, "but
Nason, yesterday, saw how many of us there were. He was
a careful, good man. He won't forget anything he saw here
—ever!"

Contemplatively he added, "But White's suggestion has
merit. This would be a much better world if it were rid
of its ingrates."

"Most ingrates don't recognise themselves as ingrates,"
I reminded the captain. "They'd put up a strong argument
as to why they shouldn't be killed."

"I suppose so," the captain said, "and most of 'em, probably, would think they'd made out quite a case for themselves. Anyway, we can't kill Graystock and Saver, much as
they deserve killing."

"You could send them out to bring in all the meat that's
left," Neal suggested. "They know where it is. If all the
meat were divided now, we wouldn't have to stand watch
to make sure they didn't steal the rest."

"That's a good idea," the captain said. "Graystock and
Saver, hand over your knives. Then go out and clean yourselves. After that, bring back what's left of the meat. There
are three pieces. Bring back the seaweed it's covered with,
too. And don't eat any part of those three pieces of meat!
If you do, I swear to God we'll throw both of you in the
surf."

Protesting, Saver and Graystock stumbled out into the

snow. There was a pallid grey light in the east, so that they could see where to put their feet. How Saver had made that journey in the pitch-dark is something Saver himself couldn't have answered. Perhaps if a man has an animal's craving for something, a mysterious inner sense guides him safely to it.

What with the snow and the high seas and the thick slabs of meat that Captain Dean gave us, we hardly moved from the tent all day. We took turns roasting slivers of meat, stoking the fire, and dozing in its faint glow—a mere breath of nothing to anyone who has known a real fire in a real fireplace; colder, far colder than the Bodleian at its coldest; but a bit of heavenly radiance to us who had lived so long in a frigid hell.

We looked, of course, toward shore, but not in hopefulness. No vessel could have approached Boon Island in that abominable storm, and we were afraid, even, to speculate as to when Nason might reach Portsmouth. We knew in our hearts that he and his little sloop, with that unexpected wind to harry them, might never have reached Portsmouth at all.

January 4th, Thursday

THE SNOW stopped, the wind dropped, the tent was warm, and we must have slept like logs; for when I woke, we were sitting up, all ten of us, wild-eyed, hair on end. I was vaguely conscious, in the recesses of my mind, that a gun had been fired: that I was still hearing its echo.

The tide was almost dead low: the sea had fallen: the wind was a light breeze, offshore, so that the tops of the swells had a slick look—and rising and falling on those rollers was a craft so sturdy, so smart, so daring in the way she slipped around those brown ledge-fingers, almost touching them, that I couldn't shout, or even speak. All I could do was stand there, empty of thought, devoid of sensation, barely alive.

The little vessel was odd-looking. She had a high sharp bow and an even higher sharp stern, and under her boom rested a broad, high-sided skiff with a narrow, flat bottom. There were five men on her deck, one lying out on the short bowsprit watching for ledges, one at her tiller, one reloading the musket that had aroused us, and two wrestling the skiff over the side.

"That's a pink," Captain Dean said in a strangled voice. "Nothing like 'em to nose in and out of a rocky coast."

Captain Dean lowered himself half-way down the seaweed.

The man on the pink's bowsprit jumped up and let go an anchor: then joined those at work on the skiff. The man at the tiller left it, took two coils of rope and tossed them into the skiff: then four men slid her into the water and jumped in.

One made fast a rope to the bow: another did the same in the stern, tossing the unattached end of the rope to the man who had held the tiller.

The man in the bow stood up, cupped his hands around his mouth and shouted to Captain Dean. His voice carried strongly to us on that gentle but frost-laden land breeze. "The dory's made fast astern. We'll pay out easy. When we're close enough, we'll throw the bow rope ashore. Get some men down there with you and lay on to that bow rope. Hold it taut so we can't be swamped."

Two of the men in the dory stood up, pushing at oars. They faced in the direction they were rowing, which seemed strange and awkward. It wasn't right, I thought numbly, for a rower to be able to see where he was going, instead of turning his back to his objective and seeing nothing, as do rowers in England.

I wondered why these Americans had to be so different, sailing something called a pink, sharp at both ends: recklessly approaching ledges in a flat-bottomed dory instead of a skiff: standing up to row so to face forward.

I looked around for someone to help the captain. Only Neal, Langman and White had come from the tent. The others must be helpless, sick, probably, from too much meat, too much smoke, the unaccustomed warmth.

The four of us joined the captain. When the man in the dory's bow tossed us the rope, we fumbled for it, caught it and clumsily took it high up on to solid rock, above the seaweed.

The dory, held bow and stern, jerked at the ropes like a fractious horse.

The newcomers picked their way over the seaweed and stood looking at us as we laboriously made the rope fast around a boulder. I never saw such incredulity as was written on their faces.

Captain Dean, testing the hitch, looked up at the foremost of those sturdy heaven-sent figures.

"You probably don't remember me," he said. "We'd pretty near lost hope——" His voice broke.

All four men stared at us, their brows wrinkled, their mouths half open.

The man Captain Dean had addressed seemed both horrified and puzzled.

"Nason said I'd find John Dean here," he said. "I'd like to——"

"I'm John Dean," the captain said. "You're Furber."

He turned to another. "You're Captain Long. I—I—I——"

He sat down suddenly on a boulder, clasped his hands around his middle and rocked himself back and forth.

Long and Furber jumped forward and hoisted him to his feet. Long patted his back. Furber held his upper arm with both hands.

"We caught the outgoing tide as soon as we heard," Furber said. "Nason said to hurry, so we hurried. You'll be all right, John!" He hesitated and asked uncertainly, "You're John Dean of Twickenham?"

"Jasper's brother," Captain Dean said. "I'll be all right when I get away from these damned breakers! Can't seem to hear a thing! Where's Nason?"

"He's in Portsmouth," Furber said. "He ran into a southeast squall and piled up on Kittery Point. Too much of a hurry to get back, I guess. He lost his sloop, but he got word to Colonel Pepperrell, and Colonel Pepperrell got word to us. We sail Pepperrell's ships, John."

"We got gruel aboard the pink, John," Captain Long said. "You'll feel different when you get some gruel into you."

He spoke to the two silent sailors, who were examining us as if we were dangerous animals in cages. "Put the captain in the dory."

"You're William Long," Captain Dean said in a shaking voice. "And Jethro Furber! I never thought I'd see the day!"

"Now, John," Captain Long said. "We'll have you out of here in a jiffy." He took Captain Dean's arm and steered him toward the dory.

"Take the others first," Captain Dean said. "They're in the tent. Had our first fire last night—breathed a lot of smoke. Tent smells pretty bad. Things weren't easy. I had to stop trying to drive 'em."

"You can't drive 'em if you're human," Captain Furber said.

Captain Dean's voice was suddenly shrill. "Hurry up and help those others. We can't tend this rope all day."

Captain Long, Captain Furber and the two seamen scuttled off toward the tent as rapidly as anyone could move across those snowy, icy rocks.

Captain Dean rubbed his face with both hands, and examined them as if surprised. "I'd know Furber anywhere. Name of Jethro. Only Jethro I ever saw. Used to keep running into him—Antigua, Halifax. Where was I? Oh yes, he sailed under John Frost. John married Mary Pepperrell. Pepperrells marry all over. Is John Frost here with Furber? Or is it Long? I met John's wife once."

I saw his mind was wandering. When I went to help him, he half-turned, put out his hands gropingly and fell heavily.

Neal tried to lift him up.

"Let him alone," I said. "Let him rest. He's been through a lot. A rest won't hurt him."

Long, Furber and their two sailors came cautiously to us, each one carrying a man on his back.

"The captain had a fall," I told Captain Long. "The fire smoked last night—tarred rope—no wood. I think he's a little tired."

"I wouldn't wonder," Captain Long said. "Now look: I'm in command here! Put Dean in the dory right now." He pointed at Neal. "Put him in, too. That's two passengers and two to row."

He signalled to the man on the pink, who tightened the dory's stern rope.

"All right," Captain Long said to Captain Furber. "Slack away on the bow cable. Hold it tight till she's half-way out."

We stowed the captain in the dory: Neal got in by himself.

The two rowers faced the pink, and when a roller lifted the dory, they dug in their oars and pushed hard. Aboard the pink the man pulled at the stern rope. The dory went stern-first as readily as bow-first.

"How many left in the tent?" I asked Captain Long.

"We couldn't see," he said. "We brought out four. Who are they?"

I looked at them, sprawled just above the seaweed. They all seemed to be exactly alike. They might have been quadruplets—bearded, foul, horrible-looking.

"One's the captain's brother," I said. "I think the others are Graystock and Saver and Gray. Gray was a gunner."

I couldn't remember what it was that Captain Long had asked me, and so shook my head.

Captain Long, seeing that I was confused, reached out and slapped my cheek, so to jolt me back to reality. "No offence meant," he said. "Who else is there? Have we got 'em all?"

"Let's see," I said, "Neal and Langman and the captain and I hauled in on the bow rope. That's four. Yes, and White. That's five. You took out four. That's nine. There must be another in the tent. Mellen. He can walk. It must have been that damned smoke. That's ten. There were fourteen to begin with."

Captain Furber nudged Captain Long. "The dory's coming back," he said.

They went as close to the water's edge as they could, watching the dory lift with the surges, rock toward us, pushed by the two sailors. When one of them tossed the bow rope ashore, the two captains belayed it around the same boulder we'd used.

The rowers climbed out and hurried back to the tent.

Captain Long came to stand beside me. "Nason told us there were twelve: that two were lost on the raft, though only one was found."

"No," I said, "there were fourteen. The cook died of lung complaint. We set him adrift. Then the carpenter died. The men wanted to eat him. We finished him up last night."

Captain Long took me by the shoulder. I saw he once more thought my mind was troubled, and was about to slap me to sensibility again. "I'm all right," I said, pushing his hand away. "You'd have done the same in our place."

Langman crowded up to Captain Long. "I was against it," he shouted. "I said it was barbarous, unchristian and a sin!"

Captain Long dropped his eyes from mine: then looked hard at Langman. "So you didn't eat him?" he asked.

"I didn't eat him as Chips Bullock," Langman explained earnestly. "I didn't eat him the day he was skinned. I only ate him the next day, when he was beef."

"That's a nice distinction," Captain Long said.

He became suddenly irascible, impatiently lifted Henry Dean, and shouted at Saver, Graystock and Gray. "Get on your feet! Stow yourself in that dory!"

He pointed a stubby finger at Langman. "Help 'em if

they *need* help; then get in yourself! Don't stand around!
All we need is a capful of wind to be stuck on this damned
island ourselves! God knows how you stood it! I couldn't
have stood it a week without losing all my anchors!"

His two seamen came back, pushing and pulling at
Mellen.

"Get him in! Get him in!" Captain Long shouted. He
tapped me on the shoulder and pointed to the south-west.
There, coming up fast, were two schooners and a brigantine,
all three of them running before the wind.

"Word's got around," Captain Long said. "And that wind
has shifted! Pack 'em in! Pack 'em in!"

Five minutes later I was hauled over the side of the pink,
her anchor was up, and we were moving to the westward.
Between us and that miserable island there was the mist of
breaking seas and the haze of cold air above salt water.
That island had visited upon us every conceivable form of
misery, disappointment and torture, but it hadn't been able
to destroy us, and in spite of my aches and my discomfort,
I felt a great peace—a blissful quiet.

Around me men spoke quietly and I heard them—heard
small sounds: the sighing of the breeze in the rigging: the
screaking of the boom against the mast: the faint rustle of
the seas along the hull. The world, after an eternity, was
blessedly silent once more. Gone forever, thank God, was
the deafening tumult of breakers, bellowing and roaring
like furious beasts determined to destroy our minds as well
as our bodies.

The brigantine and the two schooners hove to and waited
for the pink to come within hailing distance: then cruised
along on either side and spoke to us.

"Get 'em all?" they shouted. "Anything we can do?"

Long used his speaking trumpet. "We got 'em all. Ten
of 'em. If you beat us in, see there's canoes at Pepperrell's

Wharf in Portsmouth. Take word to Dr. Packer. Get barbers. Find Nason and see what he's arranged."

The skippers of the three vessels nodded vigorously: held their hands clasped high in the air and shook them.

Captain Long resumed his shouting. "Plenty of warm water! They're lousy, all of 'em! Plenty of bandages! All kinds of ointments!"

One of the skippers, perched in the ratlins, bawled, "How many days on the island?"

"Twenty-four," Captain Long shouted.

The skipper slid down from the ratlins, and I could see the crews talking and gesticulating. I knew they didn't believe it.

The three vessels sheered away from the pink and drew ahead, as if racing for Portsmouth.

A sailor brought me a tot of rum and a slice of bread. "Captain's orders," he said. The rum burned my gullet and went heatedly around in my stomach. My first bite of bread had a flat taste, but the second was better: the last better still.

The same sailor came back with a cup of gruel and stood before me while I drank it. Then he quickly took the mug from me and moved to a distance. "I'll stand here so you won't fall overboard," he said.

I didn't know what he meant until the pink skittered on the top of a wave, then sank sideways down it. On that my ears roared, my insides were contorted, and everything in me churned up and out. I hung over the pink's bulwarks while the sailor held my knees. This, I thought, was death.

Dimly I heard the sailor say soothingly, "This'll clean you out. Everyone was sick after the gruel, even the captain."

Just at that moment I didn't care what had happened to the captain. I didn't even care what happened to me. I was seasick.

Pepperrell's Wharf was crowded when the pink slid along-

H

side it at dusk. It was a mystery to me why so many
hundreds had gathered on that wharf to see a few scarecrows, but in spite of the bitter January cold there *were*
hundreds of them, women and men, too. Almost all had
lanterns of pierced tin. They were somehow different from
any such throng that might collect in Greenwich. In Greenwich there would have been beggars among them and
hangdog-looking folk, and deformed, dwarfed people, slyly
seeking pockets to pick. Those of substance would have been
smaller and would have seemed contemptuous. Almost
certainly there would have been some who jeered, or laughed
raucously at our hairiness and raggedness and queer oakum
garments.

But those hundreds on Pepperrell's Wharf stood straight,
had solidity, and all of them, without exception, were concerned about us. They were compassionate people, deeply
interested in our welfare. When I was helped over the
bulwarks and saw all those solicitous eyes, glittering in the
light from their upheld lanterns, I couldn't help gulping to
think that strangers should be so kind.

Nason came from the crowd to lower me into a canoe
with Neal. "You're going to Captain Furber's," he said.
"Captain Dean's going there, too. He's already gone." He
put his hand on Neal's shoulder. "I'll see you to-morrow,"
he said. "We're all your friends. You needn't worry about
a thing."

The canoeman took us a short distance downstream,
helped us ashore, pulled his canoe half up the bank, and
motioned us to follow him.

"Tell us where it is," I said, "and we'll go there. You
don't need to leave your canoe."

"Why not?" he asked.

"Someone might steal it."

He looked baffled: then urged us forward, between two

warehouses and across a street to a two-and-a-half-story wooden house. The door of the house was open and before it stood two women and three children, all peering in through the doorway.

Our canoeman touched one of the women on the shoulder. She stifled a cry and whirled to face him.

At the sight of us, she pressed her hand to her lips and shrank back, drawing the children against her skirts. They were pretty little plump things, and I had the thought that has come to me, against my will, a thousand thousand times since then, whenever I see a sturdy child or a woman with a large arm or heavy buttocks—the thought that, if the need arose, that child or that woman would make good eating. No wonder the women were afraid of us!

"What's the matter, ma'am?" the canoeman asked. "I was told by Captain Nason to bring these people here, orders of Captain Furber, and Captain Dean's already been brought here."

"Oh," the woman said, "he frightened us to death, just the look of him. When he stood here and started to speak to us, we screamed and ran out. He went in. I think he's in the kitchen."

"Well, go on in," the canoeman said, "and take these two with you. Treat 'em the same way you'd want Captain Furber to be treated if he'd been cast away on Boon Island for a month."

"Only for twenty-four days," Neal said.

Mrs. Furber looked at Neal: looked away, then studied him carefully. "Only!" she said. "*Only* twenty-four days! You come in the house, right this minute!"

Captain Dean was in the kitchen, as Mrs. Furber had suspected. On the fire he had found an iron kettle filled with beef stew, and had forked out pieces of beef and turnips and potatoes, and had covered the top of the kitchen table with them to let them cool.

"I'm sorry, ma'am," he said to Mrs. Furber. "When you screamed and ran out, I figured the wise thing to do was to stay here instead of running after you and maybe frightening you and the children even more."

He looked at the children in what he doubtless thought was a genial manner; but I knew too well that he was entertaining the same understandable thought that had passed through my head—that they would be tenderer to eat than Chips Bullock had been.

Mrs. Furber's initial horror was passing. "You can't have all that beef and vegetables you've put out on the table," she said sternly. "And just because you're starved is no reason you shouldn't eat like human beings." She brought a bowl and three plates, forked a moderate amount from the table top to each plate; then put the remainder in the bowl.

"Now," she said, "that's all you can have!"

"Ma'am," Neal said. "I'll ask you to put us in the room where we'll stay. We'd better eat there."

"Well I never!" Mrs. Furber exclaimed.

Neal scratched himself deliberately, first his head: then his arm.

"Well," Mrs. Furber said, "we'll put you in the barn. There's three stalls and a summer oven, and lots of hay and blankets. When you're cleaned up, we'll move you to the house."

There was a knock on the door. Mrs. Furber opened it to admit three men—Dr. Packer and two barbers.

The doctor took one look at us, then beckoned us to pick up our plates and follow him. To Mrs. Furber he said, "Bring us hot water as often as you can. And get tubs. If you've only got one, borrow two from the neighbours."

I can hear Dr. Packer's voice, after all these years, exclaiming over our sores and over our feet. "It's a miracle," he said over and over. "I've got to send word to Boston!

Urine and oakum! Seaweed? God knows! But it's a miracle, all the same!"

Warmth, blankets, soft hay on which to lie, clean bodies, shorn heads, shaved faces, white bandages, soothing ointments! I felt as the sailors of Ulysses must have felt, when freed of Circe's spell.

The Last Chapter

I WAKED, the next morning, to the sound of jingling, faint
and far off, couldn't remember where I was, and sat up
straight on my hay-stuffed mattress, half-frightened by not
hearing the unending roaring of those Boon Island breakers:
bewildered by my flannel nightgown, smelling of lavender.
Lavender, of all things, instead of the stenches of our Boon
Island tent! The jingling sound went on and on.

Captain Dean spoke up from the adjoining stall, "Sleigh
bells! People moving around! Probably there'll be a few
of 'em come to see us to-day. Probably they'll want to know
all about us. We'd better decide on what we'll tell 'em
about Neal."

"That's simple enough, isn't it?" I asked. "He learned to
read and write while working for my father. And my father
got to know him because Neal's father was in the Naval
Hospital."

"Yes," Captain Dean said. "That's close enough. Are
you listening, Neal?"

From a third stall Neal politely said he was.

"Probably," the captain went on cheerfully, "we won't
have occasion to say much. Shipwrecked sailors aren't a
novelty nowadays, considering how our good countrymen
in Devon and Cornwall make a business of getting them
wrecked. These New Hampshire people aren't much
different, probably."

Probably! Probably!

How little Captain Dean knew about America, in spite of the high opinion he'd expressed to us in the harbour of Killybegs concerning the people of Portsmouth.

How little anyone, anywhere, knows about America! About its insatiable curiosity concerning the welfare of others! About its generous eagerness to help strangers achieve the same health and happiness that its own citizens enjoy! About its limitless resources: its enormous latent strength! And above all, about its friendliness to those who deserve its friendship: its implacable detestation of false men and evil measures!

Captain Furber came banging at the door that led from the barn to the woodshed, which in turn opened into the kitchen. With him he carried a kettle of fish chowder, three bowls, a ladle and three spoons.

"Haddock!" Captain Furber said portentously. "The Woman"—and I took The Woman to be Mrs. Furber—"cooks the heads and bones in one kettle, and the onions and potatoes and fish in another. Then she makes a mess of pork scraps, and breaks up some ship's bread, and mixes 'em all up with the liquor from the bones. Every sea captain in Portsmouth claims his wife makes the best fish chowder in the world, but I'll put The Woman's up against any of 'em. It's the liquor from the heads and the backbones that grows hair on your chest!"

He ladled the stew into the bowls, then discoursed while we rolled that hot and fragrant chowder over our tongues, crunching the pork scraps through the soft and savoury ship's bread, the tender haddock and the melting potatoes. My toes, what there were left of them, would have curled, if that had been possible, at the life-giving sweetness that trickled down my throat.

"The Woman," Captain Furber said, "makes fried pies that would stand a dead Indian right up on his feet. Doc Packer's in there now, eating fried pies. The Woman wanted me to take in a few for you, but Doc Packer said No. There's a couple of nurses coming over—Governor Wentworth authorised 'em—and Doc Packer says maybe you can have one fried pie apiece along about four bells."

As a seeming afterthought he said, "There's been people coming around with stuff already, but Doc Packer says they can't come in till after he's looked at you. He says maybe some of 'em can come in after you have your dinner."

"What sort of stuff?" Captain Dean asked.

"Oh, knitted small clothes," Captain Furber said. "Linen shirts. Woollen stockings. Big parcel from Mrs. John Brewster—the one that was scalped. Good woman. Got a silver plate in her head to close up a hatchet hole. Hair never grew back, so she wears a wig. Kind of starchy-looking woman, but she softens up considerably toward those who've been in trouble. I'll have a table brought in so you can spread things out on it."

Dr. Packer came in, followed by two women in grey dresses. One, the Widow Hubbard, was short and stout and had a luxuriant moustache. The other, Widow Macklin, was tall and cheerful-looking with a cast in one eye that made her seem to be examining a distant object when in reality she was looking straight ahead.

"Now then," Dr. Packer said to Captain Dean, "we'll have off these bandages. Colonel Pepperrell sent word he wants to see you as soon as you're fit to be seen. There's some others too. They want to hear all about it. How do they think I'll get around to seeing all my other patients if I yap, yap, yap all day about you!"

The nurses brought buckets and rags, stoked the fire, swept the barn floor and set up a table for the gifts Captain Furber had mentioned.

As the doctor sopped at our legs and feet with rags dipped in the concoction in one of the buckets, he rumbled fretfully about our condition. "Hurt much?" he asked. When we said No: no more than an aching tooth, he demanded further details about the treatment our feet had received after the cutting off of our boots.

"There's something here I ought to get to the bottom of," he mumbled again and again. "You'd lost toenails when you cut off your boots, and some toes came off when you washed 'em in urine. Then you put on pieces of linen and some layers of oakum. Then you went out on the rock and kept getting your feet wet, and had no fire."

We said that was correct.

"Hurt much?" he asked again.

Captain Dean said—and Neal and I agreed—that the most painful of all was when we put our hands in water to loosen mussels. We tried to explain to him the excruciating agony that almost paralysed us after the fifth or sixth immersion; but pain, of course, can't be described.

"Mussels, now," the doctor said. "Could mussels have anything to do with it?"

We didn't know.

"And you ate seaweed every day," he ruminated. "Could seaweed be a remedy against frostbite?"

"I don't know *why* I made 'em eat seaweed," the captain said. "I knew we *had* to eat it. There wasn't much of anything else till Chips Bullock died. The fat from Chip's kidneys helped us a little. You'd better not forget to mention kidney fat if you make a report to those Boston doctors. It certainly eased the pain in our feet and legs."

"It's annoying," Dr. Packer said. "We can't go out to Boon Island and carry on experiments under the conditions you encountered, because in the first place nobody'd be such an idiot as to go there under those conditions; and in the second place, everybody that went would die before we found out anything. Exasperating!"

"How long before we'll be able to walk?" Captain Dean asked.

"Well," Dr. Packer said, "we could move you to an upstairs room to-day, if you felt you'd like to get out of this barn and into a comfortable bed."

"I don't want to," Captain Dean said. "I'd feel choked in a comfortable bed. I'd rather stay here, where we can practise walking again with only about half our feet."

Dr. Packer looked relieved. "That's the best thing to do —stay where you'll be out from under foot, and handy to the privy."

"How's my brother?" Captain Dean asked. "How's the rest of 'em?"

"Your brother's all right," Dr. Packer said. "He's just the same as you. He lost toes, the same as you did; but when they fell off, they sort of healed themselves, just like those lizards down in Antigua, that shed their tails if you so much as look at 'em."

He pronounced it Antigga, so I knew he'd sailed there— probably in one of Pepperrell's vessels.

"When can I see my brother?" Captain Dean asked.

"Since you'll stay here in the barn," Dr. Packer said, "I think I'll move him over here later to-day. I don't think much of the sailors he's with. If I tell 'em they can have a certain amount to eat, they eat three times as much."

"Saver and Graystock," the captain said. "I'll be glad to have Henry here where I can keep an eye on him."

The doctor eyed Captain Dean peculiarly. "You've got some others that'll bear watching," he said.

"I know," Captain Dean said. "Langman and Mellen and White."

"If I was you, I wouldn't trust 'em," Dr. Packer said.

The captain snorted. "I don't trust 'em as far as I could throw a whale by the tail."

From my earliest days I had seen, wherever I'd gone in England, beggars of all sorts pleading, imploring, praying for alms, for food, for cast-off clothing; but never had I seen generosity freely offered. Now, in Portsmouth, where beggars were unknown, I saw what I would never have believed, unless I had seen it with my own eyes—an out-pouring of all the good things of this earth to people, strangers, who had suffered adversity during the same storms which had howled around the sheltered homes of their benefactors.

Captain Furber complained and fulminated at the surplus offerings of money, piles of clothing, fur hats, flowered waistcoats, boots and shoes that accumulated in his best room—the room unused, except for funerals and weddings, in the front left corner of every large Portsmouth house. No matter how rapidly Widow Hubbard and Widow Macklin sorted them into piles of three—one pile for ourselves, one for Langman, White and Mellen in the Motley house, and the third for Graystock, Saver and Gray in the Swaine house —they continued to accumulate, so that Captain Furber, at Neal's suggestion, tacked to his front door a card reading, "*The Grateful Survivors of Boon Island Have More Than Enough.*"

Another thing for which Neal was responsible was the writing of letters of thanks to those who had left their names with their offerings. "People like to be thanked," Neal said, "but my father said most people forget to teach their children to say ' thank you.' So if Captain Furber will buy us some paper, I'll write the letters."

More people came to see us or call on us than I would have believed lived in Portsmouth. Merchants, sea captains, tavern keepers, King's Councillors, Lieutenant Governor John Wentworth, John Plaisted, Theodore Atkinson, Colonel William Pepperrell, Richard Nason, Robert Almory, Roger Swaine, Edward Toogood—fine men: the finest, barring my father and Captain Dean and Swede Butler, I ever met.

Every one of the men who called upon us without being

turned away by Dr. Packer was solicitous about our welfare, and in a few weeks' time I had more offers of positions than I would have had in England in half a century.

As for Neal, word had gone around concerning the manner of his father's death, and everyone who saw him was instantly seized with the idea of planning his future.

Colonel William Pepperrell and his partner Governor Wentworth came to call on our second day in Portsmouth. Everything, Governor Wentworth said, would be done for us, and at the expense of the Province of New Hampshire. We were entranced by his elegance, his affability, and the attentiveness with which he listened to our answers to his questions. His companion, Colonel Pepperrell, seemed more remote—more interested in scrutinising the ceiling than in listening to us.

Then Colonel Pepperrell came again alone. Neal, when the colonel walked in, was sitting at our gift-table. The gifts had been pushed away from the end at which he sat, and his pen was scratching diligently at one of his many letters of thanks.

The colonel went to the table, picked up one of the letters and read it aloud:

" *Hugh Gunnison, Esqre.*
" *The officers and the crew of the Nottingham Galley wish to express to you their profound gratitude for your sympathy and your kindness to them after their rescue by the citizens of Kittery and Portsmouth from their bitter days on Boon Island.*
" *John Dean, Master.*"

Colonel Pepperrell was a broad, powerful man with a bulldog face, and he waved the letter exultantly. "Look at that! I read every word of it, easier than print! Takes two men to translate *my* writing." He narrowed his eyes at Neal. "Where'd you learn to write?"

Neal stood up. "In Greenwich, sir."

"He's to work for my father," I said, " in law and insurance."

"Law!" Colonel Pepperrell cried. "Quibble, quibble, quibble! That's no life for you, my boy! Here, sit down! Sit down! Dr. Packer said he had to trim off half your foot."

"I don't know how much he took off, sir. It feels no worse than it did before he trimmed it."

"Yes," Colonel Pepperrell said. "I see!" He looked carelessly at Neal, glanced at Captain Dean and me: then seemed to come to a decision.

He spoke thoughtfully and jerkily, almost as if meditating aloud. "I talked to John Wentworth about you. Twice. Slow man, I am, like folks in Devonshire. Think slowly but make up my mind quick. Always wanted to go to America, but couldn't make up my mind to go till I was sixteen. Then I went quick."

"My brother Jasper speaks of you often, Colonel," Captain Dean said. "He heard all about you from David Waterhouse."

Colonel Pepperrell looked mellow. "Yes. Handles my accounts in England." His eyes strayed back to Neal.

"Mustn't wander from subject," he grumbled. "My boy William Junior! He's fourteen. I can write, but what I write I can't read. William Junior can't write at all, and of course he can't read my writing either. He's got to learn to write, because my other son Andrew's at sea, learning the things a shipowner needs to know. Andrew's delicate. He couldn't have come through Boon Island the way you people did."

He tilted back in his chair and ran his eyes over us, a shrewd, farseeing old man, wondering, I suspected, whether he could have endured Boon Island.

"I know a little about England," he said. "I ought to. I was born in Revelstoke, near Plymouth. I didn't like it. It's no place for a man without money. Upper classes every-where protecting themselves from lower classes, and with good reason!" He snorted. "Been thinking some of going back to Revelstoke: buying a few hundred acres in the country: being upper classes myself."

He glanced at us sharply, as if to get our reactions. I, for one, had none.

"The thing that stops me is William Junior. I've built a big business. William Junior's got to write letters to me about the business, so I can buy books and learn to chase foxes at Revelstoke! Chase foxes! Those fools that chase foxes never kept hens. If they ever had, they'd kill all the foxes before they had a chance to grow up!"

He clucked disparagingly at himself. "Wander, wander from the subject! Now here: we got no schools. Imagine that! John Wentworth says he's going to build a school with his own money, but he hasn't done it, and William Junior still can't write. Time's getting short! Nine vessels I've got—one of 'em picked you up—the pink *Joanna*." He named them, ticking them off on thick fisherman's fingers: "Ship *Frenchie*, brigantine *William and Andrew*, brigantine *Dolphin*, sloop *Miriam*, sloop *Fellowship*, sloop *Nonesuch*, sloop *Olive*, sloop *Merrimac*."

He looked proud, and he had reason. The poor boy from Revelstoke had truly prospered.

"You know what that means," Colonel Pepperrell went on. "It means having our accounts handled in half a dozen ports—invoices—letters of instruction to captains, enough letters to drive anyone crazy." He pounded the table. "William Junior has *got* to learn to write, and you, young Butler, have got to learn him."

Neal quickly wrote the word "teach" on a scrap of paper, and showed it to the colonel.

"Yes, yes!" the colonel said. "That's what I meant, but don't start me wandering! The point is, William Junior is a problem. He gets into bad habits. He goes over to Bray's and gets into the pigpens and rides the pigs. Then he comes home and hides his boots where his mother can smell 'em but not find 'em. Now then!"

He leaned forward and fixed Neal with a steely eye.

"Well," Neal said, "I half promised——"

"I know what you half promised!" Colonel Pepperrell said. "You half-promised Richard Nason you'd go with him to see where your father was lost! Well, I've had a talk with Richard Nason. He lost his sloop coming back from Boon Island—no fault of his. I've made him captain of one of mine. We'll both of us take you to where we think your father was lost."

At the look on Neal's face he turned suddenly toward Captain Dean and me. "Well, what about it?"

"If I had such an offer," Captain Dean said, "I'd say Boon Island was worth it."

"What about you, Whitworth?" the colonel demanded.

"His father would have been—probably is—mighty grateful," I said.

"Then that's all right," Colonel Pepperrell said comfortably. "We'll see a lot of each other before the two of you are healed up and ready to take one of my ships to Barbados."

Captain Dean drew a deep breath. "I'd feared something like this," he said.

"Feared!" Colonel Pepperrell protested.

"Yes, feared," Captain Dean said. "Feared that I might not be able to take advantage of such an offer. There's something you don't know——"

"You probably mean Langman," the colonel said. "Well, John Wentworth and I know all about Langman. He's jealous because you're getting all the attention—because everybody's stopped going to see him and his two cronies. As soon as he began telling everyone that you purposely ran the *Nottingham* ashore on Boon Island, Portsmouth had a bellyful of Langman. My God, Dean, this is a seafaring town! Do you think *anybody* over the age of three and a half would believe that anyone—anyone at all—would, for the sake of *any* amount of insurance, run a vessel on Boon Island in a north-easter? And in the dead of winter? Pish! Portsmouth doesn't want people like Langman and his fellow conspirators around. They've been in the Motley house, but the Motleys have ordered them out."

"Colonel," I said, "we know people like yourselves and these wonderful friends we've made in Portsmouth wouldn't believe Langman; but people in England aren't like that. Those around the docks believe anything they hear about people of property or position. They're too ignorant to investigate—to find out the truth. They have no judgment. From the first Langman has hated Captain Dean, and we've never known why. Perhaps it's because bad men always hate good men, and rejoice in their downfall.

"At all events, if Langman has started telling his lies— though he gave the captain his word of honour that he wouldn't—then he'll keep right on. He'll tell them in England, unless he's bought off. He might even have them printed. Then there's no escaping the fact that the captain will have to tell his own story, with two witnesses. Even then there'll be so many to believe Langman's lies that Jasper Dean's home and even his life may be in danger from mobs. In all likelihood Langman will drag my father into it, for my father handled Captain Dean's insurance. We're mighty grateful to you, Colonel, but I'm afraid this means that Captain Dean and Henry Dean and I must go back to England."

Colonel Pepperrell glowered at us, his eyes belying the thin line of his lips. "I never go back on my word," he said. "There'll always be room for the Deans and Miles Whitworth in the Pepperrell fleet—and when your feet are healed, we want all of you at Kittery Point, so you can see Neal Butler in the surroundings I hope he'll always call his home."

Our worst fears were justified when, a month later, Colonel Pepperrell notified us that Langman, Mellen and White were to appear before his friend Samuel Penhallow, a justice of the peace, to take oath that Captain Dean had deliberately run the *Nottingham* ashore and that Captain Dean had in addition treated Langman in a barbarous and inhumane manner.

The colonel went with us to Justice Penhallow's residence on the following day to hear Langman, Mellen and White swear to the truth of a tale that put anything in the fairy tales of Edmund Spenser to shame. Justice Penhallow looked up at Langman before writing his signature. He didn't say a word: he didn't need to. He just looked. Then he raised his eyebrows at Colonel Pepperrell. "Any comments, Colonel Pepperrell?"

The colonel asked politely, "Would I make any comments if you swore that the moon was a netful of sardines?"

Justice Penhallow signed the paper, pushed it across his desk, and without a word stood up and opened the door for Langman, White and Mellen to go out.

He came back and shook hands with all of us. "There's nothing to be done in a case like that," he said. "If you could spare the time and the money, you might prosecute him for perjury, but you'd do yourself more harm than good. That man would feel honoured to be noticed, but he'd never be noticed by anyone worthy of the name of mariner."

We took our departure from Pepperrell's Cove on a soft April morning, with the south-east breeze bringing us the sweet Maine odours of young willows, damp beaches and newly-turned earth. A shipowner couldn't want a pleasanter cove than Pepperrell's. It was shielded from the sea by the spruces of Odiorne's Point and Champernowne's Island, and from the north by the hills behind Braveboat Harbour. It was a safe anchorage, always, and I hated to leave it; but our testy good friend Colonel Pepperrell had arranged for Captain Dean, Henry Dean and myself to sail from it on one of his brigantines. Langman he avoided as he would the pestilence.

"If it hadn't been for Langman and his lies," the colonel told me disgustedly, "you and Captain Dean would be working for me to-day, instead of wasting the best time of year doing nothing! John Wentworth wanted me to provide Langman and his cronies with passage on this same brigantine, and at government expense. I'd see 'em in hell first! Let the British Navy take charge of Langman and his two dogfish, I told John. All three of 'em need a taste of the cat every day or two, just to remind 'em to be human! Drat such dod-ratted truth-twisters, and drat the fools who always believe 'em!"

The colonel eyed his son William, the problem child, with disfavour. He and Neal Butler stood beside me on the colonel's wharf. I'd always thought of Neal as a younger brother, but he suddenly seemed grown up, and to me his new friend William didn't look like a problem: he looked like a young man who'd be handy in an emergency.

On the shore behind the colonel and Neal and William stood half the population of Kittery Point, studiously scanning the cloudless sky, as if they had found themselves near the wharf purely by accident. By now I had come to know these Maine people a little, and I suspected why they were there. They wanted us to know they were resentful of any person who expected them to believe that Captain Dean would have wrecked a ship on Boon Island in a December north-easter. Under most conditions they were patient; but when aroused, they took steps.

"Seems to me," the colonel said severely to his son, "you'd be better off up at the house, learning to write."

"Yes, sir," Neal said, "but we figured you wouldn't mind if we said a final word to Miles about coming back. Also I wanted to tell him something."

"Well, go ahead and tell him," the colonel said.

"I wanted to tell him that some day I'd try to be worthy of what's been done for me—for us—here."

The colonel looked from Neal and William to Captain Dean and me. He cleared his throat. "Why," he said, "that's all right. Under the circumstances, both of you can have the day off."

"Yes, sir," William said, "and I'd like to say that if Miles will come back, there's quite a few things we'd like to show him when summer's here. It's pretty country—a lot different from Boon Island."

The colonel blew his nose loudly. "Oh my, yes," he said. "I talk about going back to Revelstoke, but I'll never do it!"

I tried to speak, but couldn't. They had us by the arms, urging and helping us into the long boat. There was a fluttering of hands and a babel of cries. The oars rattled in the thole pins; the gulls squalled and squealed overhead; the shore seemed misty and the Braveboat hills wavered a little.

Well, who could tell? God, if we're fortunate, is good to us. How many of us have our Boon Islands? And how many have our Langmans? But doesn't each one of us have an inner America on which in youth his heart is set; and if—because of age, or greed, or weakness of will, or circumstances beyond his poor control—it escapes him, his life, to my way of thinking, has been wasted.

THE END

POSTSCRIPT

In 1745 Captain Moses Butler of Kittery served under Lieutenant-General William Pepperrell in the attack on the French fortress of Louisburg on Cape Breton. He led the 7th Company, and fought with distinction at the taking of the Royal Battery, the Island Battery, and in scouting attacks on the French and Indians in the wilderness to the westward. The fortress surrendered on June 17th, 1745, and there was great rejoicing in Kittery, York, Berwick, Wells, Arundel, Biddeford, Falmouth and places farther to the eastward. General William Pepperrell was knighted. Captain Butler married Mercy Wentworth. His daughter Sarah married Joshua Nason of Arundel.

Captain John Dean so successfully defended himself against Langman's attacks that he was made His Majesty's Consul for the Ports of Flanders, residing at Ostend, and held his post for many years.

In the writing of *Boon Island* the author had generous assistance from:

Marjorie Mosser, *Kennebunkport, Maine*
Major A. Hamilton Gibbs, *Middleboro, Massachusetts*
Clara Claasen, *New York City*
David Leggatt, *Librarian, Central Library, London*
Professor J. G. Bullocke, *Royal Naval College, Greenwich*
Sybil Rosenfeld, *Society for Theatre Research, London*
Dr. Vilhjalmur Stefansson, *Hanover, New Hampshire*
Robert C. Gooch, *Library of Congress*
Henry J. Dubester, *Library of Congress.*
Legare H. B. Obear, *Library of Congress*
Margaret Franklin, *London*
John J. Connolly, *Boston Public Library*
Dorothy M. Vaughan, *Portsmouth (New Hampshire) Public Library*
Dr. Dean Fisher, *State House, Augusta, Maine*
Dr. Angus M. Griffin, *George Washington School of Medicine*
Harold B. Scales, *Portland (Maine) Water District*
W. A. R. Collins, *London*
Walter M. Whitehill, *Boston Athenaeum*
Herbert Davis, *St. John's College, Oxford*
George A. McKenney, *Kennebunkport, Maine*
And the Editorial Staff of Doubleday & Company—Ken McCormick, LeBaron R. Barker, Jr., George Shively.

ARUNDEL

" When I think of the thin, tinny novels which tumble from the press to-day, to be forgotten within a few months, I feel that *Arundel* is a permanent contribution to the literature of this country. I go around telling people to read it; but I despair—until they have read it—of making them realise its quality. It seems to me like a perfectly splendid plum pudding! No, I think it is more than that; I think it is brown bread, and roast beef, and beer! It is *the real stuff*, and while I congratulate the author upon having written it, I congratulate all of us novel-reading folk even more heartily. How anybody can lap up whipped cream when he can get *Arundel*, I don't understand! "

—MARGARET DELAND

PRINTINGS

First published ....November 18, 1929
Revised, replated and reprinted.......................................June, 1933
U.S., 1931 twice; 1933 twice; 1934 four times; 1935; 1936 three
    times; 1937 three times; 1938 three times; 1939; 1940; 1941;
    1942; 1943; 1944; 1945 twice; 1946; 1947; 1949; 1953; 1955
Braille, Library of Congress ....January, 1934
England (Bodley Head) ....September, 1936
Germany (Holle & Co.) ....October, 1936
Germany (Buchgemeinschaft) ....January, 1937
England (Readers' Union) ....December, 1938
Sweden (Bonniers) ....March, 1939
Denmark (Aschehaug) ....November, 1939
Italy (Mondadori) ....September, 1940
Armed Services Edition ....May, 1945
Spain (Janes) ....May, 1946
France (Editions de la Paix) ....Details unobtainable
Czechoslovakia (Borovy) ....October, 1947
Arundel 300th Anniversary ....June, 1953
German Book Society (Koch, Darmstadt) ....January, 1955

THE LIVELY LADY

" *The Lively Lady* is the best historical novel we have read in years. After considering soberly the works of William Stearns Davis and S. Weir Mitchell and Rafael Sabatini and the earlier Robert W. Chambers, we'll go even further. We have read no better book of its type than *The Lively Lady*, anywhere, any time. It drives, full-sailed and rail under, logging a yarn of the War of 1812 and the privateers that were America's chief substitute for a navy. There is a mighty gusto in the book, controlled and disciplined by writing of high merit. It hurries you along through frothing sea and pungent powder smoke and the grim ordeal of Dartmoor Prison with no respite in its traction. Its people are real, its situations plausible, its style a delight. To this reviewer *The Lively Lady* stands quite as high in the aristocracy of historical romance as *Hugh Wynne*, and it is quite possible that the patina of years will make it seem even finer."

—FREDERIC V. VAN DE WATER, *New York Evening Post*

PRINTINGS

RABBLE IN ARMS

" *Rabble in Arms* is magnificent. In both the beauty and the horror of his story, Kenneth Roberts reaches supreme heights and can defy comparison with any author that ever lived and wrote in any language I ever read in the original or in translation. They talk big talk of Tolstoi, Victor Hugo, Stephen Crane and a few others, but I put Kenneth Roberts up with the best of them. He is a great author who has actually written great novels." —ROBERT HUGHES

PRINTINGS

First published ....November 2, 1933
U.S., 1933 twice; 1935; 1936; 1937 three times; 1938 twice; 1939
    twice; 1940; 1942; 1943; 1944; 1945; 1948; 1950; 1953
Braille, Library of Congress ....January, 1934
Germany (Holle) ....October, 1936
Germany (Book Society) ....January, 1937
England (Collins) ....January, 1939
Australia (Collins) ....January, 1939
England (National Library for Blind) ....March, 1939
England (World Books) ....April, 1940
Italy (Mondadori) ....June, 1941
Czechoslovakia (Borovy) ....July, 1941
Sweden (Bonniers) ....February, 1945
Talking Books, Library of Congress 1945
Spain (Janes) ....September, 1946
Illustrated Edition ....October, 1947
Republished Czechoslovakia (Odeon) ....January, 1949
Republished Sweden (Bonniers, Folkbibliotek) 1956

CAPTAIN CAUTION

" It is such powerful writing as that in *Captain Caution* describing the British hulks, the prisoners and their escape that sets Mr. Roberts' work apart from that of most historical novelists."

—Saturday Review of Literature

PRINTINGS

First published ....November 7, 1934
U.S., 1934 twice; 1937; 1938 twice; 1939; 1940; 1941; 1942; 1943;
    1944; 1945 twice; 1946; 1948; 1950; 1953
Braille, Library of Congress ....March, 1935
Talking Books, American Foundation for Blind ....December, 1939
Armed Services Edition ....April, 1944
Spain (Janes) ....May, 1946
Czechoslovakia (Odeon) ....Suppressed: Iron curtain
Switzerland (Diana: German) ....February, 1948
Sweden (Bonniers) ....October, 1948
England (Collins) ....January, 1949
Hungary (Konyvkiado) ....March, 1949
Italy (Mondadori) ....September, 1951
Norway (Cappelens) ....October, 1951
Sweden (Bonniers, Folkbibliotek) ....March, 1953

NORTHWEST PASSAGE

" Towering above all else in the swirling 700 pages of *Northwest Passage* is that indestructible giant, Robert Rogers, a prodigious creation, a character bristling and sounding with life, a vivid portrait for your literary gallery. *Northwest Passage* will give you three novels' worth of entertainment."   —CHARLES LEE, *Minneapolis Journal*

PRINTINGS

First published ....June 25, 1937
U.S., 1937 fifteen times; 1938 eight times; 1939 four times; 1940 three
    times; 1942; 1943; 1944; 1945; 1946; 1947; 1948; 1940; 1952
    1952; 1954
Book-of-the-Month Club ....July, 1937
Braille, Library of Congress ....September, 1937
Talking Books, American Foundation for Blind ....January, 1949
England (Collins); Book Society; Daily Mail Book-of-the-Month
                                                                        January, 1938
Australia (Angus & Robertson) ....February, 1938
Sweden (Bonniers) ....April, 1938
Germany (Paul List) ....September, 1938
Denmark (Jespersen) ....September, 1938
Norway (Cappelen)..October, 1938
Finland (Kirja)..November, 1938
Holland (Torrentrans)...December, 1938
Japan (Mikasa Shobo)...December, 1938
Italy (Mondadori) ....March, 1939
England (Foyle's Book Club) ....May, 1939
Hungary (Revai) ....May, 1939
Czechoslovakia (E.L.K.) ....June, 1939
Continent of Europe (Albatross Giant) ....June, 1939
Poland (" Roj ") ....July, 1939
Rumania (Ciornei) ....November, 1939
France (Editions Stock: 338 printings) ....February, 1940
Brazil (Companhia Editora Nacional) ....July, 1941
Spain (Janes) ....June, 1946

Yugoslavia (Athenaeum) ....Details unobtainable
British Broadcasting Co., 8 instals..........................July-Sept., 1947
Czechoslovakia (Podrouzek) ....January, 1948
Sweden (Bonniers, Folkbibliotek) ....November, 1953
Germany (Europäischer Book Club) ....March, 1953
England (Collins Fontana) ....November, 1953
Italy (Mondadori) 4 Vol. Pavone Edition ....January, 1955
Yugoslavia (Kosmos, Belgrade) ....May, 1955

OLIVER WISWELL

" The story of the Royalists in the American Revolution has never been adequately told in fiction form. Now, after 160 years, Kenneth Roberts has undertaken this herculean task in *Oliver Wiswell*. No one excepting a man of Mr. Roberts' stature as a writer could lay before us the case of the American Royalists. It takes industry and unending research to accomplish the bare skeleton of such a book; it takes a high form of imagination, finished technique, and courage to carry the task to a successful conclusion. Yes, courage, for even after the passing of centuries, old prejudices still persist and cloud issues. It requires something greater than good writing and technique to hold up for examination a lost cause, and turn the dead past into a living present. This Kenneth Roberts has done. He has given life to people who were only names on a page of history, and summed up a case for Americans whom we had forgotten were Americans."

—INGLIS FLETCHER, *San Francisco Chronicle*

PRINTINGS

First published ....November 22, 1940
    Reprinted twice before publication
U.S., 1940 twice; 1945; 1946; 1948
Braille, Library of Congress ....January, 1941
Australia (Angus & Robertson) ....January, 1941
Sweden (Bonniers) ....February, 1941
Switzerland (Humanitas; Zurich) ....April, 1941
Brazil (Companhia Editora Nacional) ....July, 1941
England (Collins) ....August, 1943
England (National Library for Blind) ....November, 1943
Czechoslovakia (Thalia) ....May, 1946
Spain (Janes) ....May, 1946
France (Editions de la Paix) ....September, 1947
Italy (Mondadori) ....September, 1949
Switzerland ⎫
Germany ⎬ (Diana; Zurich) ....November, 1953
Austria ⎭

LYDIA BAILEY

" *Lydia Bailey* is a rich, long, never lagging book, triumphantly ranging over half the world and more than half of human hopes and follies. It shows Kenneth Roberts' special power of bringing the past to full and unforgettable life; and in its anger at political selfishness and stupidity it has a harsh, barbed meaning for to-day. If 1947 produces a better novel, it will be a notable year for American fiction."

—WALTER HAVIGHURST, *Chicago Tribune*

PRINTINGS

First published ....January, 1947
Literary Guild ....January, 1947
Braille, Library of Congress ....June, 1947
Book-of-the-Month Club ....July, 1947
Argentina (Rueda; Spanish) ....October, 1947
Brazil (Instituto Progreso; Portuguese).....................November, 1947
Norway (Cappelens) ....December, 1947
England (Collins) ....January, 1948
Australia (Collins) ....January, 1948
Braille (Clovernook; Library of Congress) ....January, 1948
Sweden (Bonniers) ....May, 1948
Switzerland (Diana; Zurich) ....June, 1948
Denmark (Aschehoug) ....June, 1948
Holland (Breughel) ....August, 1948
Finland (Aura) ....October, 1948
France (Editions de la Paix) ....November, 1948
Hungary (Konyvkiado) ....December, 1949
Spain (Janes) ....July, 1950
Italy (Mondadori) ....November, 1952
England (Collins Fontana) 1954
Yugoslavia (Kosmos; Belgrade) ....May, 1955

OTHER BOOKS BY KENNETH ROBERTS

TRENDING INTO MAINE (published Little Brown, 1938: Doubleday, 1944)

" Kenneth Roberts takes you into the kitchen, sits you down by the stove, hands you a doughnut, and stuffs you full of Arundel, Maine traditions, Maine smells, Maine people, the hardships of soldiering, the pleasures of ducks' breasts, the bravery of sea captains' daughters."
—E. B. WHITE, *Saturday Review of Literature*

MARCH TO QUEBEC (published 1938: revised 1940)

" Bringing together, in *March to Quebec*, the journals of the Quebec Expedition is an exceedingly valuable contribution to the Americana of the Revolution. . . . Many have been practically inaccessible. . . . Only a few libraries in the country have them all, and he who would buy them for himself would be obliged to spend a large sum of money and wait for a year or so before some dealer in rare books could accumulate all of them." —*Boston Evening Transcript*

MOREAU DE ST. MÉRY'S AMERICAN JOURNEY (1793-1798) (published 1947)

" Here is a cross-section of a nation in the process, to use Moreau's apt phrase, of being born." —*New York Times*

I WANTED TO WRITE (published 1949)

" The record of the reading, the assimilation, the eternal tracking down of details, the enormous correspondence, and the starts and stops of a historical novel in progress. Here is the reason why it took three years to write *Oliver Wiswell* and five years to complete *Lydia Bailey*. Here is what you go on doing, once you have learned to write." —*Atlantic Monthly*

HENRY GROSS AND HIS DOWSING ROD (published 1951)

" In October, 1949, Henry Gross dowsed a fresh-water dome at Clayhouse on a map of Bermuda, an island on which no potable spring water supposedly existed. The Clayhouse well was drilled and, on April 27, 1950, flowed 44 gallons a minute, a daily 633,60 gallons ' wasting its sweetness on the desert air.' . . . It is the greatest Bermuda story ever told."

—PARK BRECK, *Mid-Ocean (Bermuda) News*

THE SEVENTH SENSE (published 1953)

" *The Seventh Sense* is Roberts' answer to the volleys of his critics— the account of the first year's operation of Water Unlimited Inc., whose aims are to insure an adequate supply of water for the world's people, and to obtain for Henry Gross a steady income."

—ALAN NASH, *Rochester Times-Union*

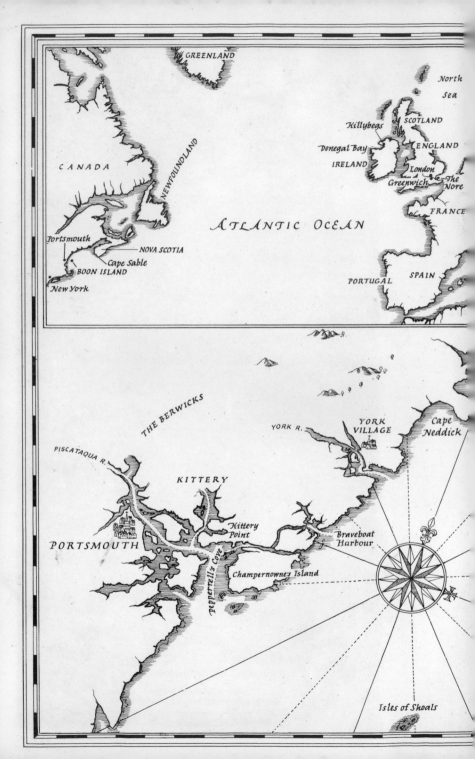